THE ENGINEER WORE VENETIAN RED

MYSTERIOUS DEVICES
BOOK FOUR

SHELLEY ADINA

Moonshell
Books

The Engineer Wore Venetian Red / Shelley Adina—1st ed.

ISBN: 978-1-950854-15-8 R111522

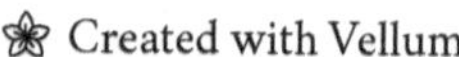 Created with Vellum

For my mother

THE ENGINEER WORE VENETIAN RED

CHAPTER 1

FRIDAY, SEPTEMBER 20, 1895

The Royal Kingdom of Spain and the Californias

There she lies." Captain Boyle's basso voice boomed through the speaking horn. "The royal city of San Francisco de Asis. And may I say, we are one of the first crews to see her like this, from the air. The Royal Kingdom's skies have only opened to airships within the last year."

The gondola of the touring-class airship *Iris* was of a progressive and unique design, having not one level, but two. Above, on the navigation level, the captain, the navigator in the person of his son Timothy, and the engineer in the person of his niece Dinah, held principal sway. On the observation level below, generous viewing ports allowed Peony Churchill, the ship's owner, and her guests to see where they were going, and to communicate freely with the crew without inconveniencing them by getting underfoot.

Captain Boyle permitted his employer access to the upper level. Everyone else was obliged to keep to the airy iron stair that spiraled up from the observation deck to the living quarters in the fuselage.

Daisy Linden stood at the viewing port with her sister Frederica, next to their hostess, and tried to take in the vista below. An enormous bay of salt water, so large that the foot of it faded into the haze on the southern horizon, lay directly beneath. Ahead, a jumble of adobe houses and shops and palm trees and other greenery tumbled pell-mell down the hills on which the city was built. Crowning the highest hill, and seeming to grow out of its very rocks, was the mighty cathedral of San Francisco de Asis, golden in the long rays of late afternoon.

"There is the Viceroy's palace." Barnaby Hayes pointed with his good arm. "Just below the cathedral, with all the arched windows and cantilevered terraces."

"It is not so much a palace as a city within a city." Peony Churchill's gaze was as transfixed as Daisy's own. "It covers practically the whole hill. How is one to find one's acquaintance?"

Barnaby chuckled. "It is quite likely that they will find us. We seem to be the only occupants of the skies at present."

But Daisy was not so much interested in cathedrals and palaces, nor even the acquaintance that Peony and Barnaby claimed in this strange place. She leaned into the speaking horn. "Captain, may we see the Barbary Coast from this vantage point?"

"No, miss," came his basso tones. "We have just passed over the waterfront at Buena Vista Cove. With Miss Churchill's permission, we will come about so you may have a better view, and I may find enough space to moor beyond it, for I have no hope that a proper mooring mast may be found."

"Permission granted," Peony said, then squeezed Daisy's hand. "We shall get the lie of the land, and know what we are up against in the place where your papa was last seen."

Daisy gave her a grateful smile. For they had been given information in Bodie—which lay behind them now, on the other side of the mountains—that indicated Papa intended to work his passage north from here on a steamship. The only place to secure such employment was on one of the most dangerous waterfronts on the entire continent. To muster up the courage to go down there and make inquiries would take every bit of fortitude she possessed.

To say nothing of the Thaxton pistol in her reticule.

Daisy had no illusions about the difficulty of finding a clue as to which ship Papa had taken and his eventual destination. They were operating on the assumption that their father, Professor Rudolf Linden, R.S.E., had regained enough of his memory to make his way north to Victoria, in the Canadas, where many months ago they had all been bound as a family in order for him to take up a position at the university there.

But a band of Californio soldiers had intervened—had shanghaied him, beaten him, and imprisoned him, to the point where he had forgotten his own name and great swaths of his own life. He did not even know that Mama was dead. Or that Daisy suspected grief had hastened her passing. Or that his two daughters had been pursuing him across the whole of the Wild West, existing on hope, the kindness of strangers, and the slenderest of clues.

Barnaby Hayes had told them all he could of their father, for he had shared a gaol cell with him in the south of the king-dom, before the Rose Rebellion. And more recently, on the way here, he had told them of Evan Douglas, who had been another prisoner in the cell. Mr. Douglas was now one of the most powerful men in the land and engaged to be married to the daughter of a wealthy landowner.

Of all the things Daisy might have hoped or expected during the course of their search for Papa, their being received at a royal palace had not been one of them.

Iris made a graceful turn and soon the harbor came into view below—a forest of masts and steam funnels and ships jostling together, moored cheek by jowl and fighting for custom. The Barbary Coast was famous for fighting—and thievery. For opium dens and the smuggling of black powder. It, Bodie, and Port Townsend in the Canadas held the dubious distinction of having achieved fifty different ways to die before dawn.

"Gracious," Freddie said faintly. "How is one to make sense of it, never mind find news of one man?"

"I do not know," Daisy said on a sigh. "But we have managed so far. Dinah is confident he will be heading north, so perhaps that narrows the field a little. And here, at least, we may find friends who may be able to help."

"I hope you are right," Freddie said, allowing herself to be encouraged.

Or at least, allowing Daisy to believe she was.

An exclamation of surprise issued from the speaking horn, and *Iris* once again leaned into a turn.

"Captain?" Peony said into its brass circumference, clutching at the rail with the unexpected change in course. "Is something wrong?"

"No indeed, miss," came the rejoinder. "But the sharp eyes of our navigator, here, have told me that progress has indeed reached these shores."

"In what form?" she asked, her attention once again on the view below.

"Observe that island in the water, miss—not the flat rock with the large house upon it to the north, but the island with the floating bridge. On the charts it is called Isla Yerba Buena, and by all accounts is uninhabited except by birds. It appears to have been turned into an airfield recently."

"Evan," Barnaby said with a nod of conviction.

"Bring us in, Captain," Peony said. "For if my eyes do not deceive me, the armed and mounted party even now setting foot upon the bridge is our welcoming committee."

As they floated down to the island on a short approach, Daisy could see Barnaby keeping a close eye on the party approaching across the water.

"Those horses seem to me to be exceedingly well trained," she murmured to him. "I have never known a horse to walk anywhere but upon solid ground."

"That bridge appears to be made of pontoons, but even so, the swell is heaving them up and down," Freddie said. "Someone is sure to be tossed in at any moment. You do not suppose we will have to ride them, do you?"

"Those are not live horses," Barnaby said in wondering tones. *Iris* dropped lower, and as she hovered a mere fifty feet above the grassy airfield, they could see the approaching horses in more detail. "They are *mecaballos*—only these seem to have been adapted for civilian use."

Mecaballos! Of course they were. It was not their harness flashing in the sun, but their mechanical bodies.

"Cut the engines, vanes vertical," they heard Captain Boyle say, and *Iris* settled into position in front of the lone mooring mast.

The ten-year-old Boyle twins, Luke and Rebecca, scampered down the gangway and made her fast, and tied her stern down with their own mooring irons.

Peony inclined her head toward Barnaby. "Mr. Hayes, since you claim friends here, will you escort me to meet this rather terrifying delegation?"

"I would be honored," he said with a gallant bow. "But first, someone must help me with my jacket."

She did so with grave solicitude, draping it over the left arm, still in its sling. He was gaining strength and movement every day, but Daisy thought a gunshot wound must be very painful, no matter how well treated it had been by their friends in Bodie, and by Mrs. Boyle since.

Escorted by a watchful Captain Boyle, flanked by Dinah and Timothy with hands resting lightly on their Colt revolvers, they disembarked to await their visitors.

A track covered the short distance from the water, and one rider separated himself from the others, leaning over the gleaming metal withers of his mount and urging it up the gentle slope and out on to flat ground. He tore off his black-brimmed hat and waved it with all the excitement of a schoolboy.

"Evan!" Barnaby snatched off his own bowler to wave in acknowledgment and half-walked, half ran out from under the shadow of *Iris*'s fuselage.

"Well met, old man!" Evan Douglas, privy councilor to the Viceroy, was not the sober personage of middle age that Daisy had been envisioning. He leaped from the back of the *meca-*

ballo, lithe as any athlete and hardly older than Barnaby or Peony themselves.

"Easy—" Barnaby stretched out his good hand before Evan could seize him in a hug. "Got shot in Bodie. By George, what a sight for sore eyes you are!"

Evan seized his hand instead, his face alight, his eyes taking in every detail of his friend's well-being. He wore a suit of fine black wool, its short jacket decorated wondrously with black embroidery, its trousers trimmed down the sides with silver medallions joined by fine silver chains.

"I don't believe anyone has ever been so welcome." Belatedly, he seemed to realize that Barnaby was not alone. "Do introduce me to your friends, and then I will take you to meet my Isabela and the others."

"With pleasure. Evan Douglas, Minister of Magnificent Devices, may I present Miss Peony Churchill."

"Goodness me, such a title." Peony offered her gloved hand and curtseyed as he took it. "Mr. Douglas, I have heard much of you."

"You may blame the Viceroy for my title, Miss Churchill. I had nothing to do with it. I know of your mother, and both Lady Hollys and Mrs. Fremont have spoken highly of you. I had a letter from Gloria just a few days ago, in fact, informing me that you were in the country."

"In which case one is obliged to call," she said, her dimples flashing.

Goodness, Daisy thought. *I would not dare to speak that way to a privy councilor of a foreign nation! But Peony is markedly unlike anyone else, and people seem to forgive her nearly anything.*

"One certainly must call," he said with a laugh. "And your friends?"

"Mr. Douglas, may I present my crew. This is Captain Alturas Boyle and his wife Persis. First Engineer Dinah Boyle, their niece, and Midshipman Samuel Boyle, their nephew. Navigator Timothy Boyle, their son. And these rapscallions are their children, Lucas and Rebecca Boyle."

Evan shook hands, clearly aware that Captain Boyle was giving him the once-over. "It is a pleasure to welcome you to San Francisco de Asis, Captain, Mrs. Boyle. And your crew. You have the distinction of being the first civilian ship to moor here."

"Mrs. Fremont's ships have not yet come?" the captain asked. "I understood that one of her vessels had preceded us."

"Yes indeed," he agreed. "At present it is serving as a school for aeronauts. You will see them practicing lifts and landings there." He pointed a little south of where the pontoon bridge terminated on the other side.

"How many students have you, sir?" Dinah asked with interest.

He hesitated. "Three."

"Three!" she repeated in disbelief. "Gracious, there were thirty in my graduating class alone."

"We are but planting seeds as yet," he said. "Classes are taught by the president of the Viceregal Society of Engineers herself. My fiancée is a student, and the youngest member of the palace guard another. Here is a name you will remember, Barnaby. Captain de Sola's eldest son is eighteen and was so determined to become our third student that he abandoned his obligatory trip to Spain and has postponed his formal education indefinitely."

"Flying will educate him better than anything," Dinah said with a nod.

"But you have not met our young ladies," Barnaby said, smiling at the young woman's conviction. "Evan, may I present Miss Daisy Linden and her sister Frederica."

Daisy dropped a curtsey, and Frederica another. "We are honored, sir. Imagine our amazement at the manner of your transport across the water. In the Texican Territories they called them *mecaballos*—mechanical horses."

Evan looked pleased at Daisy's knowledge. "Indeed they do. I have heard May Lin use the term, too. They are surprisingly adaptable. Machines are merely a hobby for me, but May Lin—I beg her pardon, Madam President of our fledgling society of engineers, has taught me more than all my professors at university ever did. Repurposing the *mecaballos* was my first project. But come. Isabela will be storming up here on her own mount if I do not bring you along."

"Bring us along … where, sir?" Peony asked.

"Why, to the palace," he said in some surprise. "His Serene Highness saw you from the council chamber and you can imagine the disarray the excise meeting fell into. He is anxious for news of Mrs. Fremont."

"Is he, now?" Peony murmured with some interest.

"The Viceroy," Captain Boyle murmured back. "Fancy that."

"Shall we attend you, miss?" Dinah asked her employer.

"I should like the captain with me, but as for you and Timothy, you ought to go where duty and interest call you," Peony replied. "In short, were it up to me, I should say you ought to do as you like."

"Now, miss, that is no way to maintain discipline," Captain Boyle said firmly. "The two of you stay with the ship, if you please. I should not like Mrs. Boyle and the young ones marooned out here without protection."

"They are quite safe," Evan said earnestly. "A detachment of soldiers guards the shore side of the bridge, and the harbormaster has assigned a patrol to circle the island."

"The same harbormaster who manages the ships in Buena Vista Cove?" the captain inquired.

"Yes."

Captain Boyle gave a nod. "Then my engineer and navigator will remain close to *Iris*. Armed, sir, with your permission."

Evan inclined his head in a nod, as though he did not want to argue with a guest, then offered his arm to Peony. "Shall we?"

Daisy half wished she could stay with *Iris*, too, and paint the vista she'd seen from the viewing ports, which was so unusual and awe-inspiring it must be committed to pigment and paper without delay. But already Barnaby was offering her his good arm. She could see that Freddie was agog to embark on this adventure—in a moment she would be edging close enough to Mr. Douglas to ask if she might ride his *meca-ballo*, as she had done in Santa Fe. So Daisy smiled at the detective, settled her hat, and together they set off across the field.

CHAPTER 2

FRIDAY, SEPTEMBER 20, 1895

8:40 p.m.

In the old days before the Rose Rebellion, had May Lin wished to examine a visiting airship and take in its modern wonders, she would have tossed her head and done so without so much as a by-your-leave, and helped herself to a bit of its lovely technology into the bargain.

But the old days were long behind her now.

Sometimes she was glad about that. For the most part, the country no longer wanted to kill every witch on the river. Nor did the Viceroy now wish to invade the Texican Territories, as his father had. She could ride out to see the finishing touches being put on Gloria and Captain Stan's school for girls, first of its kind, now crowning the top of a hill just outside the city. Or she could demonstrate an invention to the slowly growing members of the society of which she was president, and of whom she was far more proud than she should be.

But then there were days like today, when she had to

endure the tiresome ceremonies of the viceregal court, which included this crowded fiesta upon one of the cantilevered terraces of the palace. May Lin had no objection to food, mind you. But prelates and clerks and the busybodies perpetually watching and tattling wore her out.

Earlier, the party of people from the airship moored on the island had made their bows to His Serene Highness Carlos Felipe, Viceroy of the Royal Kingdom of Spain and the Californias, Defender of the True Faith, and General of the Armies of Heaven. Having heard them numerous times before, she had nearly fallen asleep during the recitation of all his titles.

On the way across the pontoon bridge she had designed when she and Evan had had the airfield built, she had met them all, had seen them loaded into a pair of carriages belonging to the de la Carrera y Borreaga family, and had promptly ridden off ahead of them on her *mecaballo*.

Perhaps they thought she had been bringing word of their arrival to the Viceroy, since she'd joined him in his formal welcome in the great reception chamber. But in reality it was an excellent excuse to put the *mecaballo* through its paces and enjoy the cool wind ruffling the red silk roses she wore twined in her crown of glossy braids.

May Lin never forgot that she and her mother before her were witches. Never let anyone else forget that without the help of *las brujas*, Viceroy Carlos Felipe's kingdom would have been lost to a usurper. And now, while she might be outranked by many others sipping wine and enjoying their *barbacoa* on the terrace, she had the royal ear—and his respect as well.

She respected him, too. Liked him, even. When she wasn't wishing for a horsewhip to take to his fine, arrogant behind.

"You look as though you have been drinking lemon juice." Isabela de la Carrera y Borreaga joined her, her red rose tucked behind one ear in a bewitching fashion.

"I would welcome lemon juice if only I could drink it in my laboratory," she murmured back under cover of the music of guitar, trumpets, and fiddle.

"The rules of hospitality must be observed, no matter how painful," Isabela teased. "Come, you have hardly eaten anything, and you must keep up your strength. Besides, my *novio* wishes to hear you praise my progress with the airship's ropes this morning."

"I can do that with a good conscience, at least," May Lin allowed, as the petite beauty towed her over to the groaning tables of food.

She would never grow used to the quantities of food that the nobles consumed. This one fiesta alone could keep the witches of the canyons of the Sangre de Cristo de Colorado fed for a week. She chose her portion carefully—vegetables and salads, and a slice of beef. When she laid down the carving knife, causing the nearest prelate to visibly relax, she looked around to find that Isabela had already been claimed by Evan.

In her place was one of the visitors—that quiet little personage with the demure brownish-red chignon and the speedwell-blue eyes that held despair.

May Lin could spot despair at fifty yards, having seen it often enough during the war. And in the village before that— her own reflection in the polished silver bowl she had once used as a mirror.

"Will you have some beef?" she offered politely, and scooped it on to the girl's plate without waiting for a reply.

"This is what they call *barbacoa*?" the visitor said, gazing down at it.

"It is, and it will be a source of offense to His Serene Highness if you do not eat a little of everything."

"Oh, dear," the girl sighed, and moved along the table to do as she was told.

"Try some," May Lin said. "It is really very good."

"I cannot think of eating when my mind is so wholly occupied with—" She cut herself off. "Other matters."

"The mind cannot operate at all without food to fuel it," May Lin, ever practical, told her briskly. "Eat, or I shall know the reason why."

A ghost of a smile curved the girl's mouth. "You sound just like my Aunt Jane." She followed May Lin to the terrace wall, which commanded a stunning view over the city, all the way to the Barbary Coast. She seemed to become lost in the prospect—in the lamplit streets, in the warm lights in the houses, in the lanterns in the distance, rocking on the bows of the ships.

"Eat," May Lin reminded her, and she did.

"My goodness." She swallowed a bit of beef. "It is delicious."

"I never tell a falsehood." May Lin reconsidered. "On the subject of food."

A raucous burst of laughter seemed to engulf the little group near the royal table, consisting of their honored guests and Isabela's father, who enjoyed a good joke.

"You are May Lin, are you not?" the girl asked. "I am Daisy Linden."

"Yes, I remember. You are the artist."

The girl looked startled. "Goodness. What a memory you have."

"We do not have guests from foreign parts so often that I mix them up," May Lin said.

"And you are the engineer." Daisy smiled. "I have a young friend who is also named Lin. I believe she and you would like each other."

"Lynn is not such a common name in these parts. It is English?"

"No, L-I-N. She is a Canton girl, too. She is looking for a relative, but …" Daisy sighed and took an enormous forkful of salad.

May Lin hazarded a guess. "You became friends because she is looking for a relative, and you are as well?" The English spy Barnaby Hayes had shared the story with herself and Evan.

Daisy began to take a greater interest in her dinner. "It makes sense to search together, does it not? Especially in the Wild West."

May Lin was intrigued in spite of herself. "But I saw no Canton girl with your party. Is she still aboard ship?"

"No, she is in Santa Fe. At least, I think she is. I hope she and her friends will come here." Her cheeks colored in the light of the festival lanterns strung overhead. "She and a boy named Davey stowed away on the flying conveyance of a—a snake-oil salesman. After that, it seemed a good idea to travel together."

A Canton girl looking for a relative was one thing. That occurred fairly often in this port city, where the steamships brought people from the Middle Kingdom down the coast from Victoria daily. But a Canton girl who would stow away on a flying machine?

May Lin found herself wishing she might meet such a person, and congratulate her on her ingenuity.

"And this friend?" she asked, because that blush told her the story so far lacked a few pertinent details. May Lin liked her stories to be resolved. Stories, and mechanical projects, and … and … She glanced at the royal table, but his back was to her and he was talking with that Churchill female.

Bah.

"The friend who owns the flying conveyance and has the power to make a woman blush?" May Lin prompted, when Daisy did not speak.

The girl's color deepened even more. "Goodness. You are a plainspoken person, are you not?"

"When I lived in the canyons, plain speaking was normal among us. Sometimes it could save a life. Now that I am at court," May Lin said, "it can be useful still. Like a saw, to cut through all manner of male fabrications and smoke screens. And like a gentle hand, to remind another that it may be healthy to speak of that which makes us blush."

"What makes you blush, Madame President of the Viceregal Society of Engineers?"

She must not look. Indeed, she must not.

Blast.

Somehow her unwilling gaze was dragged toward him once again. Only this time, as though he felt it, he turned. His dark eyes swept the crowd, then found her and Daisy at the edge of the terrace, the lights of the city behind them.

He bowed to them, an inclination of no more than an inch.

And then Miss Churchill said something, and he returned his smiling attention to her.

"Ah," said Daisy Linden, following her gaze there and back again. "I see we have something in common."

No. This was May Lin's secret alone. "Tell me about him. This snake-oil salesman."

"He does not really sell snake oil," Daisy said awkwardly in the wake of this rebuff. "He concocts herbal remedies. He nearly graduated from Harvard with a degree in chemistry, but when he blew up the building by accident, he was expelled."

May Lin was impressed. She had no idea what Harvard might be, but blowing up buildings was right up her creek. "I should like to meet him."

Now the girl left off blushing and only looked miserable. "I do not know if I will see him again. We have not seen one another in some weeks. More time has passed than I expected when we parted. And so I wrote to him before we left Bodie, but I fear I may have been ... too precipitate in my expressions of—of—" She ground to a halt. "Oh, bother it. I told him of my feelings and I think it may have been a mistake."

"Would your feelings have frightened him off?" May Lin asked. Plain speaking was getting them somewhere.

"I fear so," Daisy whispered. "My sister says that the repairs to his conveyance are simply taking longer than expected, but ..."

"Repairs will do that," May Lin said encouragingly. She was not often in a position to comfort someone on matters of the heart. *Las brujas* had a much more practical and enjoyable way of relating to the lovers they took. She tried to imagine

Ella Bilbao weeping on her shoulder about Honoria, and could not.

"Never mind," she said at last. "A man who could be frightened away by honest feelings is better left to his own devices."

"I am sure you are right," Daisy said faintly. She cleared her throat. "How long have you served the Viceroy?"

She could not help it—May Lin's gaze turned cool. "I do not serve anyone. It pleases me to assist him. He does not command any *bruja*."

If Daisy had been sad before, she was truly distressed now. "I beg your pardon, madame. I did not mean to offend."

"I am no madame. You may use my name, if you please, like anyone else, riverman or prince."

To May Lin's surprise, Daisy did not turn and leave her, but smiled bravely instead. "I should like that. I am drowning in a sea of titles as it is."

"They begin to grow on you after a while." May Lin leaned on the lacy stone parapet, very much aware of the drop of fifty feet to the flagged courtyard below. "When in doubt, Isabela can be depended on to help. That girl could have been a leader among the witches had she been born to a different family. And Lady San Gregorio, she is one of us also. You see her there, on the Viceroy's other side, with Ella Bilbao, her love and companion."

"They are both so beautiful," Daisy said. "So happy. Her ladyship is half-sister to the Viceroy, I understand?"

"Yes, his father used her mother against her will, and Honoria was the result. She was the spy called Joe, who was imprisoned with Evan and Barnaby Hayes and a man called Dutch in the south."

"Ah," Daisy said on a slow breath of understanding. "Now it is becoming clear."

"You may go to any of those three should you require something. Isabela, Honoria, and Ella are the pillars who hold up the Viceroy, despite what his hovering cloud of churchmen think, gliding about in their black robes, silently watching and making sins out of every little thing."

"So my sister and I might apply to one of these ladies for help in finding a clue as to my father's whereabouts?" Hope was brightening her face to prettiness. "Perhaps you know that he was the man you spoke of. They called him Dutch in the gaol. Our last information was that he planned to work his way north on a ship from the Barbary Coast."

Now May Lin understood the reason for her absorption with the view. "Please do not tell me you plan to go down there."

The despair, which had been dissolved by interest and hope, now returned to the girl's gaze. "I must. You do not understand—we must find him. He has lost his memory."

"How?"

"He was beaten by—" She dropped her voice as one of the grandees passed by. "By the Californio soldiers. And impressed into the work crews to build the dam."

The dam that Alice and Ian Hollys had blown up, with the help of May Lin's own inventions. But better that remain one of her secrets, too.

"He remembers nothing? Not even you?" she asked instead.

"I understand that bits and pieces are coming back, but in the meantime, he is wandering lost and alone in this strange country, and it breaks my heart to think of it."

May Lin had never known a father, but the loss of her mother was still a ragged hole in her own heart. This young woman could hardly march down to the docks to ask questions. She would be stolen and used just as brutally as ever Tia Clara had been, and then killed. Nor could May Lin go there any longer. While she was perfectly capable of protecting herself, she was too recognizable, with too many enemies in the church who would seize their advantage in a moment, and blame some poor longshoreman for the crime.

"Do you suppose I might ask one of the ladies for an armed guard?" Daisy asked, clearly becoming alarmed at May Lin's protracted silence.

"No sailor in his right mind would speak with you under those circumstances," May Lin said. "And if they did, they would lie, in hopes of payment. No, I have a better idea. I will put about your story among the Canton dock workers and laundresses."

Daisy looked as though she hardly dared hope that such help could be given simply for the asking. "Would you? I have a picture of him, if that would help."

"It would indeed. I can have copies made. There is a skilled artist in the Canton district who has invented a kind of daguerreotype camera for the purpose of replicating documents. The more people who see your father's face, the more memories might be jogged."

"Oh, thank you." Daisy clasped her hands around her napkin, which she had been twisting into a tortured spindle. "How can I ever repay such kindness?"

May Lin could think of a hundred ways, but she chose the one upon which all the others depended. "Try not to be killed while you are here. That would make a good beginning."

CHAPTER 3

11:30 p.m.

aisy could hardly believe that help had been offered so practically, so without ceremony, after they had been in the city barely half a day. It was almost too good to be true.

But no, she could not think like that. Not when May Lin, as prickly and unpredictable as she seemed to be, had seemed honestly to wish her and Frederica well. And her parting shot —about not being killed—was surely just hyperbole. No guest of the Viceroy could be in real danger in a city that, outside of the waterfront, was so beautiful and festive, could they?

May Lin, so slender in regal red robes embroidered in glossy black silks, was a study in contrasts, to be sure. Oh, how Daisy wished she had the courage to ask her to sit for a portrait! The confidence in the tilt of her chin, the pride in the set of her head with its crown of roses, the intelligence in those eyes that missed nothing ... what a delight they would be to paint. And she had a tiny pot of Venetian Red with her that would be perfect for that robe with its waist-cinching sash. The red would go down first, and then once that had dried, she could mix in just a bit of blue for the shadows, and—

"Daisy!" She jumped, and came out of her abstraction to meet Freddie's exasperated gaze. "You were a thousand miles away," her sister said, turning to look out at the harbor in the distance. "There, perhaps? The Barbary Coast."

"Earlier, I was," she confessed, "but my mind was much more agreeably engaged just now. I was imagining how I might paint May Lin."

"The lady who leads the society of engineers?"

"The very one. But Freddie, listen. She has offered to help us. We may not go down to the docks ourselves—"

"We certainly may not."

"—but she will put out the word among those who work there, to see what breadcrumbs may come back to us. I am to give her Papa's portrait so that she may circulate copies. Is that not wonderful news?"

Freddie's eyebrows were by now rising practically into her hair. "What did you do that prompted a stranger—well placed, I will admit, but still, a stranger—to make such a kind offer? My goodness, Daisy, no one has even brought up the subject yet with the Viceroy."

What did his knowledge or ignorance have to do with anything? "I do not think the Viceroy needs to know of our search, do you? He has a country to manage. After the war, the fate of a missing man is likely all too common a concern for many families, even yet."

Freddie gazed at her, perplexed. "Why should he not be told, if his privy councilor has been?"

"Because Papa knew Mr. Douglas in gaol. To my knowledge, the Viceroy never met him. If Mr. Douglas offers his help, I will accept it gladly, but we needn't bother a prince with—"

"Daisy!" came Peony Churchill's lovely alto voice. They turned from the view to see her on the Viceroy's arm, passing through the flower-covered arch to the terrace and pacing companionably toward them. "I have been telling His Serene Highness about your search for your dear papa."

"Too late," murmured Freddie, as they both dropped to the flagged stones in deep curtseys.

"Please rise, ladies," the young man said. "While certain formalities must be observed, the need to curtsey every time you see me is not one of them."

Goodness. He sounded like an ordinary man, not a prince at all. "Thank you, sir."

"Between us, Evan and Barnaby and I have put His Serene Highness into the picture, Daisy," Peony told her.

"I must say, you remind me a great deal of my Tia Clara," the prince said to them. "She braved more difficulties and dangers than any woman I have ever known, and all for love of her child."

He really was a handsome young man, if a little thin. In the light of the lanterns his cheekbones cast intriguing shadows on his cheeks, and his glossy black hair fell over his forehead in studied disarray. He was dressed in a manner similar to Evan, in a black wool suit with a short jacket and the ever-present silver medallions, with the addition of a blindingly white formal shirt and a red sash that crossed his chest on the diagonal. A gold starburst with an inscription hung on a smaller red ribbon between his collar points.

He seemed quite taken with Peony. But then, was there anybody who wasn't? Poor Barnaby. Daisy hoped his heart was less vulnerable than his body had been in recent days.

"She must have been a very great lady, sir," Freddie ventured. "Your Tia Clara."

"She is indeed." The Viceroy smiled, his dark eyes sparkling. "But she would laugh at the thought of it. She is a river witch, you see. One of the fabled *brujas* who helped me save my kingdom. I suspect you and she would have much in common when it comes to bravery and ingenuity."

"My goodness, sir, what has Miss Churchill been telling you?" Daisy managed, hardly knowing where to look.

"Only what I have heard from fairly reliable sources," Peony said with airy confidence, "such as myself. Now, sir, you must tell them what you told us."

"I am commanded," he said, with such a comical look of helplessness that Daisy nearly smiled through her horror at Peony's familiarity. "Indeed, for friends of Evan and Barnaby I would do anything in my power. You believe your father to have taken ship at Buena Vista Cove?"

Daisy nodded. "To the best of our information, sir."

"Then I will send a company of men in the morning to make inquiries of every shipping office and captain's cabin on the waterfront."

Goodness! The ease with which royalty could command what would have taken her and Freddie the rest of the month to attempt, even leaving out the part about being killed.

But she had not forgotten May Lin's opinion on the subject. "Sir, you are too kind. But—"

"Think nothing of it. I owe your friends much more than I can ever repay."

"But—"

"Miss Churchill, I believe I hear the orchestra once more. Will you favor me?"

"Sir," Daisy said, raising her voice before she lost his attention for the rest of the evening. "I thank you with all my heart, but Madame May Lin has already put plans into motion. I—she—I would not wish you or your men to be inconvenienced when the matter is already being seen to."

He had turned at the mention of May Lin's name, and at the end of this breathless recitation, one eyebrow rose. "You have spoken to May Lin of this?"

"Yes, sir."

"And what solution does she offer?"

"M-much the same as yours, sir, only on a smaller, more discreet scale."

"Be specific, *senorita*, if you please."

Now she was the one commanded, and dared not disobey. "She proposes to put the word out among the working people of the docks." May Lin had not told her to keep it a secret. So Daisy elaborated further. "The Canton people, sir, such as longshoremen and laundresses. To see if information may be gleaned from them."

"There are Canton people on the docks?" he asked after a moment.

"Apparently, sir."

"It seems a roundabout way of gaining information that your men could elicit in a single morning," Miss Churchill said. "Daisy, did you accept her offer?"

"I did." Then, anxiously, "Was I wrong to do so?"

The Viceroy shook his head. "Not wrong. But there are more efficient ways to accomplish a task than the covert and roundabout. May Lin, you see, is a skilled engineer, and is all efficiency in that sphere. Outside of it, I think she remains more witch than courtier."

Peony gave a merry laugh.

"I thought her admirable, sir," Daisy said, concealing her irritation at that laugh as best she could. "And you said yourself that it was not courtiers who helped you recover your kingdom, but witches."

Daisy distinctly heard Freddie draw in a horrified breath. Wide-eyed, Peony touched her mouth with her fingertips.

The Viceroy inclined his head. "Touché," he said. "Miss Churchill, shall we?"

Peony had time to cast a worried glance over her shoulder at Daisy before the prince took her into the brilliantly lit reception room and swept her into a waltz.

"Do you think he will still help us?" Freddie slipped her hand into Daisy's and squeezed it, as though to offer comfort.

"I do not know." Somehow she had managed to commit a *faux pas* by speaking the truth as May Lin had. "I wish he would not. May Lin says that an official inquiry would only elicit bribes and lies."

"And you believe her?"

"It is difficult to know whom to believe." Turning her back upon the dancing, she gazed out toward the harbor, and beyond it, to the east. The waning moon rose in a sky that was still as empty as it had been this morning, save for the stars. "But does it not seem more likely that a witch would know more of discovering information than a prince?"

A witch would discover information different from that of a prince, but such was the only certainty Daisy could manage. It was a relief when Detective Hayes joined them on the terrace, and she could think of something other than having a man's back turned upon one.

"What are you ladies doing out here?" Barnaby asked. "After all that fuss buying clothes in Reno, it seems a shame not to show them off."

Daisy did like her new gown, a tawny silk confection with lace flounces as fine as spiderwebs about the modestly low neckline, and the new cap sleeves made of the same lace. It had been worth every penny of the gold piece she had handed over to the modiste. Her poor striped blue could now do as a day dress, after all it had been through. But as for dancing …

"You are not dancing, either, Detective," Daisy pointed out.

"I cannot, as you know very well." He gave a rueful smile as he indicated the sling. "Miss Churchill is quite right to abandon me for greener pastures."

That was taking forbearance too far. What woman of principle would not rather stay with the man she had been nursing for days and days, even if it were only to entertain him as they watched the dancing together? Peony had given every indication of a *tendre* for Detective Hayes.

Then again, Daisy had never been asked to dance by a prince, and Peony probably had.

"Daisy has just committed the deadly sin of telling a prince the truth," Freddie confided to the detective. In a few words, she brought Daisy's foolishness to life for him.

But he only laughed. "He has heard speeches every bit as truthful from other friends who mean him well. And if he does not see that now, he will after a bit of reflection. Do not trouble your head about it, Daisy. After all, you did no more than agree with him."

"But is there no way of stopping an official interrogation

of the people on the docks?" Daisy asked, coming back to the main point. "May Lin was quite firm about its less than desirable results."

"I suppose not, at this point," he admitted. "In any case, Evan tells me that in two days' time, he and May Lin are to meet with a number of the bishops on the subject of steam landaus. She may not have time to speak with any of the Canton people until afterward."

Daisy nodded, though her stomach sank in disappointment. "Perhaps by then, anyone with information to share will think themselves safer with a laundress than a soldier."

"Detective … there are steam landaus here?" Freddie asked, fixing upon the trivial in a most maddening fashion. "I have not seen even one—only horse-drawn carriages. Even the water carriers for fire are pulled by enormous Clydesdales. I feel sorry for them. These hills are steeper than the dales of Yorkshire."

"Landaus are not in common use yet, but it is only a matter of time." Barnaby leaned his back against the terrace wall, watching the dancers within.

Under the sparkling chandeliers, Peony's new burgundy silk ballgown made a contrast to the more traditional gowns of the other women with their beribboned tiers of flounces. The fishtail of gold ruffles in its split back swirled in and out as the prince guided her adroitly among the other couples.

"First they must have actual roads instead of cart tracks," Barnaby went on after a moment, "after which the landaus may travel without falling into mudholes from which they cannot be extracted. Evan has been quite vocal upon the subject."

"They may pilot their landaus into the sea for all it

concerns us," Daisy said impatiently. "Every day we wait for information, Papa may be drawing farther away from us."

"Daisy," Barnaby said gently, "do not take it into your head to go down to Buena Vista Cove and make inquiries yourself. It is far too dangerous."

"I am well aware of that," she told him. In truth, she would not dare go without one of the aforesaid armed guard. "Perhaps I may go with the soldiers."

"I daresay you would only be in their way," Freddie said. "And we do not speak the language."

Frustration crested like a wave in her chest, and she turned abruptly to gaze out in the direction of the harbor. "Then what may I do?" Tears welled in her eyes, but she blinked them back. *Oh, Papa! Where are you? Will we ever see you again?*

"I would practice my waltz steps, if I were you," Barnaby drawled. "For here come two young grandees with white gloves and eager expressions. It appears that, since you are honored guests of His Serene Highness, the two of you are about to be asked to dance."

CHAPTER 4

SUNDAY, SEPTEMBER 22, 1895

3:30 p.m.

Saturday was a day filled with entertainments and culminating in another dinner and ball, none of which Daisy and Freddie could see their way out of. May Lin seemed to be the only one who could, for she was nowhere to be seen. On Sunday afternoon, Daisy and Freddie and the two youngest Boyles, Luke and Rebecca, took tea on a rug laid on the trampled grass of the airfield. The weather was too warm to stay aboard ship, though Daisy was less interested in tea than in painting the vista from this unusual island vantage point. Even as she watched, a rolling bank of fog seemed to be engulfing the city like a silent avalanche. How was one to paint it—to capture the eerie nature of it as it blotted out homes and hills?

Transfixed by the difficulty of executing what she saw— ought one to gently sponge away the pigment, or simply apply it more sparingly?—she heard Freddie's shouts of laughter as she and the twins started a game of badminton. Their parents, as well as Timothy and Dinah, had gone into the city with Peony and Detective Hayes. His Serene Highness had offered one of the palace's guest houses to Evan's party of friends, and so they had gone to inspect it. It was sure to be delightful, but Daisy would only have tortured herself with unfinished business had she gone.

The only person she really wanted to speak to was May Lin, but that lady was again not to be one of the party. With any luck, the reason for her absence was because she was meeting with her acquaintance in the humbler portions of the city. Though how could that be? The portrait of Papa that Daisy had painted from memory for just this purpose was still tucked in the back of her sketchbook.

Daisy sighed, and turned her gaze once more to the fog.

And below it, saw a lone rider on a *mecaballo* boarding the pontoon bridge. A lone rider with such erect, proud carriage and mastery of her mount that Daisy recognized her even at this distance.

May Lin.

"Freddie!" she cried.

"Daisy—look!"

Freddie's voice rode over her own, and something in its tone brought Daisy to her feet, laying aside her sketchbook and brush to run to the opposite side of the field, where the water of the great bay beyond sparkled in the sun.

And above the water, coming in on a long approach, was the most familiar and welcome sight in the world. From a buff-and-scarlet striped fuselage depended a most extraordinary conveyance—half apothecary shop and half steam landau. But now, as it drew nearer, she saw that it was less apothecary shop and more … what? Gondola?

"My goodness, he and Tobin have changed the conveyance almost entirely," Freddie said, waving in excitement. "I wonder if it may still be detached and piloted once it is on the ground?"

But Daisy could not answer. For welling up in her being was a joy, a relief, a jubilation so intense that she could not speak if she tried. He had come! William Barnicott had received her letter sent from Bodie, and, instead of fleeing the country as she had been imagining so pathetically, had understood her feelings and come! Perhaps he even shared them. What a miracle. Could any sight be more wonderful?

Her corset seemed to squeeze her heart and her lungs simultaneously, forcing her to take deep breaths lest she faint from sheer happiness.

"Does this field have more mooring irons?" Freddie's practicality brought her down to earth with a bump.

Still, it took a moment to find an answer. "Yes—under the wheels of the mast."

So it was that she and Freddie had the pleasure of catching the ropes that fell from the undercarriage of the balloon, drawing the conveyance to the ground, and knotting them about the irons. Daisy's heart beat practically out of her chest as the pilot's door was flung open and William leaped out.

"Daisy! Freddie! I nearly fell out the port when I saw you. How is this possible? Whose ship is this? Are you well?"

Freddie ran into his arms for an enormous hug.

But Daisy hung back, assailed by a sudden attack of nerves and blushes and the dousing certainty that her happiness of moments before was merely a delusion, that after all these weeks, any affection he might once have felt for her had cooled to that of a brother.

Freddie squealed and snatched first Davey and then Lin into a hug as they slid out of the doors in turn.

"What, no greeting for me?" William grinned at Daisy, that mischievous triangular grin that had figured so often in her daydreams. "I got your letter. We lifted at dawn, and here I am."

That smile could not lie. Nor could the warmth of happiness that sparkled in his sherry-colored eyes.

"William," she choked out, and in a moment was in his arms, sobbing against his chest as though her heart would break. So warm he was. So solid, so safe.

"What is this?" he said tenderly, smoothing her hair. "Has something happened? Have you had bad news about your father?"

"No," she wailed in a fresh paroxysm of tears. "I am just so happy to see you."

With a chuckle, he held her close until the storm passed, and then fished a handkerchief out of the pocket of his driving coat. "And I am very glad to see you. Your letter could not have been more welcome."

"Was it?" She blew her nose and mopped her face. "All of it?"

"He especially liked the spoony parts," Davey called scornfully, from where he was inspecting the details of *Iris*'s underside. "But is it really true that Barnaby Hayes was shot?"

"Come here, you rascal," Daisy said, "and greet me properly. When he comes back, Detective Hayes will show you his sling, and if you are very good, his wound."

"Topping!" The boy wriggled in her arms and gave her a smacking kiss. "Who are they?"

The Boyle twins stood on the gangway as though prepared to defend it to the death against the interlopers.

"Come and be introduced. But first, I must greet Lin."

The girl allowed herself to be hugged, and then at the end, Daisy was gratified when her thin arms slipped about her waist and she hugged her back. "I am glad that you are not shot, too," she said shyly.

"That makes two of us, though it was a close call," Daisy confided. "Freddie and I will tell you all about the standoff at the stamp."

"That sounds like one of the *Tales of a Medicine Man* by An Educated Gentleman," Freddie said. "Though it is only now that I can say so. At the time, I was certain I was going to die."

"That's my kind of story," Davey told her as they approached the gangway.

"Mine too," Lucas said. "I already heard it, though."

Daisy indicated the children. "Mr. William Barnicott, may I present Miss Rebecca and Master Lucas Boyle. And this is Master Davey—" Daisy stopped. "Do you know, Davey, I do not believe you have ever told me your surname."

For a moment, it looked as though he might refuse to do so now. Then he tilted his chin defiantly. "My mum said it were Fletcher. My dad and her were married legal and proper, even if he did scarper after."

"I have no doubt they were," Daisy said, absorbing these facts. "Your mother, I believe, was a woman of scruples and would have accepted nothing less." She returned to her introductions as though William's eyebrows had not lifted so high they had disappeared into the tumble of curls on his forehead. "And this is Miss Lin Yang."

"Yang Lin-Bai," Lin corrected her. "You must say it properly."

Daisy repeated it, and Rebecca gave a curtsey, odd though it looked since she was wearing an aeronaut's canvas pants, and Lucas bowed.

"Mr. Barnicott," Rebecca said shyly, "may we look at your conveyance? For I have never seen anything like it."

William laughed. "I cannot say I have seen anything like it, either. It began as a traveling shop attached to a balloon, but I am not quite certain what it might be now. The children will show you."

And off they scampered, trailed by Freddie, whose sense of delicacy had clearly dictated that Daisy and William ought to be left alone.

"Would you like some tea?" Daisy asked. "This pot is cold, but I can make another."

"I would, if I may watch you."

"Watch me?" She stood, teapot in both hands, gazing at him in puzzlement. "Whatever for?"

"For the simple pleasure of it," he said baldly. "And it will comfort me while you tell me all about the standoff at the stamp. I will have proof of your survival in a pot of hot tea."

"Come along to the galley, then," she said. "I will show you the delights of *Iris*, tell you all about her owner, and harrow up your soul with our adventures in Bodie."

But before she could set foot on the gangway, they heard a familiar shivering sound, and across the field the silver legs of the *mecaballo* flashed in the sun.

"Good heavens!" Daisy said. "I completely forgot."

Half an hour ago, the sight of May Lin had been all that

she wanted. But with the arrival of William and the children, it had gone completely out of her mind.

"Miss Linden," May Lin called in greeting. With the manipulation of several levers, she brought the mechanical horse from a full gallop to a graceful rocking halt in front of them.

Davey whooped and tore over to see. "What a fine rider you are, miss! Is this one of the river witches' *mecaballos*? Why, it's only got hooves. Where are its scythes?"

May Lin slid to the ground. The wind caught her red robes with a snap, and ruffled the silk petals of the two red roses pinned over her ear. Her hair, worn loose today, billowed out like a blue-black sail. Thirteen-year-old Lin gasped, and not for the first time, Daisy wished she could seize her paintbox and sketchbook and capture the beauty of this woman.

May Lin regarded Davey with gravity. "I see you are acquainted with the *mecaballos*, sir. Where did you see them?"

"In Santa Fe, miss. The Navapai ride 'em, innit? They got them from the witches after the Rose Rebellion. Is that what you did?" May Lin smiled a predatory smile and Davey gulped. "Beg pardon, miss. The roses—are you *una bruja* your own self?"

The smile warmed to real approval. "I do appreciate perspicacity in a man. I am indeed *una bruja*." She bowed, one hand still upon the withers of the mechanical. "May Lin, sir, at your service."

A soft sound came from behind Daisy. Lin, hearing her own name on another's lips.

Daisy turned, looking from one to the other. At the delicacy of the cheekbones, the shape of the mouth. At the whorl of hair over the right temple, causing a wave in an otherwise smooth, straight fall of hair. At the pride in the carriage, coupled with reserve about the eyes.

But surely such traits were common.

"Madame President," Daisy said, "may I make known to you Master Davey Fletcher, and beside him, Yang Lin-Bai."

May Lin's gaze locked upon the girl's face, and a shiver ran over Daisy's skin that had nothing to do with the pleasant breeze off the bay.

"I did not introduce myself correctly," the other woman said softly. "There are some things it is often wiser to keep to oneself, is that not true? But not among friends. I am Yang May Lin."

A silence blew among them, filled with the cries of sea birds and the creak of the ropes. Lin stared at the newcomer, searching her face as though it were a map and she had lost her way.

"You will find that Yang is a common enough name in these parts," May Lin went on as though there had been no pause. "Daisy, will you introduce me to the gentleman?"

Daisy recovered herself and did so. Then she went on, "May Lin is the president of the newly established Viceregal Society of Engineers, William. I must confess I told her of your unfortunate history with chemistry and laboratories."

"Which I appreciated immensely." She shook William's hand with a return of the wicked smile. "I should very much like the recipe."

"I will cudgel my brain to produce it," he said with a laugh. "Though I hardly think you will find it useful here."

"One never knows," May Lin said airily. "Daisy, I have come to fetch the portrait of your father. With His Serene Highness and the rest of your party engaged, I find myself at liberty for an hour, and may speak with my printer friend in the city."

Daisy put the cold teapot down and snatched up her sketchbook. She slipped the portrait out of the back and handed it over. "Thank you ever so much. Though I must warn you that the Viceroy told me last night he would send a detachment to question people on the docks."

"Yes, I know." Carefully, May Lin tucked the small painting into the leather wallet attached to her belt. "But that does not signify. My questions will be directed to a different set of people. Would you like to place a wager on which will produce more useful results?" Again that catlike smile.

"I should not dare," Daisy said. "However, it has been my experience that women talk amongst themselves, and networks of news form that are invisible to the captains and princes of this world."

"Mrs. Captain Stan would agree with you," May Lin said with a nod.

"Who is that?" Freddie asked.

"When the river gave her to us, she was called Meredith. And when she became the Iron Dragon and started the Rose Rebellion, she was called Gloria. Had the prince actually married her, she would have been called Vicereine."

"Are you talking about Mrs. Fremont?" Rebecca Boyle demanded, from the gangway a few feet off. "She ent no dragon, and don't you be casting such names at her."

May Lin gazed at the girl, who visibly straightened her spine to glare back. "Are you a friend of hers, child?"

"I am. We all are. She sold Miss Churchill this vessel."

"We won't hear a word against her," Lucas added, with a

stormy frown, as though he wished he had a revolver to hand at that very moment.

"You will find that she wears the name proudly," May Lin told them gravely. "And you are brave to show your loyalty so openly. Perhaps too brave. For there are those in this city who are no friends of hers. Keep faith in your heart, and keep watch."

Their eyes widened as though she were a prophet, with her robes snapping about her in the wind.

May Lin turned to Daisy. "I will return the portrait to you as soon as the ommatographs are made. And perhaps we might add another errand to that one. This girl is the one you told me of, isn't she?"

Daisy nodded, and touched Lin's shoulder as she said to her, "I hope you do not mind, but I told May Lin that you were looking for your family."

"I don't mind," Lin said, moving out from under Daisy's hand. "But it makes no nevermind. I am right back where I began, and I know she's not here."

"Have you been here before?" May Lin asked in some surprise.

Lin shrugged. "I grew up here. The padres at the mission school nearest the Canton district taught me my letters and numbers. English, too."

"Did they." It was not a question. "As it happens, I am to meet a number of padres at Nuestra Señora de las Estrellas tomorrow. I go to them so that they do not give the appearance of having been summoned by a woman. They prefer instead to put me in my place. If you would overlook this behavior, perhaps you would like to come with me, and inquire of the teachers there? They may have news of your relative if it has been some time since you lived here."

"It has," Lin allowed cautiously. "Go with you?" Anxiously, she looked to William, though Daisy could not imagine that she required his permission. Lin did not ask anyone for anything. Especially that.

"Will she be safe?" William asked.

"With me?" May Lin's brows rose. "I am advisor to the Viceroy."

William flushed at having been misunderstood. "I beg your pardon, ma'am. Of course she is safe with you. I meant—in San Francisco de Asis generally. I know of its reputation. Where women are concerned." He stumbled to an awkward halt.

"Things have improved in that quarter," May Lin said, the mask of offended arrogance falling away so completely Daisy almost wondered if it had been there at all. Perhaps she donned it in the company of men, and took it off when speaking with women. "Women are rarely attacked in the streets now if they happen to go out of doors unescorted. That said, I will have two members of the prince's guard with me just to be prudent. The mission is close to the oldest part of town, where new ideas have not penetrated quite as thoroughly as they have in the palace."

"Then I will go with you," Lin said shyly. "Thank you."

May Lin nodded. "I will send one of my escort to fetch you at nine of the clock. I am due at the mission at ten. I have allowed them two hours to fuss about the Viceroy's wishes for the future, and then we may escape to see my friend the printer. By then, I hope that the ommatographs will have been produced and I can distribute them."

"Thank you, May Lin," Daisy said, impulsively taking her hand in both of hers. "We are so grateful for your help."

"Would you like to come as well?" May Lin squeezed her hand and let it fall. "The padres will not allow a woman into the cloister or the school, but the church is very beautiful and open to all." She tilted her head toward the abandoned paintbox on the blanket, and the now dry but half-finished painting. "There is a particularly lovely ceiling—the reason it is called Our Lady of the Stars."

"I should be delighted," Daisy said at once. Fancy being invited to paint for two hours instead of snatching moments here and there! "Freddie?"

"I—I think not," Freddie said. "Too many—people for me."

Churches usually meant churchyards, which meant graves, which meant the souls of the dead. She ought to have thought more carefully before she spoke, and saved Freddie this embarrassment.

"Of course, dearest," she said hastily. "I am sure Miss Churchill will have a plan for some amusement, and you may join them."

May Lin made a sound halfway between a cough and a hiss, then seemed to recover. "Until tomorrow, then."

And without waiting for a reply, she put her foot upon a peg and mounted her *mecaballo* in one smooth motion. A lever here, another there, a puff of steam, and she wheeled it about with some trickery of the knees. The silvery singing of its limbs faded away down the slope.

"I wish I could ride like that," Davey said with envy.

"If you ask her, she might teach you," Lin said. "She seems a generous person."

"Maybe," he said in a tone that conveyed his disbelief that

she would bother. "Say, Daisy, any chance of tea? We ent had a bite since Reno and my stomach is sticking to my backbone."

"Good heavens." Daisy put away her sketchbook, stuck the two brushes through her chignon so that she could wash them in the galley, and picked up the cold teapot once more. "Come along aboard *Iris*. Rebecca, Lucas, you too. Goodness knows when we will see your family, but your mother can be counted upon to have the makings of a proper lunch."

CHAPTER 5

MONDAY, SEPTEMBER 23, 1895

9:05 a.m.

Despite what she had led Mr. Barnicott to believe, and despite her recently conferred rank and status, even May Lin did not dare go about San Francisco de Asis on foot. Of course she would be set upon, though perhaps the danger was not as great as it had been in years past. While a Californio woman might now venture to the market on her own, a Canton woman was still fair game.

Even one who advised the Viceroy.

Her conveyance based upon the design of the spider that had once scaled the walls of the river canyons was not yet finished. So today May Lin made do with the next best thing: the *mecaballo*, with Daisy's young friend up behind, and an armed escort on either side mounted on live animals. They made quite an impressive procession, and people cleared the way before them not out of respect for her, but because she had put the scythes back on the mechanical's legs.

Once May Lin was up, the girl had mounted the mechanical with no assistance from the men, finding the postillion foot pegs with the ease of one with previous experience. She had tucked her Navapai dress up under her legs without being asked, so that it did not get caught in the relentless mechanisms of the hindquarters, and had the sense to take a firm hold on May Lin's leather belt.

"You have ridden before," May Lin remarked as they dismounted the pontoon bridge and began to navigate the crowded, busy streets.

"Yes," the girl said. "In Santa Fe."

"And you are not afraid?"

"You are not a poor rider, so no, I am not afraid."

May Lin laughed as the mechanical settled into a smooth scissoring gait that did not halt for man or beast. May Lin's curiosity about her companion was increasing with every step. She stopped pointing out landmarks, and in the same tone, inserted a question. "On what street did you grow up, Lin?"

"Stouts Alley, ma'am."

"Ah, we have already passed it."

"I know."

"Perhaps when my meeting is concluded, and you have canvassed the teachers at the mission school, we might collect the ommatographs from my colleague and return there."

"Why? My aunt, the person I am looking for, is not there and I do not really want to visit with the neighbors."

"How do you know she is not there, or that the neighbors have not had news of her?"

"Because she left San Francisco de Asis years ago. Before I was born. The brute she was engaged to marry took her dowry and threw her from his house."

Could this be a more common event than even May Lin had believed? "Why on earth would he do that after she had come all the way from the Middle Kingdom?"

"He wanted the gold more than a wife, my father said. Papa came later, to find her, but he never could. And then last winter, both he and my mother died."

Last winter. "Of the typhoid?" Hundreds had died, both Canton and Californio, and the old Viceroy had evacuated his precious son to Rancho San Gregorio for safety. May Lin had been safe in the river canyons then, with nothing more to fear than the occasional incursion of Californio soldiers, quickly and silently dispatched. "I am very sorry, child. I lost my mother, too, but not of typhoid. I miss her dreadfully."

At her waist, she felt Lin take a firmer grip upon the belt, as though bolstering her resolve.

"How did she die?"

"Snake bite. Even Tia Clara could not save her. But she died as she had lived, free and on her own terms. I miss her, but I do not mourn her. She taught me everything I know about engineering." May Lin laughed, unable to keep it free of bitterness. "Had circumstances been different and this kingdom not so pigheaded and old-fashioned, she might have been the Minister of Magnificent Devices herself."

"Is the prince pigheaded?"

Was he? Those brown eyes, sparkling with intelligence and keen interest in her plans. Those long-fingered, tanned hands on the blueprints, pointing out this connection and that possibility. That maddening, bred-into-the-bone arrogance.

"Oh, yes. He is the worst of all, though in a different way. He is too aware of his rank and breeding, and as you can imagine, I have no patience with it."

"William Barnicott thinks Daisy is pigheaded, but in a different way, too. Stubborn. Fixed upon her goal. But he loves her anyway."

May Lin tightened her grip on the guidance handles. "I am not speaking of love."

"No, ma'am. There is the mission, up ahead."

It was. And there were the padres, gathering at the gates like a murder of crows.

May Lin brought the *mecaballo* to a graceful halt just close enough to force them to step back into the grounds, and slid to the flagged pavement without assistance. So did Lin, and as though they had rehearsed it, they both shook their skirts into order.

"You remember how to get to the school?" she said to the girl.

"It has only been a little over a year. I remember very well."

"Off you go, then. Daisy will be painting in the church this morning, so perhaps you and she will run into one another."

Lin did not answer. She did not push through the flock of prelates to cross the leafy, sun-dappled courtyard, but instead trotted down to the street door of the school building and was admitted by the porter.

With a sigh, May Lin turned to the man waiting with a frown of impatience, and bowed. "Good morning, Bishop," she said in the Californio tongue.

"Señorita La Presidente," he said politely, and without further ceremony, turned and indicated she should follow him into the small refectory. The tables had been pushed together to seat them all. Happily for them, the presence of a woman could be tolerated because it was not a private space.

The most aggravating hour followed, which could only be

likened to a man with a tow line attempting to pull a disabled steamboat upriver against a spring current. How was it possible for men of this day and age to be so resistant to changes that would only do the country good? It was not as though a steam landau were an airship, for goodness sake, and guilty of flying in the face of God. It would be as ground-bound as any vegetable cart, puttering down a road minding its own business and doing no more harm than occasionally, perhaps, frightening a cow.

She had taught herself to pilot the landau that had come in the hold of the ship built by the Meriwether-Astor Airship Works. She ought to have piloted it over here instead of the *mecaballo*, and shown the wretched prelates that it was not to be feared. Ah well. There would surely be a second meeting, and she would demonstrate then.

In the silence of the present obstinacy, however, she schooled her voice in encouraging, positive notes. "Perhaps your grace would be kind enough to visit the headquarters of the Society, and allow me to show you how harmless a landau truly is. Perhaps you might even enjoy an outing in it—or at least, a turn about the courtyard of the building."

The bishop's eyes widened, but she could not tell if it was fear of such a prospect, or astonishment that she had the nerve to suggest sitting so close to him within a landau's confines.

"I think not," he said frigidly. "I believe this meeting is over. Madame, I understand that a subcommittee wishes to speak with you upon another matter, so I will take my leave." With that, he rose from the head of the table, bowed the requisite number of inches to indicate his awareness of her station and proximity to his prince, and left the room. Most of the padres hurried after him, their sandals slapping anxiously upon the stone floor, their cinctures with the three knots swinging.

With a sigh, May Lin turned to the four remaining monks, who gathered around her in a manner most unlike the others she had met. Why, they were close enough to touch.

The floor seemed to shiver at the very thought—or perhaps that was her own feet, which suddenly felt a desperate need to propel her out of here.

"Padres?" she asked politely, stiffening her knees against the urge to fight her way out of the little circle. "Are we to remove to another room so that they may prepare the tables for the midday meal?"

"We are certainly to remove you," said the one in front of her. "If it is not a sin to waste the bishop's time in this manner, it certainly should be."

"I will see myself out, then," she said, striving for civility. "Please excuse me."

But he did not. "You are a blight upon the face of this city," he hissed, so close that a fleck of saliva landed upon her cheek. "God has commanded us to act, and so we shall."

If they thought to threaten her, they were about to be sadly disillusioned. She slipped her hands into her sleeves and laid them upon the hilts of her knives. Strapped to her forearms in flat leather sheaths, they were invisible from the outside. With a discreet flick of her thumbs, she could unsnap the short leather straps holding them in place and draw his life's blood in less than a second.

"Shall you act in keeping with the rules of gentle San Francisco?" she inquired. "Or of Our Lady of the Stars?"

"Do not sully their holy names!" snapped the monk behind

her. "Pray instead to a merciful God that your death will be quick." His hands closed around her upper arms. Over her shoulder, she got a whiff of the raw onions he must have eaten at breakfast.

Her instinct was to whirl and slash. She could disable all four before they even realized she was armed, but there was yet time for that. She took a preparatory breath, and swayed as the ground seemed to dip.

She couldn't be lightheaded. She had eaten well this morning, and had left her little poison taster in perfect health. Then what—

The earth jerked.

The man behind her gasped, and the one in front glared at her as though this were all her fault. "Have you cast a spell upon us, witch?" he snarled through clenched teeth.

"Yes," she said flippantly. "Intelligence very often seems like magic or prophecy to the terminally stupid."

He hauled back his arm to strike her—

She gripped the handles of her knives—

And the very ground beneath them gave a roar of rage.

A great tearing jerk ripped the stone floor out from under her feet. The man beside her went down, cracking his head on the flags, and she landed on him. With a kick, she rolled away, her hands still caught in her sleeves. By the time she gained her feet, she had freed them, secured her precious knives, and dropped into a crouch.

Only to see out of the corner of her eye something falling. She dodged it—a stone—great mother river, the walls were buckling inward! Had someone bombed the mission? Were they at war?

The outside wall slumped toward her, raining adobe

bricks and plaster everywhere and casting up a huge cloud of dust. Coughing, her eyes filling with tears, she tried to stay on her feet as she cast a panicked glance at the ceiling with its heavy black beams—

The monk who had imprisoned her arms shouted and lunged at her, but a bench slid into his legs of its own volition and knocked them out from under him. The statue of Our Lady at the front of the room leaped from its pedestal and embraced the unconscious monk on the floor.

A trickle of blood pooled between the stones—

—which were tilting out of their masonry as though the floor were a kind of lizard, flexing and lifting its scales as the muscles rippled underneath. May Lin gawked at the spectacle of the stone floor writhing up and down like a snake.

Door, fool! Move!

But there was no longer a door, only a pile of stones.

With a tremendous crack, one of the overhead beams buckled and split.

May Lin screamed and leaped for a gaping hole in the wall, where somehow, inexplicably, the sun still shone, though the grape trellis that formed the *ambulatorio* down one side of the courtyard lay in a tangled heap on the ground. The scent of crushed grapes and agonized stone assaulted her nose for a split second before the floor cracked open under her boots.

She was moving at such a speed that she could not stop.

With a shriek, arms windmilling, her toes gripping the stones fruitlessly, she hung suspended in the air as the crack zigzagged right through the wall to the street and split the building open. Then the earth gave one final shrug and tossed her into the crevasse like a rag doll.

Before she even hit the bottom, the earth jerked the other

way, closed its maw, and all the light vanished as it swallowed her whole.

DAVEY, leading the way fifty feet ahead of William and Daisy, was keeping an eye on the mission bell as a landmark through the streets. They had not left as early as May Lin's party, having decided instead on a more leisurely walk since they had no meeting to go to. Daisy hoped to meet her afterward, and accompany her to the home of the man who made the ommatographs, to see if he had had any news.

She heard a roar, as though a steambus were bearing down upon them.

How could there be a steambus when the roads did not even permit a steam landau? Her hand in the crook of William's elbow, she turned in alarm. What—

The ground jerked under her feet. Instinctively, she clutched William's arm with both hands, with the result that they were thrown to the right, pitched over a low adobe wall, and landed practically on their heads in someone's front garden.

Stunned, Daisy could only gasp, grip the vibrating earth, and gape at the sky, in which clouds of smoke—no, dust—no, both—were swirling and writhing.

"William!" she gasped. "Davey!"

William groaned, prostrate in the crushed remains of an herbaceous border.

Daisy pushed herself to her feet as the chimney of the house in whose garden they had landed crumbled in a waterfall of bricks. "Davey!" she croaked, her throat filled with dust. *"Davey!"*

The air had turned brown in the sunlight. And through it, she heard a great clang and a groan, as though the mission bell had fallen out of its tower and rolled away.

～

PEONY CHURCHILL MADE the final touches to her toilette and proceeded out to the main salon, where Barnaby Hayes waited with ill concealed impatience. But the moment he saw her deep raspberry walking suit, the hem of its coat embroidered ten inches deep in black soutache, a smile found its way to his mouth.

"I suppose it is worth the wait, if one is to accompany a lady so fetchingly dressed."

Pleased, Peony raised her arm to adjust her black hat with its pink and black feathers. Just as she did, the ropes jerked and *Iris* bounced like a balloon.

"Goodness," she exclaimed, staggering like a drunken sailor over to the speaking horn. "Captain? Is something wrong?"

"I should say so, miss," came a voice so horror-struck that she instinctively turned to the viewing port.

Dinah and Timothy pounded up the circular staircase and into the salon. "Earthquake, miss," Timothy reported. "Happens here, evidently. Dad says he's never seen such a bad one."

Peony's mouth dropped open at the spectacle that met her gaze. Where at breakfast there had been a prosperous city going about its business a few hundred feet across the water, now there were only heaps of rubble. And—what on earth—

She blinked, as though to clear her eyes. "Is that *a ship in the street?*"

But no one answered. The four of them gripped the sill of the wide viewing port, floating above the maelstrom, trying to take in a city that was still moving.

Still falling.

Still dying.

A great cloud of smoke or dust or whatever breath of hell could waft up from the underworld rose, obscuring the view.

Or perhaps—

Peony dashed the tears from her eyes and tried to blink San Francisco de Asis back into clarity.

"Our friends," Barnaby croaked. "Where in the name of heaven are our friends?"

CHAPTER 6

The first thing May Lin realized when she opened her eyes was that it was just as dark as when they were closed. Had she closed the drapes when she'd gone to bed? She didn't, usually. She liked to watch the moon wax and wane.

And then she remembered.

Buried alive.

A wave of panic surged out to her very extremities, and in her mind, she leaped to her feet and ran. In reality, she stirred and groaned, weighed down by what she couldn't see. Her fingers flexed, tested their surroundings.

Rubble. Small rocks. Hardnesses, laid in regular rows to either side.

Wet bricks.

Her head hurt, but her hands, scraped and stinging though they were, still worked. She drew up her knees, releasing a small avalanche of rocks and earth, and pain flared. She must have bounced a few times on the way down into the crevasse, and been struck by falling stone. She wiggled her toes. Flexed her ankles. Took a deep breath.

Sore, and probably bleeding, but not broken.

Another blessing—she was not buried. For past her face there flowed a current of air, bearing with it choking dust and the smell of water.

Somewhere in the darkness beyond her feet, someone moaned, a keening sound of confusion and despair.

"Who is there?" she croaked, her throat filled with dust. She coughed. "Can you hear me?"

The earth jerked, sending her prostrate body an inch sideways in the shallow, wet channel. She held her breath, but no chunk of rock fell on her head. There was a flapping sound, as though an ornithopter had taken off, then silence. A trickle of gravel sounded to her right. Whatever object had fallen was holding.

"Is someone there?"

Where was she? Who was down here in the dark with her? A murderous monk? Oh heaven, she had just given away her position. How was she to get out?

When would—

Lin!

She must get out! The girl would be hysterical from terror. She mustn't lie here in a sewer hoping that the next brick—or a monk with one in his hand—would not find her. She could not wait for rescue, for no one knew she was down here save the monks.

The ones who had escaped were probably delighted with the situation. It would save them having to dispose of her body.

She must get out of here and find Lin before the monks decided that the girl could not live, either.

Calm. Think. Sit up.

The flapping sound again. The sound robes would make, or sandals. Closer.

Breathing hard in an effort not to panic and scream herself into madness, she wriggled out from under a pile of dirt and rocks. Her robe stuck to her back, soaked through. She knew that water found its own level. Which way was it going?

Crouching, hoping whoever was down here with her would pass her in the dark, she laid her hand flat in the trickle and found it did not even cover her fingers. Still, she felt the gentle push of its current. She lifted her wet palm and sniffed.

Not sewage. Rainwater. A tunnel, then. Under the mission. Interesting. Where did it go? And more important, how far could she get before she found it blocked?

Again, the moan came, a sad treble that did not sound like a man, even an injured one.

"Are you hurt?" she said.

Again, the sad sound, and a scrabble as a rock turned. A scrabble that did not carry much weight. With a sudden conviction that this was no monk, she moved toward the sound and reached down. Her hands closed around a warm body.

Which shrieked, and struggled, and flapped for all it was worth. May Lin's arms remembered what to do. She slipped her right hand under the windmilling claws and tucked the feathery body under her left arm.

"Shhhh," she said to the chicken. "It's all right. I won't hurt you." She ran her hands over its back and tail. A hen. Barely. It was so small it rested in the curve of her hand. "Poor thing.

Were you supposed to be their lunch before the ground opened up and threw you down here?"

The attempts at struggle slowed to a stop with the soothing sound of her voice. Years ago, she and the other children had cared for the village chickens. Mother Mary had told her she had the knack of getting a bird to trust her. In the past, that had not boded well for the birds, for they were a food source.

This one was different.

"No one is going to eat you," she said to the bird, stroking her feathers. Its flapping was now reduced to trembling. "I'm not leaving you down here. We'll get out together. I will call you Perdida, for you are as lost as I."

The trembling lessened, and after a moment, Perdida's feet relaxed. May Lin comforted herself in the warm little hen's trust, and took stock of her situation.

She had been running for the street when the crevasse had opened—or rather, the roof of the tunnel had collapsed, taking the floor with it. The last thing she remembered was seeing the earth close over her head before she'd been struck. Bad luck. She might have been able to climb out.

Lin had been in the mission school, roughly in the direction from which the tiny current was coming. She and Perdida must follow the tunnel upstream and beg Mother River's help through her tiny tributary.

One step was enough to tell her that she was lucky not to have been smashed like a pumpkin, what with all the piles of fallen rocks and brick. Using her free hand, feeling her way, she fumbled along a few yards.

Was that—?

Light!

The outlines of rocks and wet brick seemed to glimmer in the faintest light. How had this part of the tunnel held and the part under the refectory failed so catastrophically? That question was unanswerable. The reality was that she must get out of the catastrophic part as fast as possible.

Another jerk of the earth sent her reeling into the curved wall of the tunnel. One hand clutching the chicken to her chest, the other flat against the bricks, she held her breath and prepared to die. A vibration ran under her feet and a thundering sound came from far away.

Up the tunnel, where the light was?

She dared to take a few more steps. Here the light was strongest. She looked up. Not daylight. But somewhere up there was a window that admitted it. And across a square aperture in the floor above lay a wrought iron grate.

At least three feet above her straining fingertips.

Should they go on, up the tunnel? Or try to get out here? Hm. The fewer layers of masonry and rock between the two of them and daylight, the better. Decision made, May Lin bent to dip a reverent finger in the rivulet of water.

Thank you, Great Mother River, for sending me Perdida. Thank you, little stream, for guiding me this far. May your journey to the sea be unfettered and free.

Gently, she set Perdida on a rock, then gathered herself and jumped. Her fingers bumped the iron grille, but could neither lift it nor push it aside.

Very well, if it would not come to her, she would go to it.

The earth jerked again, but not before she felt it coming this time. The tremors seemed to come in pairs, one lighter and one heavier, but there was no telling just when they would come. Dirt filtered out of the ceiling, and down the tunnel a brick fell, smashing to bits in the rivulet.

Perdida gave a choked alarm, but did not bolt. Evidently she had thrown in her lot with May Lin.

She had better work faster. This tunnel might not hold forever.

May Lin gulped and addressed herself to the grate once more. This time when she jumped and struck it, it hopped in its groove, as though the last tremor had unseated it. Gathering herself once more, she jumped and got her fingers through the grille.

She swung, and with each swing, flung the weight of her body upward, to push the grate. One, two, three, she wrenched at it, hopping the grate farther out of its grooves until a space opened wide enough that she might get a hand or foot through.

She swung to the ground, picked up the hen, and lofted her toward the opening. Flapping, the chicken struggled through, then perched on the grate, looking down.

"Look out, little one." May Lin unwrapped her sash, knotted one of the knives into it, then leaped again, throwing the knife through one of the holes. Perdida flew out of sight.

Don't leave me. I wouldn't leave you.

With a second leap, May Lin hung from the grate long enough to pull the knife back through. Wrapping the sash around one hand and her waist, she pulled herself off her toes, swung upside down, and slid a foot through the gap.

Now her second foot. Then knees, thighs—

Her own weight levered her torso up, and she pushed the grate aside the rest of the way. She sat up, panting with the effort. She had not used her stomach muscles like that in a long time—palace living was making her soft. When she had her breath, she rolled over, collected knife and sash, and put them back where they belonged.

Perdida perched upon a barrel, and in the light filtering through the barred window above, May Lin could see her clearly for the first time. She was pure white. Except for her wings and feet, which were feathered, she seemed to have long hair, like a cat. Purple eyes gazed at her. Her earlobes were blue. Her face and beak were black as the skin of a Nubian aeronaut. Was she from that country?

"You are no ordinary bird, are you? I've never seen your like."

Perdida seemed content to accept her compliments as May Lin looked about their new and improved prison. There were other barrels besides the one the bird perched upon. Barrels. Crates. Shelving, crammed haphazardly with ancient … books? She flipped one open, expecting an elderly treatise on the monks' religion. Instead, she found geography, its maps showing a world with open edges and leviathans swimming in seas whose width could not be estimated. May Lin shook her head. Old and a century out of date, and yet not made useful, even as fuel in a brazier during a cold winter.

But in one way these old books were useful. Could she and Perdida really have had the luck to emerge into the cellar under the school?

Was a little more luck too much to ask—such as finding the door open at the top of the stone stairs? She scooped Perdida up and climbed the narrow steps, hugging the wall and hoping every second that there would not be another tremor to fling her over the side.

The door had been torn from its leather hinges and lay flat

upon the floor. Through her boots, May Lin felt the flagstones on the landing vibrate, and braced herself against the jamb.

This jolt was much harder than the previous ones—or perhaps it merely felt so, now that she was closer to the surface. From below came a thundering crash.

A cloud of dust floated up out of the open hole where the grate had been.

May Lin's breath seized in her lungs. She lost her self control, and, clutching Perdida to her chest, bolted through the gaping doorway and down the stone-flagged corridor.

Heaps of rubble where the walls had caved in finally brought her to a panting halt. Not a soul could she see through the still rising dust. The school had only one floor, and one classroom was empty, all its contents flung upon the floor and pinned down by fallen masonry. In the other, the roof had fallen in altogether, red tiles smashed upon the wooden tables where students had learned their letters.

Had everyone taken refuge in the street? Or had they suffered a burial much the same as hers?

Please, no. Not Lin. And the young woman, Daisy. Let them be all right. Let him be all right.

But she could not think of the prince now, for he was almost certainly not thinking of her. His city lay in ruins with the catastrophe increasing every time the earth shook. The whereabouts of one obstinate witch had to be the last thing on his mind when his people were even now screaming in terror and moaning for aid.

Another jolt, and panic again propelled her through the gap in the outer wall. The stones turned under her feet and she fell into the street, instinctively rolling so that Perdida would not be hurt. When the earth stopped its trembling, she found herself on her back, staring up through the dust into a pair of dark eyes.

"I knew you would come," Lin said, her dusty cheeks stained with the tracks of tears. "What kind of chicken is this?"

CHAPTER 7

12:10 p.m.

"Here, miss." Davey offered Daisy a hand and pulled her to her feet. "Ent this an awful thing? What's happening?"

"It is an earthquake," William managed, prone in the rubble for at least the third time since the initial shock. "Are we all alive?"

"Freddie," Daisy croaked, hauling him up. "I must go to Freddie."

William dusted the dirt from his trousers, and located his hat some distance away. "She is with Peony, no doubt faring much better than we."

"We do not know that. We must return to the island at once."

"Return?" Davey squeaked. "What about Lin? She could be dead! What's happened to her?"

"An excellent question." William slapped his hat against his

63

knee, releasing a shower of dirt. "The mission is closest. We must find her first."

"Are you mad?" With both arms, Daisy gestured at the fallen buildings, the clouds of dust, and the flames beginning to lick at the building up the street, which was made of wood, not adobe brick. Before she could finish, the earth jerked again, sending all three of them to their knees with cries of terror. Somehow, the little house in whose garden they had landed remained standing.

Belatedly, she realized her reticule containing her Thaxton, her sketchbook, and her paintbox was still on the ground. She slipped its strings over her wrist even as the tremor faded under her knees. "We must return to the island *at once*, before we are all killed."

"No. Davey is right," William said. "We know where Lin has gone. We cannot leave her."

She had gone with May Lin, and a more capable protector Daisy could not imagine. She climbed over what had been the garden wall and shaded her eyes as she looked out over the bay. In the distance, *Iris* floated serenely at her moorings, looking entirely unaffected by the fact that for much of the city, the world had ended.

Her entire being yearned toward the ship, her arms aching to hold her younger sister close and assure herself that she was safe. She must be safe. There were no buildings on the island, and the airship was securely moored. Nothing could fall on it. In truth, Freddie was probably safer at this moment than anyone in the city, including the Viceroy. Or herself.

What would Freddie say if Daisy abandoned Lin to her fate and came running to her side when she was perfectly well?

"Yes," she said at last, a prickle of shame coming to her dusty cheeks. "Of course you are right. Come. It is only a few blocks, but it may take us some time to get there."

Between bracing themselves for imminent death every time the ground jolted, to dodging fallen bricks and collapsing houses and assisting one or two people to safety, it took nearly an hour to reach Nuestra Señora de las Estrellas.

"The bell did fall down," Davey breathed. "Look."

The church tower had fallen, and the bell had smashed a hole in the courtyard, burying itself nearly to its shoulders. What had happened to the starry ceiling? Daisy would never paint it now, and it seemed utterly irrelevant. A relic of a world long past.

"Look, under this section of wall." William began to throw fallen bricks out of the way. "It is the *mecaballo*."

"So they did not leave before the disaster." Daisy tied her reticule to her belt, and joined him and Davey to clear bricks and stone from the fallen horse. "If they did not come back for it, what prevented them? William, they could be hurt."

"How bad is the horse hurt?" Davey wanted to know. "Can we ride it?"

"We may be safer on our own feet," William said. "But let me see if it will ignite."

It seemed the *mecaballo* needed repairs greater than any William could make. No matter what adjustments he tried, it remained upon its side and would not respond.

William had no choice but to give up. "We cannot spare any more time. Every minute could bring Lin closer to death, if she is trapped under the rubble."

Davey's face crumpled. "Don't you say that."

"Prepare yourself," William said gently. "You have eyes.

You know her chances are not good if the earthquake struck while she was inside."

Daisy touched William's arm. "There, in the courtyard. Is that a monk? Will you ask him if he knows where they are?"

She did not know if the rules of the cloister would hold during a disaster. But she did not care. Rules or not, females allowed in or not, she was not about to be separated from him. They climbed over what was left of the wall and hailed the monk.

"Padre, have you seen Madame the President of the Viceregal Society of Engineers?" William called as they approached, giving the bell a wide berth. On one side of the courtyard, the entire grape arbor had come down, and on the other, while the main building itself seemed to have held up, papers blew in doorways like leaves.

"Eh?" The monk's eyes were bewildered, his hands plucking at his sleeves.

William repeated the question in a tongue that could only be Latin. The conversation was brief, and the monk wandered away, talking to someone who was not there.

William turned back toward them, his face so white that Daisy's heart seemed to freeze in her chest.

"She is dead," he said. "May Lin. He did not know anything of our Lin."

A pang of horror, of loss, shivered through Daisy's body. May Lin, that beautiful, vibrant woman, dead! How could it be possible for a witch to survive the Rose Rebellion and yet succumb to an earthquake when the three of them had so far survived it? How had it happened? Where was her body?

"We must find her," Davey said stoutly. "She can't be far, innit?"

For one horrible moment, Daisy thought he meant May Lin. The loss of a friendship that would now never be hers lodged in her heart.

"Lin knew we were coming along behind." Daisy forced the halted gears of her mind to work again. "Would she have gone to the church to wait?"

William turned to gaze upward at it, now reduced to merely a square building, its bell tower gone and one corner torn open to the sky. "I hope not. The fall of the tower seems to have collapsed the ceiling."

"We must look." Davey sprinted off.

William shouted, "Come back! It's far too dangerous!"

But Davey did not, and above them, a plaster saint tilted out of its niche as the ground shook again, and crashed to the ground.

DAZED, May Lin blinked up into the apparition's face and marshaled her resources to speak. "Where did you come from?"

"I have been waiting in the street," Lin said. "The padres have fled, but before they went, they told all the children to stay in the open so that the roof did not fall on us."

May Lin pushed herself to her feet. "Just like a man, to dispense advice and flee instead of offering protection or even help."

"Most of the children have gone home—if they have one now. What happened to you?" The girl asked, eyeing her torn robe and the dirt in her hair. "And how did you come by that chicken? Did you steal her from the kitchen?"

"I believe the kitchen floor may have collapsed into an underground tunnel," she told her. "The chicken and I found each other down there." Then she could not help herself. She pulled the girl in for a hug, and after a moment the girl returned it. "I am very glad to see you," May Lin said into her hair. "I was very nearly killed, and I thought you would have been, too."

"We are both difficult to kill, it seems," Lin said, wriggling until May Lin let her go. "Is that what happened? You fell into a tunnel?"

"Yes. I don't know how I survived." She pushed away the memory of the earth closing over her head and gazed up the street instead. It was difficult to tell where they were, but at least the mission wall gave her a sense of direction. "Let's go."

"Yes, we must find the others."

May Lin had forgotten all about the others. "Who, Daisy and her party? Lin, we cannot. We have no way to know where they are." The ground shook once more, and, grasping Lin's hand, she ran up the street to a crossing, where the open space was larger. People milled about aimlessly, able to do nothing but watch as homes and businesses shuddered and crashed. Some men had formed a chain, Canton and Californio working together, passing rocks and bricks in buckets as they attempted to dig someone out.

Where were they to go? The palace was too far away, and the Mother only knew what disasters had occurred there. But perhaps she had friends who were closer.

"We will find my friend the printer, and if we can, take refuge with him for now."

"But what about Daisy and William?" Lin protested. "They

knew we were to be here, and where to meet us. We must stay in one place and wait for them to find us."

"And have a building fall on your head?" May Lin demanded. "It is too dangerous out here."

"But that is how I found you." A mutinous frown was forming between the girl's brows.. "William always says he will find us. If we are lost, we are not to go looking for him or to wander off."

"The Mother only knows where William or anyone else is, or if they are dead or alive," May Lin said tersely. "Come along, or I will leave you to wait alone." The girl cast about, in one direction and then the next, but there was nothing to be seen but dazed strangers and heaps of fallen brick. Dust and fire. Shock and fear. And under their feet, the restless, agonized earth that could no longer be trusted.

May Lin set off, following the wall that had once surrounded the mission. There was no sound of rapid footsteps behind her. She smothered the impulse to go back and force the girl to come with her, for her own safety. But what good would that do? There might be some advantage in staying together, but if she chose to try to find her friends, that was her business. May Lin was doing exactly the same thing, but with a slightly greater chance of success.

She hardened her heart and walked on.

She came to the corner, where a saint had fallen out of his niche and lay smashed in the street. Stepping around the pieces, her focus on her path, she walked straight into a broad chest.

"You!" roared a male voice, and beefy arms snatched her off her feet. She was flung over his shoulder with a thump that nearly knocked the breath from her body. Perdida shrieked and tumbled to the ground, her wings unable to support her. May Lin's face was mashed into a broad back covered in rough brown homespun, a white cord at his waist.

What abysmal luck had sent her straight into the path of the monks who had been about to kill her before the earthquake had intervened?

"I was told you were dead, but God has sent you to me to make sure of it."

May Lin did not waste her breath contradicting him. She unsnapped her knives, let them slide into her hands, and pushed them silently into the monk's back, one through the kidneys and one into a lung, burying them to the hilts. With a scream, he flung her off his back. By some miracle, she retained the wit to tuck and land on her feet in a defensive crouch, knives at the ready.

The injured monk staggered, blood leaking from his mouth. "Get her! Kill her!"

She might have been a match for one man, or even two, but here were three burly, well-fed monks all attacking at once. Her knives clattered to the ground as first one got her in a headlock, then another took an arm and the third took her feet and held them fast, no matter how hard she kicked and struggled.

"Leave her alone!" A slight figure in white flew at the nearest man like a fury, pummeling and kicking. "You won't take her! Stop!"

With one swipe of his hand, the monk on her left knocked Lin to the ground. In horror, May Lin heard the sickening sound of her head striking a fallen brick. "Stop! You've hurt her, you beast!" She renewed her struggles, desperate to break free and fly to the girl's assistance.

"The saints give me patience, there are two of them?" A smoother voice rode over the grunts and curses of the others as they felt their bruises. "Take the girl, too, and come with me. We haven't much time. The prince will need me urgently. Friar Jose, see to your fallen brother."

Bishop del Fuego. Why had the floor not opened up under *his* feet instead of hers?

"Why are you trying to kill me?" May Lin cried. "Forget about the steam landaus—they are nowhere near as great a threat as this! We should be working together to help the people!"

"To perdition with the people," the bishop growled. "There will be more. Shut up, or I will have the girl drowned before your eyes."

Drowned? Cold fear engulfed her as she tried to work out what he meant. They were nowhere near the waterfront. They were going down a set of steps behind the bishop's private chapel, then into another tunnel. But this one was in much better repair, and seemed to have been carved out of living rock, not clay and lined with bricks. In what seemed like an hour, bouncing and breathless as the monk ran at a shambling trot, they emerged into the daylight once more.

May Lin craned her neck, trying to see what they'd done with Lin. The scent of seawater and tar assailed her nose, the hollow thump of the monks' sandaled feet on wooden planks her ears.

And suddenly she realized where they'd brought her.

The Barbary Coast.

They were going to sell her and Lin to the pirates, and she would never see the prince—or anyone else—again.

CHAPTER 8

12:40 p.m.

"We must be calm." Daisy clasped her hands together to keep from wringing them, and dug her nails into her skin to stop the incipient attack of hysteria.

Just before their arrival, the building that had housed the mission school had collapsed; a cloud of dust still spiraled into the air. It was the only thing that moved; the fallen stones were eerily silent and motionless after the cataclysm, spread across the street. Daisy could not tell if any lived or died. Had the children fled before it happened? Had any children even been inside today?

"Davey, what did Lin tell you, exactly?" William coughed as the dust caught in his throat.

"She said she might visit a teacher." Davey's face was white with dust and fear. "She ent under there, is she?"

"We cannot know." William tried to wipe the tracks of

tears from Davey's face, but the lad shook him off and pulled away.

"Lin!" he shouted into the pile of rubble higher than their heads. "Lin, are you in there?"

But there was no reply, only the shouts of the men forming rescue chains up the street.

"We must think," Daisy said. "May Lin is dead. Lin may have escaped before the walls came down. If she did, where would she have gone?"

"To the church, to wait for us," William suggested.

"That's what I said before," Daisy told him, somewhat aggrieved that he was only now coming to this conclusion.

"Yes, but we did not know she had another errand until Davey said so just now. Come. Let us return. She may be there already."

But a crowd was gathering in the mission courtyard as though they thought they might find help from the padres. Lin was not among them.

"If she was coming here, she'd be here already," Davey pointed out with a child's irrefutable logic. "What now?"

Daisy could not seem to make her brain work with any kind of logic, childlike or otherwise. Her mind felt thick and numb with fear. "What would you do if you were Lin?" she asked the boy. He knew her better than anyone.

"She used to live here, innit?" he said after another attempt to scan the courtyard for her small figure in its Navapai dress. "I s'pose if she didn't come here, she'd go somewhere she knew. Take refuge with someone. It's too far to walk back to the island in all this."

"With old neighbors, perhaps?" William nodded slowly.

"That seems reasonable. We must look, if only to satisfy ourselves that we have done all we can to locate her."

"But she may indeed have gone back to the bridge." That is what Daisy would have done. What she wanted to do, immediately, if not sooner. To find refuge with Freddie.

"If it is holding at all, and not in pieces in the bay, she will be waiting for us when we get there," William said. "But for now, we must be certain we have eliminated the closest possibilities."

And before Daisy could argue that the best possibility was the island, he stepped through a breach in the courtyard wall and made his way out to the street. Under no circumstances was she going to be left behind, so she scrambled out after him and Davey. The wall turned a corner and took them the length of the block, where at the corner, another statue lay smashed. And perched upon its detached head, rather as if it were an enormous egg, was a small white bird.

No, not merely a bird. A hen, hunkered down and clinging to the saint's carved ear for all it was worth.

Daisy had come to appreciate the hens at Mr. Hansen's house, back in Georgetown. In the horror and madness of that visit, the birds had represented a tiny oasis of beauty and calm. She and Freddie had come to value simply sitting on the back porch of his house to watch them, and they'd missed them when they departed for Santa Fe.

The strange little bird—was this hair instead of feathers?— made no complaint when Daisy scooped it up; rather, it pushed its head under her arm as though seeking her protection. "Hello, little lost thing," she murmured to it. "Are you as frightened as I am?"

"Daisy," William said impatiently, already ten feet away.

"What are you doing? Put that poor creature down and come along."

She was perfectly willing to come along, but nothing on earth would induce her to leave the tiny bird there in the street. She fit comfortably in Daisy's palm, yet it was too late in the year for chicks. What kind of hen was she?

"She won't survive the day," she told her companions as she caught up. "If she isn't killed by a falling brick, someone will make a meal of her by sunset."

"It's not big enough to make a meal," Davey said, giving the bird a critical once-over. "What is it? Some kind of parrot? It's got blue ears."

"It is a chicken," Daisy told him with dignity. "And *she* is coming with us."

"Suit yourself," William said, and forgot the matter as they crested a slope. "There is the Canton district. We will ask for the printer May Lin was going to see. Perhaps someone will have seen Lin."

To reach the Canton district, it was necessary to slide down a crumbly slope and cross a fairly broad creek that might even be an inlet from the harbor. Under normal circumstances, perhaps there might have been a bridge, or a boat. But not today.

"Blimey," Davey said, once he had got his hanging jaw back in operation. "I s'pose we just climb over 'em?"

"I suppose we do," William said, his voice hushed. "Be careful."

Three sailing vessels lay crushed in the water, as though a giant had picked them up out of the harbor and, bored, dropped them as he walked away. Daisy opened her reticule and slid the hen, protesting loudly, into it. "I apologize, but I need both hands, and I will not risk dropping you." Then she slipped her head through the strings so that the reticule bumped against her chest.

At which point she realized that she was no longer wearing her hat. Goodness knew where it was. Likely buried under another fall of bricks.

The three of them scrambled down the short slope, then across the shifting, creaking bridge formed by the broken ships, helping one another over the slanting and splintered decks. Davey straddled a bit of detached gunwale. "It's faster like this—watch me!"

"Davey!" William shouted, already too late.

The curve of the gunwale deposited the boy neatly on the grass twenty feet below. William looked at Daisy and shrugged. "After you."

Had this been Bath, she would have refused in high dudgeon, exclaiming some nonsense about dignity and danger. But the climb down was broken and treacherous, the gunwale smooth and inviting. Daisy threw a leg over, implored protection from heaven, and let go.

"Well done," Davey said with approval when she landed with a bump at the bottom, and when William landed beside them a moment later, they took stock of their new prospects. Davey, who seemed to have designated himself the leader of this expedition, pointed. "That way. More solid ground." The water meadows had been scored and chewed by crevasses torn in the grass, necessitating jumps from tussock to tussock. On the far side, William came to a stop.

"I believe we are now in the Canton district."

They might as well have been in another world. Perhaps they were. For instead of adobe brick, the buildings were an aerie of metal struts and girders, rising and falling like a lacy wave six or seven storeys high, following the contours of the hills and outcroppings of rock. Within the girders and in fact part of them were homes and shops, made of wood. Shingled roofs turned up at the eaves to form channels where rain was diverted into cisterns. From each cistern a pair of pipes went through a wall, presumably conducting the water to some useful purpose.

There were streets, certainly, between structures, and moving busily from the ground to each level were square platforms of a kind that Daisy had never seen before. Puffing engines operated pulleys, moving the platforms with such speed that the clothes of the passengers blew gently in the breeze of their going.

Children chased each other from level to level, now gathering on the south side to point at the spectacle on the Californio side of the creek. People strode along catwalks with purpose, and in the streets, it seemed teams were forming to assist with rescue efforts.

"How have they survived without damage?" William wondered aloud. "I cannot see a single fallen building."

Another tremor jerked the ground out from under them. They staggered. The little hen, who had been squirming in her efforts to escape, popped her head out of the velvet mouth of Daisy's reticule with a squawk.

And the Canton buildings swayed gently. The old-fashioned hoop skirts Daisy and Freddie's grandmother used to wear had swayed like that as she walked—graceful and rhythmic and utterly unconcerned with their surroundings.

The tremor faded away into silence.

The buildings settled. People who had ceased walking,

working, and visiting while they waited for the tremor to pass, started up again. A red clay pot that had been left unattended rolled off the end of a catwalk and fell four storeys to smash upon the ground. A man in a black linen robe and trousers came out with a broom and tidied the pieces away.

"There's your answer," Davey said, watching the man. "How can people live in buildings that move like that?"

"Better than the Californio people, it seems," William said. "Come. Let us ask the man with the broom if he can direct us to the printer. And keep your eyes open for Lin."

The man, a grandfatherly sort, looked the three of them over as though astonished they had come from the water meadow unscathed. William asked, "I beg your pardon, sir, but do you speak the Texican tongue?"

"Of course," the man said. "And the Californio tongue, if that is more useful to you. But you do not look like Texicans or Californios."

"We are neither," Daisy said. "We are the guests of Yang May Lin, the Pres—"

He bowed.

After a moment, so did William and Davey.

Daisy curtseyed. "—the President of the Viceregal Society of Engineers," she finished when she came up. "My name is Daisy Linden. May I introduce William Barnicott, and Davey Fletcher."

"I am Zuo Jen Wei, and I am honored to meet the friends of the esteemed Yang May Lin." The man bowed again, as though the mention of her name required the civility.

William bowed back. After a moment, Daisy curtseyed.

"Please tell me, you three, how you come to be here when

the capital is suffering so painfully in this disaster? Surely the esteemed May Lin has not sent you?"

"The esteemed May Lin is dead," Davey said with brutal matter-of-factness—so brutal that Zuo Jen Wei was too shocked to bow a third time. "She was meeting with the padres when the earthquake struck." The man's face lost all its color, as though Davey had struck him.

"We do not know the details," Daisy put in hastily, "but the padres say it is so."

"It *cannot* be so." Zuo Jen Wei turned to call through the doorway behind him, and in a moment a lady came out, her eyes wide with horror. "This is my wife."

William and Davey bowed, and Daisy curtseyed.

When the lady straightened from her bow, there were tears on her cheeks. "The honored May Lin is dead? How can that be?"

Daisy could not answer her, for she wondered the very same. "After her meeting with the padres, she planned to come here to meet a man. A printer of ommatographs. Do you know of such a person?"

"We do." Zuo Jen Wei pointed to a structure on the next block. "There, on the third level, with the flowers at the door. But why should you seek him if she is dead?"

Why indeed, when there were so many dead and suffering? But in the mountain of things she could not help, there was one thing left that she could.

"It is a very long story, but in brief, there are two reasons. One, my father is missing, and May Lin hoped the printer would assist us by distributing ommatographs of his portrait among the people on the waterfront in hopes that someone would recognize it." Daisy drew in a sudden breath.

"Daisy? What is it?" William said.

"The portrait of my father." Daisy's throat closed as tears welled into her eyes. "May Lin had it with her. And now I have nothing to give the printer."

The increasing series of disasters—physical and emotional—caught up to her at last, and she burst into tears. William slipped an arm about her shoulders, and Madame Zuo clucked and fussed and produced a handkerchief out of her sleeve, which Daisy accepted with a wail.

"Buck up, Daisy," Davey said. He touched the reticule strung around her neck, causing the little hen to squawk and wriggle. "You've got your paints, innit? You can paint another one."

Daisy mopped her face on the lovely silk fabric square. Blew her nose. Took a shuddering breath. Bless the boy for thinking when despair and fear seemed to have worn her down to her very lowest ebb.

Madame Zuo patted her shoulder and indicated she might keep the handkerchief. Daisy tucked it in her reticule, much to the outrage of its occupant.

Zuo Jen Wei gawked at the strange sight. "Pardon my familiarity, Miss Linden, but why do you have *wuguji* in a bag upon your person?"

"Wuguji?" Davey tested the word on his tongue.

"A black-boned chicken. Their skin is black, too, like the soot on the bottom of a pot."

"I—I do not know." Daisy regarded the incensed individual struggling to get out of the reticule. "She needed help, and so I am giving it as best I may. I could not leave her in the street to die."

Madame Zuo went into the shop and in a moment

returned, not with another handkerchief, but with a wicker basket the size of a handbag, such as one might put spools of thread in. "She is better in here, where she can breathe and see, and keep her dignity. I have put leaves in for her to eat. She will eat cooked meat, too, and fish, but I have none to hand."

Daisy's eyes filled again at this kindness in the midst of so much misery. "Thank you, Madame."

"What of the second reason?" her husband asked as the bird was transferred from one conveyance to the other, shook her feathers in the manner of ridding herself of indignity, and addressed herself to the leaves with vigor. Madame closed the lid with some stealth, before the bird noticed, and slipped its woven loop over a button attached for that purpose.

"We came with another friend, a girl of thirteen named Yang Lin-Bai," William said. "We lost her in the maelstrom and are hoping she might have come here, to a place she knew as a child."

"Yang Lin-Bai," Madame Zuo said, startled. "Daughter of Yang Ju-Long?"

Daisy exchanged a glance with William. "We do not know her parents' names. Is hers familiar to you?"

"Aiyah, if only it were not. That poor child—we thought surely she must be dead. She ran away after—" Madame shook her head sadly.

"After her parents died of typhoid?" William concluded gently.

"Yes," Zuo Jen Wei said, surprised at his knowledge. "They lived in Stouts Alley. But you will find nothing of her there."

"Still, we have to try," William said. "Daisy, if you would speak with the printer, then Davey and I will go to Stouts

Alley. With your permission, sir and madame, we will meet back here when our inquiries are completed."

"Of course," the man said.

"I must paint another portrait of Papa," Daisy said. "Madame, I hesitate to ask assistance of you a third time—"

"Three is a lucky number. You must sit at our table," the lady said with a smile. "And I will tell you what I know of the Yang family. Husband, take the young men to Stouts Alley. Friends of our esteemed May Lin must not go unescorted from door to door like peddlers." Her face crumpled for a moment, before she regained her self-control and motioned Daisy in to the shop. "I will introduce Miss Linden to the printer when the painting is finished."

"You may not find him inclined to assist you," Zuo Jen Wei warned her. "He may already have joined a rescue party."

"I must still try. Will an hour be sufficient, William?" Daisy asked anxiously. "You will not be longer, will you?"

"No," William said. "Good luck."

"Luck has abandoned the city on this day," Daisy heard Zuo Jen Wei say sadly as he led the way down the street. "The Californios ... they were foolish enough to build their church and their palace upon the dragon's eye, and it was only a matter of time before the dragon stretched himself and shook them off."

CHAPTER 9

12:45 p.m.

e must do something to help." Peony, Freddie, Barnaby, and *Iris*'s crew all crowded the airship's wide viewing ports, unable to tear themselves away from the dreadful sight. "Look— Dear heaven, *look!*" Peony pointed.

The great cathedral of San Francisco de Asis, built on the hill and adjoining the viceregal palace, seemed to shiver in the smoky golden light. Then, as slowly and gracefully as an actress fainting in one of the flickers, its spire collapsed and fell.

Mrs. Boyle gasped and began her prayers over again.

At this distance they could not see what was happening to the rest of the church, but a cloud of dust rose into the air that Peony could swear was the size of a nave. Had the prince been inside, praying for the welfare of his people? And what of that nice Mr. Douglas and his pretty fiancée?

"I agree, Peony," Barnaby Hayes said, horror hollowing his

voice to a whisper. "We must help. But with so many needing assistance, where ought we to begin?"

Thank heaven and all the angels that you did not go with Daisy.

But that was horrible of her, when poor Freddie was standing right next to him, a mewling sound coming from her throat as she—a true heroine—did her best to stifle her tears. And then she could stifle them no longer. "Daisy!" the girl wailed, and turned to sob in Mrs. Boyle's comforting embrace.

They would never find Daisy in all that destruction. Bleakly, Peony gazed at the place where the cathedral's spire had been, then northward along the shore, toward where she understood the mission to be. How could they find her, her friend Mr. Barnicott, or the children? Peony could only hope that, since they were together, they were helping each other to safety. At a time like this, one could do nothing but focus on the possible, for anything else would drive one mad.

Because she did know where *some* of her recent acquaintance might be found. Neither Claire nor Gloria would ever forgive her if she did not make the attempt to locate Mr. Douglas and assure herself (and by extension, her friends) that he was unharmed.

"We must lift and go to the palace," Peony said at last, for they could not stand here all day in perfect safety while people suffered and died. "We must discover whether the prince and Mr. Douglas are alive, and if they are, assist them in any way we can."

"Assist them how, miss?" Captain Boyle rasped. "The city did not boast a modern hospital the last time I was here—the monks looked after the sick. We might ferry the injured, if nothing else."

Peony nodded slowly. "We must do something, so let us begin there. Freddie, do you agree?"

The girl turned glassy, tear-filled eyes to Peony. "We are not going to try to find Daisy and William? And Lin and Davey?"

Peony turned up her hands. "Where? We none of us know the city, and what Captain Boyle might once have known is damaged past recognition. How can we even begin to look? Don't you see, Freddie? We must go where we know our acquaintance is to be found. And that means the palace."

"It is possible that the palace remains undamaged," Barnaby said kindly to Freddie, who had turned white to the lips. "The Viceroy may assign men to help us search for Daisy and our friends."

"Do you think so?" The faintest glimmer of hope seeped back into Freddie's eyes.

Peony did not in the least think so, but she allowed Detective Hayes to make comforting noises in the affirmative.

"Come, let us change into the most practical garments we own," she suggested. "Captain, prepare *Iris* for lift."

Within fifteen minutes, the twins had cast off ropes and *Iris* had left her safe moorage on the island, with only Mr. Barnicott's peculiar conveyance left to keep watch. As they rose into the sky, they could see dust clouds and fire rising from both the western and the distant eastern shores. To the south, what looked like a long rip in the earth ran straight as a badly tailored seam before it buried itself in the hills. Peony, stationed at the viewing port in the navigation gondola, could hardly see the homes and hills of the city below for all the dust and smoke.

"I believe the easiest place to land is on one of the palace terraces, Captain," she said over her shoulder.

"Aye, miss." Captain Boyle adjusted the propellers' speed and she felt the deck press up against the soles of her boots as he brought the ship in on a short approach.

The wide, square cantilevered terrace where she and the Viceroy had spoken last night to Daisy at the ball was empty. It seemed to be stable enough—for if the cantilever were going to collapse, surely it would have done so by now. The gangway went down at an acute angle, for the fuselage was bigger than the landing space, and they had to hover a little. The twins tied them down to the balustrade.

The potted palms near the doors had tipped over, the poor trees sprawled on the stones. And when Peony disembarked, it was to find that the doors themselves had shattered, as though the huge terracotta planters had been flung against them first, and then back outside, where gravity had asserted itself.

"Captain Boyle, please stay with the ship until we have found those we seek. I am not certain of *Iris*'s safety should there be another tremor. The terrace might collapse."

Mrs Boyle let out a yelp, her eyes huge as she cast about, as though it might happen in the next few seconds.

"Frankly, I do not see why the terrace is still standing," Detective Hayes remarked. "This does not feel like a good plan at all."

Before Peony could make an irritated retort—he was the spy, for goodness sake, could he not contribute something? Must she be the one coming up with all the plans?—Captain Boyle said, "Rebecca, Lucas, we will take up the gangway and run *Iris* out to the end of her tether. If the terrace does fail, she'll be jerked down, but should float free of actual destruction. Persis, my dear, I beg you to stay aboard. The gondola is the safest. Twins, your duty is to see to your mother's safety while I stand watch."

The three of them climbed the gangway without argument. And perhaps the smallest hint of haste.

She should float free? That's a slender estimation to pin my ship's safety on. But there really was no other way. Nowhere was safe, and it was best to have refuge close by should they need to run for it.

"Peony, you and I and Freddie will search," Detective Hayes said.

"And I," Timothy told him. When Captain Boyle growled, he shook his head. "Dad, if their friends are injured, they will need another man to help carry them. You need Dinah to pilot the ship more than you need me."

"I should go," Dinah objected. "I am the oldest."

"You are my chief engineer," her uncle said firmly. "Timothy is right. If we must take sudden flight, or make adjustments to become a hospital ship, it will be your responsibility, not his."

Face like a thundercloud, Dinah had no choice but to obey.

"Right," Detective Hayes said briskly. "If we are not back in two hours, send Dinah to search for us." He checked his pocket watch. "It is twenty minutes past one."

Captain Boyle checked the temporal device upon his own arm, and nodded.

"Mark each door," Dinah said, forcing the words out between stiff lips. "So I may follow you if necessary."

"Good idea," Detective Hayes said. "Miss Freddie, does Daisy have some spare graphite?"

She fetched a stick of graphite for each of them. Peony did not know how Daisy would receive this rifling of her art supplies, but this was a matter of life and death. As she passed through it, she marked an *X* on the white wall next to the door frame at eye level, then glanced at Dinah.

The young woman nodded, and they set off. Behind them, Dinah and her uncle boarded. In a moment, the gangway slid up, and the mooring rope began to spool out.

The ballroom looked forlorn, coated in dust and empty of its brilliant company, its tables of food, its orchestra. A few chairs lay on their sides. Halfway across what had been a polished dance floor, Peony realized that Freddie was not with them.

She turned to see her still standing in the doorway, frozen. "Miss Freddie?" she called. "Are you coming? We have no time to lose."

"I—I am not."

"But why?"

"I am sorry," the girl called, her voice thick with tears. "I cannot."

"I thought you wanted to help Daisy," Peony said, at a loss.

"I cannot!" The girl whirled back out on to the terrace, presumably to beckon *Iris* back down and seek the safety of Mrs. Boyle's comforting embrace.

Peony shook her head in speechless disbelief. Very well then. If she wished to upend all their plans and stay where it was safer, so be it. Peony had no more patience to spend on her. She crossed the ballroom, marking the doorway into the reception room. Here was chaos for certain, with more potted palms sprawled on the red and gold carpet in heaps of dirt, windows broken, and the royal canopy torn from its moorings, lying drunkenly across the throne.

She reported to Detective Hayes and Timothy that their party had been reduced by one. Then she marked the door behind the throne and they passed into the prince's living quarters.

"Where is everyone?" Timothy asked, taking in each cavernous, ornate room as they passed it. "Have they all run off?"

Peony hoped so. The alternative did not bear thinking of.

In what was clearly the Prince's own bedroom, they came to a halt in the doorway. Peony gasped, then coughed as she got a lungful of dust.

The exterior wall of the huge, once lavish room had fallen clear away, leaving the prince's private quarters open to the sky. The legs of his bed were made in the shape of crouching lions. One lion hung over the precipice, snarling at the ground two hundred feet below. A pair of pigeons perched on the gold headboard startled at their appearance and flew off.

"Is that ... what is that?" Detective Hayes said. "No, Peony, do not go in. The floor may not be stable. Timothy, is that blood? There, on that sheet on the floor nearest us."

"It looks like it, sir," the young man said. "The prince could have been hit by falling bricks."

"In that case, where is he?" Peony asked. Her stomach rolled uneasily as she felt the first internal tremors of actual fear. Of the realization that this was not a flicker, or a dream, or anything approaching an adventure. Freddie might have had the right of it—this was real. People she knew could be dead. The Viceroy, that lovely young man, so handsome and gallant, might be lying under a broken wall somewhere in his own palace, his dancing brown eyes closed forever.

Worse, in her haste she might herself be the instrument of Daisy's death, by not coming to her aid in time.

Peony felt a little sick. This was too much.

But no. She must stick to the course she had chosen and hope for the best. "We must find someone who can tell us where the prince is. We must find Mr. Douglas at once."

More rooms, and now the damage became more acute. Fallen people had been buried in masonry, their lifeless bodies left behind in the panic. She scratched more crosses on door frames, until Peony was running, her companions behind her, from room to room, from study to library to sitting room, running from the horror of a foot protruding here, a hand there, reaching from a heap of stones pleading for help that would not come, a pair of sightless eyes forever open on the horror of those last moments.

Another tremor struck, jerking the floor out from under Peony's feet. She hung on to the door frame while the detective flailed his arms and clutched at her, both of them managing to stay on their feet enough to ride it out.

Someone gave a muffled shriek, and while the pendulum of the cracked clock standing against the wall swung wildly, the time forever stopped at a quarter to eleven, Timothy located a person huddling behind the sofa. It was a maid in what had once been a black dress and white apron, the skirts of which she had flung over her head as she crouched in terror.

Timothy spoke to her softly as he brought her over to them. At first she could not stop crying, but as she realized that they were neither ghosts nor angels sent for her soul, he was eventually able to get a few broken sentences from her.

"Everyone who can has run out into the main courtyard, away from falling walls," Timothy reported. "She does not know where the prince is, nor Mr. Douglas."

"What rescue efforts are being attempted?" Detective Hayes demanded. "Some of those people we saw might have been saved had there been an organized effort."

A rapid question, and a broken answer.

"There was no time, she says," Timothy translated. "From childhood, everyone is taught to run outside. No one stays within. Except her, for she was searching for a loved one. I will ask her to guide us in exchange for our help. Perhaps Mr. Douglas and the prince are already in the courtyard."

The maid wasted no time, and broke into a run in answer to his request. Down a flight of stone stairs, then another, then she flung herself at an arched door bearing an iron studded cross.

It did not open. She shrieked something at Timothy.

"We must go through the vestry, but it is blocked," Timothy reported.

"There must be a dozen ways to get to the courtyard," Peony snapped. If she didn't get outside herself, she was going to go mad.

The maid took them back up the stairs, down a pair of intersecting corridors, and then, to Peony's infinite relief, out a door that opened on to an enormous courtyard. The loggias had fallen in, dragging thick grapevines with them, and agitated doves and sparrows wheeled overhead as though they had been thrown out of their roosts and could not find a safe resting place. But two hundred people at least milled in the open space, weeping and calling the names of others. People embraced as newcomers joined them.

A man in a butler's livery wandered from group to group, calling, "Tonia! Tonia!" hopelessly, as though he no longer expected a reply. The maid shrieked and ran into his arms, and he covered her face with kisses.

At least they had accomplished one good thing today. Peony blinked the moisture from her eyes.

But if she had thought to see the prince organizing rescue parties, or at the very least exhorting the people to take courage, she was doomed to disappointment. Where in heaven's name was he? For there were two of his privy councillors, each clutching the other as though to let go would mean collapse. And there, behind them—

"Mr. Douglas!" she exclaimed. "All of you, come with me."

With Detective Hayes and Timothy acting rather like the cowcatcher on a locomotive engine, Peony pushed through the crowd, using elbows and hips in a most unladylike way. The closer she came to the ministers, the more the people seemed to be crowding in to demand help. They burst out from between two shouting gentlemen and Peony practically fell into Evan Douglas's arms.

"Miss Churchill!" he exclaimed, setting her on her feet. "Barnaby. What on earth?" He looked up to see the curve of *Iris*'s fuselage looming behind the roof of the damaged palace. "How…?"

"We are moored to the ballroom terrace, sir," Timothy said. "We've come to offer our help."

"That's brave of you," Evan said. His face was white, his hair and clothes nearly the same, so covered in dust was he. Two of the jingling chains on his trouser legs had been torn off, and his shirt would never be clean again. "If only I knew where to begin."

"With doctors," Peony said briskly, recovering herself all at once. "Are the injured being seen to?"

A spasm passed over Evan's face. "Did you not see what happened to the church?"

"We saw the spire fall," Detective Hayes said. "What does that have to do with doctors?"

"Everything," Evan said simply. "The people go to the mission *asistencias* for healing. The padres there are well versed in herb lore and skilled in surgery. But ... the church collapsed. And with it the *asistencia*, burying heaven only knows how many monks. I have just had a report of survivors. They are bringing them now." He drew in a breath. "I'm afraid I am all the palace has at the moment, and that is not saying much. My training is in hurts of the mind. Though I can attend the hurts of the body to some degree, some of these people need surgeons."

"Where is the nearest operating *asis—asistencia*?" Peony asked. "We can take the injured there in *Iris*."

Evan looked as though he could hardly believe his luck. "Are you serious?"

"I do not waste time with flippancy when lives are at stake, sir," she said, with a smile to warm the reproof. "There is another mission in the city, is there not? Nuestra Señora de las Estrellas?"

Evan shook his head. "We sent a runner first thing. The mission has been destroyed. Half of it swallowed by the earth, from the runner's account."

"Wait—that is where May Lin and Daisy were going this morning," Detective Hayes exclaimed. *"Swallowed?"*

Evan froze as the recollection seemed to hit him, and he scrubbed his face with both hands. "May Lin's meeting. To discuss the landaus." His head dropped into his fingers and he groaned. "The runner reports a crevasse running through the courtyard and into the building at least twenty feet deep. They have not yet numbered the people who fell into it. I cannot bear it."

"We will help you bear it," Peony said, gripping his shoulder and hoping it would give him strength. "Where is the Viceroy?"

Evan lowered his hands and recovered himself enough to pat hers in thanks. "I do not know. I have every soldier I can spare searching, but have not yet had a report."

"His bedroom is open to the sky," Timothy said, "and the bed is hanging halfway out."

"You were in his room?" Evan asked, his eyebrows rising.

"It was on the way," Peony told him. "But Mr. Douglas, there was blood on the sheets. I fear the prince may be injured, possibly wandering the corridors, out of his wits."

"It won't be the first time," Evan muttered, then shook himself. "The soldiers will find him. And in his absence, and with the incapacity of those two ministers over there, as senior minister, I am in charge. So." He took a breath. "We will accept your kind offer and convey as many of the injured aboard your ship as will fit. I will fetch Isabela and her parents. My future father-in-law is showing symptoms of heart palpitations from trauma, and I want him out of the city as fast as may be. The nearest mission of a size to support an *asistencia* is San Gregorio, so I will send you there. Let us hope they have not suffered as we have."

"San Gregorio," Detective Hayes repeated. "You're sending us to Joe?"

For the first time, Evan smiled. A real smile, wiped clean of despair. "Lady Honoria San Gregorio to you, you dam-destroying miscreant. She will be delighted to see you, and Ella will cover your face with enough kisses for both of them."

Ella? Who was this person who took kissing Detective Hayes so for granted? Peony felt her hackles go up, and then chastised herself for a fool. She had no right. And now was far from the time to indulge herself when so many were hurt and needing their help.

"We will depart at once," she said. "Timothy, return to the ship and instruct the captain to land here in the courtyard. There are enough men unhurt that they can hold the ropes until the injured are taken aboard."

"Yes, miss." He took off at a run, and a scant quarter of an hour later, the hundreds of people weeping in the courtyard let out a roar of panic, and scattered for the walls, trampling the fallen grapevines in their haste to get out of the way.

The airship settled above the flagstones like a queen upon her throne.

Evan and Barnaby seized two of the ropes, and the former shouted orders into the crowd. Several men came forward, cautious as deer, to grasp the other ropes, gaping upward at the lovely gondola and the flawless curve of the fuselage above their heads.

It took well over an hour to assist, convey, and otherwise chivvy the injured and those caring for them on to the ship and into its salons. Belatedly, Peony realized that this was likely the first time any of them had ever been on an airship. Hmph. Well, if it could take them to where they could find healing and care, perhaps the palace's inhabitants would change their minds about flying in the face of God. Perhaps there would be a revolution of the technological kind, and airships would become part of life rather than simply permitted by the new law and consequently avoided.

A man using a broken tree branch as a crutch was helped up the gangway by a boy, and that seemed to be everyone. Until Peony became aware of a heated argument taking place at the bottom of said gangway.

"Isabela, please. You must accompany your father and mother, and see that Senor Ignatio receives the care he needs."

"And leave you here facing death and destruction? Certainly not!" A small, shapely, and undeniably beautiful young woman set her fists on her hips, the roses in her hair practically trembling with indignation. "We are to be married, Evan. That means we face the disasters of life together as well as its joys."

Isabela de la Carrera y Borreaga, Evan's fiancée, whom Peony had met last night at the ball. She could understand Evan's need to see the woman he loved safe and out of danger. At the same time, Peony would like to see any man she had chosen try to leave her behind while he faced so much as a speeding steambus without her.

She glanced at Detective Hayes, catching him in the act of glancing at her. Heat seeped into her cheeks, and to counteract it, she stepped forward to lay a hand upon Isabela's silken arm.

"Lady Isabela."

The girl jumped and whirled, as though she had believed herself and Evan to be utterly alone. "Senorita Peonía. Help me to convince this so obstinate man that we must not be parted when there is danger."

"I would, my dear, but I fear an even greater danger."

"What is that, Miss Churchill?" Evan's eyes held concern.

To Isabela, she said, "With your father incapacitated, there is no one aboard my ship with any authority over the Californio citizens." Peony lowered her voice. "You will shortly be the second lady in the land, and may speak with your father's authority. Should there be those aboard whose pain or pride makes them ... unruly ... it would add to the safety of everyone on board if there were someone who could keep order."

Isabela glared at her. "Is this a ruse to separate me from my beloved?"

"Certainly not. It is the literal truth. None of these people save you have traveled by airship. There may be some panic, and your leadership would go a long way toward quelling it."

"I have been successful in my aeronautical lessons," the young woman admitted reluctantly. "Am I at liberty to go anywhere I please?"

"Even the navigation gondola," Peony promised recklessly. Isabela, she had no doubt, could handle Captain Boyle.

"Then I will go, to assist my prince's people and keep order," she said at last. "Not because I am a foolish lamb who must be hurried out of the way when *el terremoto* strikes!"

"Thank you, my lady," Peony said fervently. "We will lift at once. Good-bye for now, Mr. Douglas. We will return as soon as we can."

She ran up the gangway so as not to have to witness the passionate leave-taking of Evan and his bride-to-be. There was a distinct possibility they might not see each other again.

And when Detective Hayes jogged up the gangway to allow Rebecca and Lucas to perform their duties before lift, she allowed him to believe that the color in her cheeks was because of his friend's public show of affection.

Not because she wished that the detective would kiss her with that kind of feeling. No, indeed.

1:10 p.m.

The reek of mildewed canvas and the excrement of rats was nearly overwhelming—enough to stop May Lin's breath in her throat. She pushed herself off the wet boards of the *lazaretto*—the storage locker in the bow of the boat into which they'd just been dumped—and rolled her companion over.

"Lin? Are you all right?"

A tear leaked out of the corner of the girl's eye before her lashes fluttered up and she gazed into May Lin's face. "Oww. Where are we? Why do the padres treat us like this?"

"Not you. It is I whom they hate."

"But why?" Lin pushed herself up to a sitting position. "Because you are a Canton?"

"Partly. But mostly because I am a woman, and a witch. They cannot bear to see me so close to the Viceroy, so they are taking advantage of the earthquake to do away with me."

But they had been ordered to kill her before the crevasse

had opened up in the refectory. At this very moment, the bishop was probably singing hymns of praise for God's cooperation, as he did a victory dance back down the tunnel to what remained of his residence.

"But I've done nothing to offend," the girl said sadly.

"Only come to my aid," May Lin told her. "For which I thank you, even though I might question your sanity."

"We are in this together," the girl said. "And we will get out of it together."

"You are right." May Lin pulled her to her feet. "Let us take stock of our situation."

"How? It's dark."

"Your eyes will adjust in a moment."

The *lazaretto* was dark, but May Lin's eyes were keen. The light coming through chinks in the hull showed the pile of rotting sail, the pulleys and tackle, an an overturned bucket.

"Are we in the hold?" Lin asked.

"This boat is not big enough for a hold. This is the *lazaretto*, the place where the dead are kept if they die at sea." She pointed to a long crate. "See? A coffin."

"A *lazaretto*. That's what they call a prison ship, too," Lin whispered. "There is no land here to waste on gaols or housing prisoners, so they use derelicts in the harbor." She swallowed. "If the prisoners are found guilty of their crimes, they are taken out to sea and the ship sunk."

A cold shiver plunged through May Lin's stomach.

"We must scream for help," Lin said. "Surely someone will come."

"Certainly," May Lin replied. "The watchman topside, and his club, with which he will beat us into silence."

"We can't just sit here and wait for them to sink us," Lin snapped. "We have to escape."

May Lin agreed wholeheartedly, but a thorough search of the *lazaretto* revealed that not only was the hatch locked down tight, the space had been reinforced to contain capital offenders. No one was getting out of here until someone unlocked the hatch.

With a sigh of frustration, May Lin arranged herself on the bucket opposite the short flight of ladder-like steps leading up to the hatch, while Lin huddled on the end of the coffin. "What are you doing?"

"Preparing myself," she told the girl. "When the hatch is raised, I will leap and disable whoever is coming down. It is our only option."

"That padre who threw us in here was awfully big. He carried you for a mile at least."

"I have ways to compensate for size. And strength."

"Have you killed a man before?"

"Yes." She had had her knives then, and bombs, and pistols. Depending only on one's bare hands evened out the odds rather more than she would like.

"With these?" The girl unwound her woven wool sash and May Lin nearly tipped over in her astonishment.

"Where did you get my knives?" She took them, nearly unable to believe her own eyes, and slid first one and then the other into their sheaths on her forearms. The snap of the closure as they were once again secured where they should be was the best thing that had happened in this whole awful day.

"They fell on the ground when they grabbed you, and I picked them up." The girl frowned. "I should have used them on that monk. Then maybe he wouldn't have tossed me over his shoulder so easily."

"You should not. Concealing them was the smartest thing you could have done." For the first time, May Lin felt a lightening of the black cloud of despair she had been fighting since the moment the earth had jerked out from under her feet. "You didn't happen to see what happened to Perdida, did you?"

"Is that the chicken? No, she fell on the ground and then the monk grabbed me and I couldn't see her anymore."

Poor Perdida. Out of the frying pan—perhaps literally—and into the fire.

"They won't find us quite so helpless when they come back," she told the girl grimly. "Well done."

"I would have told you before, but—"

"Yes, you should."

"I'm sorry," she said meekly.

"To make reparations, you must tell me about yourself." She resumed her perch upon the wooden bucket. Who knew how long they had to wait, so they might as well use the time to become acquainted. "Our lives are in each other's hands. I should like to know the person on whom my survival might depend."

"If I tell, then you have to."

"Agreed. You first."

The girl wrapped her sash about herself, knotted it, and settled back on the coffin. "I was born here, in the month the wild roses bloom. Thirteen years ago. That's why I know so much about it. I lived with my parents in Stouts Alley, and went to school at the mission. I learned the Texican tongue there, and was taught the Canton tongue at home."

"Not the Californio tongue?"

"Oh yes. But I could never get my mind around it very well."

"And your parents? What were their names?"

"My father's name was Yang Ju-Long, my mother Chu Chunhua."

May Lin sat up straight, and the half of her mind that had been focused on the hatch above their heads snapped to attention.

"I told you that he had come from the Middle Kingdom in search of his sister when my mother was expecting me," Lin went on.

"His sister." May Lin said, her voice a little hoarse. "Who came to Gold Mountain to marry someone."

"A bad man. He took her dowry and turned her out after—after behaving to her like a husband when they weren't married."

"He raped her."

Lin turned her face away, a pale oval in the gloom. "My father never put it like that. He had the story from the brute's housekeeper, before he was forbidden to go back to the house. It was a large house, up on the rocks, with a view of the bay."

May Lin focused on her breathing. "And the man? Is he still living?" One hand slipped into the opposite sleeve to touch the hilt of the knife.

"I do not know. He was when I left. My parents caught the typhoid last winter, during the floods, and died. I did not want to go to a flower house or to work on the railroads, so I ran away."

"Where?"

"Just ... away. Out of the Royal Kingdom, because they

hate us here. I found work as a laundress in Reno, and ended up in Georgetown, where I met William and Davey."

"The friends you came with in the odd conveyance."

"Yes. We helped Daisy and Freddie solve a murder there. And in Santa Fe we helped a man whose bride had been stolen from him. But lately, Daisy and Freddie have been in Bodie, while William and Davey and I were with the Navapai, in their village on the cliffs above Santa Fe."

"I know that village." But Daisy and Freddie had been in Bodie? The gold mining town where there were so many murders that people greeted each other in the morning with, "Has there been a man for breakfast?" She tried to imagine the oh-so-proper Daisy Linden there, and failed. "And what were you doing in Santa Fe, if they were in Bodie?"

"The shaman's son, Tobin, is a clever engineer. He was making adjustments to the conveyance, so we missed all the fun. Daisy and Freddie were nearly killed. She sent us a newspaper account of it."

"The Wild West is not a safe place for young ladies on their own, as both you and I know. Tell me, what was the name of your father's sister? The one rejected by her prospective husband?"

"She was called Yang Jiao-Lan. That means—"

May Lin drew a deep breath of certainty. "Beautiful orchid."

"How do you know? You have no accent—do you speak the Canton tongue as well?"

"I know it because it was my mother's name."

Slowly, Lin's head lifted from her contemplation of her own story to meet May Lin's wide-eyed gaze. "Your ... mother?"

"She was rejected by her husband-to-be, but not before he raped her. She found her way across the mountains and fell in with the river witches. She was the greatest inventor the canyons have ever seen. Everything I know about engineering comes from her—she had the best education in mechanics her family could afford, back in the old country, before she came here."

"Then you are—" Lin looked her up and down. "Your father isn't that brute in the house with the view, is he?" She waved her hand in the direction of the Canton district, so close and yet so very far away.

May Lin laughed. It was not a nice laugh. "No. My father was a cowboy out of Texico City. He drove cattle through Santa Fe every year, and my mother would hop the eastbound freight to see him. Once she even took me."

"Is he still alive?"

May Lin shook her head. "There was a fight in a saloon and he was shot. He wasn't even part of the fight—he was playing Cowboy Poker in the back." After a moment, she said, "Aren't you going to ask me?"

"Ask you what?"

"Why your aunt and my mother should have the same name? The same story?"

Lin shrugged. "There are a lot of Yangs here. And many women are forced by men. Even me. Almost. Once."

May Lin touched the sheath of her knife again. Let any man touch this child now, and he would regret it. "Let me ask you a different question, then. Why do you suppose we are both called Lin?"

"It was my father's mother's name."

"And my mother's mother's name. Are you seeing it now, Yang Lin-Bai?"

The girl's face went slack. "You are— Are we—"

May Lin nodded. "We are first cousins. My mother was your father's sister, whom he came all this way to find. She never knew, you know. That he was looking for her."

"And he never knew where she had gone," Lin whispered. "Truly? We are cousins?"

"I have no birth certificate to show you."

"Nor do I. But the names cannot be a coincidence." The girl stood and laid her hand on her arm. "We are *family?*"

The tremulous hope in her eyes brought unexpected tears to May Lin's own. "Yes," she whispered. "I can see my mother's eyebrows and chin when I look at you."

"And I can see Papa's nose."

"I do not like my nose."

"Blame our grandfather. Papa did not like his, either."

May Lin began to laugh, and that made the tears start, and before she knew it, the girl was in her arms, the two of them laughing and crying together.

And somewhere deep in May Lin's heart, a terrible wound began, just a little, to heal.

FREDERICA LINDEN FELT Peony's censure from across the ballroom, even as she turned and fled back out on to the terrace. There were some things that she could not bring herself to do no matter the price … and venturing out into so much death and destruction was one of them.

They would know she was there. The dead. They would

want her to carry messages, and would drive her mad with their grief and rage, and she simply could not bear it.

She was frantic enough not knowing if Daisy were dead or alive or lying injured in the street. She must do something. But she felt paralyzed by fear and indecision. She dared not lean on the balustrade of the cantilevered terrace, in case a tremor tossed her off. She clung instead to *Iris*'s mooring rope. What madness had made her and the detective agree to stay with Peony this morning when Daisy had left? Well, she suspected she knew Barnaby's reasons. But she did not share them.

She ought to have remained on the island with Mr. Barnicott's conveyance, where if Daisy were alive, she would know where to find her, and where the only ghosts were those of its original inhabitants. They ignored her as they went about their business gathering acorns and fishing the way she assumed they had in life. Could it be that acceptance of one's fate led to a calmer afterlife, even if they had been killed two centuries past?

She would never know. All she knew was that those who had been killed in this palace—today, and in the years since it had been built—had not accepted anything, promises of eternity included. She must stay as far from them as she could, even if it meant looking like the worst kind of coward.

And she must decide what to do, for she could not stand here like a sleeping automaton while Daisy was lost.

The Boyles left her alone, returning to the navigation gondola to keep watch amid the comforting presence of vanes and levers and helm. Clinging to her rope, Freddie gazed down into the gardens below, where trees had been torn out by the roots and lay sprawled on lawns that once had been carefully clipped. The fountain had collapsed, and even the water feeding it had stopped. Presumably the pipe to it had broken somewhere under the ground. Behind her, the ubiquitous grape vines, as big around as her wrist, had managed to cling to the wall of the palace, but bunches of grapes had been torn loose and lay smashed upon the stones below, their juice beginning to dry now as the heat of the day increased.

Sudden movement in the garden caused her to put aside a little of her fear in favor of curiosity, and lean out to watch.

Two men carried the unconscious form of a third, dressed only in a pair of pants and a shirt, out of the palace and under the surviving trees. Was he injured? Were they taking him to the padres for medical care?

Then Freddie's gaze sharpened. Why, she knew him! She'd been introduced at the ball. But why were two men carrying the Viceroy out of the palace, dressed like that? He hadn't even any shoes on, and there was no help to be found in the gardens.

A third man stepped out of the shadow of a pine while his companions laid the prince on the ground to rest their arms. He pulled a neckerchief from his companion's throat, balled it up, and stuffed it in the unconscious prince's mouth, then whipped off his own and tied it over the gag. It was not to staunch any bleeding, then, but to keep the prince quiet should he wake up.

Good heavens. They were abducting the Viceroy in broad daylight!

She yanked on the rope, and the resulting dip in the ship's trim caused the captain to look out. With frantic signs, Freddie indicated they must lower. When the ship was in reach, she ran up the gangway and burst into the gondola. "Captain Boyle! The prince is being kidnapped!"

His brows rose. "Indeed, miss. What would you like me to do?"

That was a poser. "Help him, of course!"

"And leave my station? What if Miss Churchill should return? Who will fly the ship?"

"She will, I expect. Captain, they're down in the garden at this moment, kidnapping him!"

"That is not my nevermind, young lady," he said gravely. "Nor yours, either. The affairs of princes are their own. My affair is to be here when my employer needs me, and to look after you."

"But—" She waved her hands in frustration, then rattled up the circular stair into the main saloon and along the corridor to the cabin she shared with Daisy. She snatched up her Colt, and was buckling its harness around her hips even as she ran back down the gangway. What luck that she had had practice in escaping the eagle eyes of the dormitory monitors at school by shimmying down the vine outside her window. The grapevines were even more sturdy than English ivy, and took her weight without complaint.

Maggie Polgarth had gone with her on a number of those nocturnal adventures, raiding the kitchen for cake, or for a fish head to slip under the bonnet of Penelope Frayne's landau so that it would set up a terrible stink when she ignited the boiler. Maggie, she felt perfectly sure, would approve of Freddie's tearing across the lawns in pursuit of the prince and his kidnappers, and of ignoring Captain Boyle's shouts for her to come back.

The fact that the men were burdened with his unconscious

form made up for the minutes she had lost equipping herself. She caught up to them at a gate in the stone wall that surrounded the palace. The gate gave on to a set of steps so steep they were practically a ladder down the rocks to the street below. Freddie was forced to wait some anxious minutes until the men had reached the bottom with their awkward burden and were on their way once more before flying down after them, her boots barely touching the stones.

And then she was out in the streets of the stricken city, the last place she wanted to be. The air was full of dust and smoke and the pale forms of the dead and the shrieks of the living. If it had not been so horrifying, she would have said it was the perfect environment in which to pull off an abduction.

One of the men, the one who seemed to be in charge, yanked a wheelbarrow out of someone's front garden, and the two at the prince's shoulders and feet dumped him into it. After this the going was faster, though they had to keep stopping to balance the barrow, and to wheel it around heaps of fallen stone.

Freddie followed them, keeping well back, until the neighborhood began to change. Instead of houses and shops, the buildings were larger. Warehouses and offices, some in ruins, some still standing. Soon even that changed, and she was forced to dodge into the doorways of saloons and flower houses, shaking off importunate hands at the point of her revolver and ignoring the catcalls of the desert flowers milling about in the street, waiting anxiously for the next tremor.

The Barbary Coast.

Heaven help her. Had Papa been here? She must stay alive long enough to find out, but first things first.

Her cold fingers gripped the Colt.

The three men abandoned the wheelbarrow when they reached the docks themselves. One of them pulled a canvas hammock down off an abandoned wagon full of goods, and rolled the prince's unconscious body into it. With the ropes at either end wrapped around their arms, the hammock slung between them, they trotted after their leader, their boots pounding hollowly on the planks of the pier—one of the few left standing.

They must be putting him on a ship, here in the last place anyone would ever think to look.

She must help him. She was the only one who could.

Freddie dragged a deep breath into lungs that wanted to contract with terror, ducked out from under the misty, pleading hand of someone reaching through the hull of the steam vessel moored a few feet away, and zigzagged down the pier after them.

CHAPTER 11

1:35 p.m.

Zuo Jen Wei's prediction turned out to be correct—the printer stared at Daisy, looking from her face to her hand, which held the ink sketch and its hastily applied washes, in a kind of disbelieving disdain.

"When so many are injured and need help, you wish me to make ommatographs?" he repeated, as though he had not heard her perfectly well the first time. "Now? And distribute them?"

"Not *now*, of course," she said, because she could hardly say anything else. "You will wish to join the rescue parties. We are doing the same. But—"

"I am relieved that we agree." He shook his head and rounded the end of the counter, swinging what appeared to be a sack of supplies and tools to his shoulder. "Leave it, and perhaps in a few weeks there might be time for such a task."

"A few weeks!" Daisy shook her head urgently. "I do not have a few weeks. My father could be on a ship even now."

"There are fathers and daughters and mothers and sons across the creek who do not have even a few minutes," he told her tersely. "My wife is in the back. Leave it with her. I must go." And he strode out the door, his sack jouncing on his shoulder.

Daisy pressed her lips together, but still, a sob burst out of her in a great hiccup. She could not blame the man. Of course he must go to the aid of the suffering. But could no one spare even a moment for Papa, after she and Freddie had come so far and endured so much?

In her basket on the counter, the chicken tilted her head, one purple eye examining Daisy. "I am well, little bird. But everyone I love seems to be lost."

"Surely not everyone." A dark-eyed woman about ten years younger than the printer came through the curtain that led to the back of the shop. "Have you just been speaking with my husband?"

Daisy nodded, then remembered her manners. She curtseyed.

The woman smiled. "No need for such civilities when we are all in such a state. I am Madame Yuen. And you are Miss Linden. I am very good at eavesdropping, you see." She gazed at the occupant of the basket. "Do you offer the *wuguji* in lieu of payment?"

The silky little bird squawked. Daisy grasped the basket firmly. "No indeed. She is my companion, for the moment. She is not to be eaten."

"Very well. Perhaps she will bring you good luck. Now, you were to leave something with me?"

Daisy no longer held out any hope that anyone would see the portrait, or if they did, that it would do any good at all.

Still, she slid the square of lovely toothy paper that Madame Zuo had given her across the counter. "This is my father. I believe he came to the Barbary Coast, attempting to work his passage on a ship. His destination might have been Victoria, in the Canadas, but we are not certain of his route."

"I see. And when was this?"

"Within the last week, I think." Daisy sighed, and pulled out the silk handkerchief to dab at her nose as the tears heated her face once more. "My sister and I have been searching for him since July."

The lady's gaze took her in, shimmering with sympathy and even a little admiration. "You are brave."

Daisy's lips flickered in her best attempt at a smile. "I think we are reduced now simply to stubbornness. In each place we go, we find just enough hope to keep going."

Madame Yuen looked past Daisy to the door. "There is little enough hope here this morning." The door closed, and a tiny brass bell rang. "Ah Mah," she said, "you were not to go out in the streets. It is too dangerous."

The elderly lady who had come in said something in the Canton tongue.

"She says she has lived through many an earthquake before," Madame Yuen said to Daisy. "This is my grandmother."

Daisy curtseyed, and the older woman bowed.

"This is why we build here the way we do," Madame Yuen went on. "Our grandparents' generation is all too familiar with the shifting of the dragon in the old country. Those who build houses have learned to adapt to a certain restlessness of the earth. It is familiar to us."

The old lady caught sight of the portrait on the counter,

and picked it up. She asked a question of Daisy, who looked uncertainly at Madame Yuen.

"She asks who this is," the latter translated.

"It is my father," Daisy said to the older woman. "I had hoped to have ommatographs made to show to people. Someone may have seen him. But the time is not appropriate."

A short exchange followed between the two women. "You do not need ommatographs, she says. Why, Ah Ma?" A moment later, Madame Yuen translated. "My grandmother sells dumplings on the waterfront every morning, when it is more likely that violent men will be passed out on the piers and working people will be hungry. She says she saw this man five days ago."

Daisy felt a great leap of her heart, and she barely prevented herself from seizing the older woman in a hug, and then demanding everything she knew. "Is she certain?"

"Yes, for he was wearing a greatcoat of this very shade of blue." Madame Yuen tapped the portrait. "In this warm weather, she thought he was mad."

"He is not mad," Daisy said. "He has lost his memory. The coat is all he has in this world. I would not take it off, either, were I he."

Madame Yuen spoke to her grandmother at some length, presumably conveying this information.

"Where exactly did she see him?" Hope was pushing so insistently on Daisy's breastbone she could hardly breathe.

"He was, as you say, boarding a ship."

"Which one?"

"She does not remember—" Daisy let out a gasp of disappointment. "—but she remembers that it was a Texican woman's name. She heard someone hail the ship—she does not read the English letters. If the harbor master is still alive, you might be able to find out its name and destination."

"Do you think the harbor master might still be alive?" Daisy was feeling a little light-headed. Five days ago, Papa had been here! They were on the right trail!

"She cannot know, but she will take you there."

"Now?"

The old lady nodded. Daisy grasped her hand. "But you must not. It is too dangerous. The earth is still shaking."

"That does not bother Ah Ma. I will come with you." Madame Yuen hustled into the rear and reappeared a moment later with a paper parasol and a basket two or three sizes larger than the one in which the little *wuguji* reposed.

"A parasol, Madame? Do you expect rain?"

"No." She pressed a lever near the handle shaped like a fish, and a slender spike shot out of the other end, locking into place. "Earthquakes or no, one does not go to the waterfront unprepared."

Daisy opened her reticule, tucked the second portrait into it, and showed them the grip of her Thaxton pistol.

Madame Yuen's polite smile widened into real appreciation. "Shall we?"

Daisy followed the two women to the elevating platform outside, and they were swiftly deposited at street level. On the corner opposite stood William and Davey. Urgently, she waved them over.

"William, this lady—Madame Yuen's grandmama—has seen Papa boarding a ship! We are going this moment to the docks. If I can find the harbor master, I will ask him its name and destination. Is that not wonderful news?"

William and Davey both bowed to the Canton ladies, who

bowed back, and Daisy completed the introductions. "It is indeed," William said. "I wish we could share news as good."

Their guides set a brisk pace.

"No sign of Lin in Stouts Alley, then?" Daisy asked as they hurried after them.

"None. Either the neighbors had not seen her, or they affected not to understand me. Perhaps they thought me intrusive."

"Or a spy," Davey said helpfully.

"It amounts to the same thing," William told him. "I hope we will have better luck at the harbor."

As they descended the hill, a view opened up out over the bay, with the forest of masts and sails half a mile away now reduced to chaos. The island they had left this morning in such good spirits floated just beyond.

But something was missing from the landscape besides the churches and buildings that had been there earlier, before the cataclysm. And with a sudden chill tiptoeing down the back of her neck, Daisy realized what it was.

"William," she said hoarsely. "Where is Peony's airship? *And where is Freddie?*"

WITH HER KNIVES restored to her, May Lin's mind began to work along its usual efficient channels. The hull of this old tub might be battered and filthy, but it was watertight and could contain prisoners. So any hope she might have had of finding a chink and carving their way out was dashed. Such a tactic would take hours of concentrated work, anyway, and she was not certain they had hours. For as the afternoon lengthened and the spots of light that entered through knot-holes over their heads inched along the deck, it was clear that no one had plans to give them any food or water.

"That tells me they will dispose of us soon," she mused aloud to Lin. "Why waste provisions? They are probably going to sail on the tide."

"It was high tide or a little before when we were tossed in here," Lin said. "The piers above the waterline were dry, not wet."

An excellent observation. One that May Lin had not made, despite her familiarity with water. "Very soon, then. We must prepare ourselves to act."

"A surprise attack when they open the hatch?"

She and Lin were sitting side by side on the coffin, which was built to be sturdy and contain bodily fluids during long voyages. May Lin marveled at how comforting was the sensation of a child leaning against her, even allowing her arm around her shoulders, sharing her slender body's warmth as the day cooled. Equally marvelous and strange was how protective May Lin felt toward a girl who was practically a stranger, yet so familiar, now that her features had been illuminated by memory.

Her family. All she had on this side of the world. It was a miracle they had found each other.

She would protect this girl with her life. And oddly enough, she had the feeling that it was mutual. The girl had given her trust in a moment—all of it, like a gift handed over in a rush of joy. She would never betray that trust. Never.

Come what may.

"They might not open the hatch," May Lin said, forcing herself to contemplate their situation once more. "They may simply cast off and set a course for the— What did you call it?"

"The golden gate," Lin reminded her. "That is what they call it in the Canton district—though not in a child's hearing. I think it means something rude. This ship—"

"Boat. It's a three-masted lugger. Not very big."

"It must go at the turn of the tide. At low water, there are too many rocks in the golden gate for ships to pass through, even empty like this one. And then we must get through the place where the water is roiling and rough. I must warn you that I am no sailor. I can tolerate a river well enough. But the sea makes me sick."

"If you are sick, that will make no difference in here," May Lin said with a moue of distaste. "From the smell, you will not be the first."

"But how will we get out of this *lazaretto*?" Lin asked, clearly trying not to sound afraid. "If they plan to sink the boat?"

May Lin had been wondering this very thing, even as she had inspected the hull earlier. "It is my opinion that a second boat will go out with us, to take off the crew. Then they will either bomb her or hull her to force her to capsize. In either case, I hope you can swim."

"I can."

"Good. So can I. But that is a last resort, for we will not last long in water so cold. Our first plan is to hope they are foolish enough to open the hatch, giving us our moment to attack. Let us take our places. It cannot be long."

The most practical plan was to stay out of sight of anyone descending the ladder. His ankles and knees would then be exposed to her knives from behind. May Lin and her young cousin had no more settled there than they heard the thump of booted feet on the gangway. They crossed the deck, coming toward them. Her blood leaped and began a dizzy race through her veins as she unsnapped the knives and let the hilts slide into her hands.

She counted four sets of boots, maybe six. Two sets were clumping closer … closer …

The lock was opened with a clank and the hasp thrown back. Someone flung up the hatch cover and May Lin was blinded by the light of late afternoon. But that did not stop her. Her knives flashed up—

—and nearly pierced a dead body swaddled in canvas. It thumped down one step, then rolled and fell three feet to the deck.

A shout of laughter rang out. "Some company for you!" someone called, to a chorus of whistles and derision.

The body subsided in a lifeless heap as the hatch cover slammed down, plunging them into gloom once more. The hasp and lock clanked into place. Sailors shouted, and the anchor chain rattled as it was hauled up. And a moment later, Lin groaned as the lugger rocked in the grip of the outgoing tide.

They had lost their chance. May Lin choked back a growl of frustrated disappointment.

Another groan.

"Lin? Are you going to be sick?"

"That wasn't me," came the whispered reply. "Whoever that is, I don't think they're dead."

May Lin could make certain of it with one swift stroke of her knife. But what were the odds that this captive was an enemy of the padres, too? An enemy of the church was likely to be a friend of theirs.

She slipped the knives into their sheaths and secured them. Then she crept around to the base of the steps. "Are you alive?" Her fingers found a thick, hastily constructed seam. "Lin, look. They've sewn him in." One of her blades took care of the clumsy stitches and was re-sheathed. Then May Lin pulled the canvas away, like opening a pod of peas. She still could not see the prisoner clearly. Her eyes had not adjusted yet from the assault of daylight. "Can you speak?"

A gasp. "Who is there?"

A man. Young. "Are you hurt?" May Lin demanded.

"Y-yes. Where … am I?"

"You are on a prison vessel bound out of the harbor. I do not know our destination. Is anything broken?"

"How would I … know?"

May Lin paused, her skin tingling with shock. That voice. It couldn't be. No.

"Wiggle your fingers and toes," Lin suggested.

A brief, rustling silence as the person seemed to experiment with his appendages. As he did, May Lin's nose detected the scent of oranges. No, lemons. And lavender. How strange to smell that familiar scent here in this cesspit. It was almost as though Fate were giving her a final gift before she doled out her death: Her cousin revealed to her, and the prince's scent, and then farewell for ever.

May Lin's eyes widened as her brain snapped to its conclusion like a distracted soldier being prodded by a rifle. She drew a quick breath and tried to calm the sudden gallop of her heart.

"Fingers and toes … work," the young man said. "But pain. Was I … beaten?"

"You were thrown down the stairs," May Lin said. "Can you move your head, Your Serene Highness?"

Lin gasped. So did their new companion.

"Dios mio," he said, his voice rising to a squeak in surprise. "May Lin? What … in the name of Mother River … is happening?"

CHAPTER 12

2:15 p.m.

Frederica Linden could no longer see what the sailors aboard the wreck of a boat had done with the prince, who had still been rolled up in the canvas hammock. But from her hiding place behind a haphazard stack of barrels on the pier, she could hear their shouts as two of them climbed the yards, where they began to unfurl the largest of the ship's three reddish-brown sails.

Another man pulled up the gangway.

Dear heaven, what should she do?

"Looking for a ride, little lady?" A miasma of sweat and rum assaulted her nose just before a drunken man the size of a steambus grabbed her left arm. "I got plenty for ya. What's your price?" He made a lewd gesture that caused Freddie's entire body to recoil.

She did *not* have time for this.

The sail thundered down and the man at the bow cast off the first rope.

Freddie jerked the Colt out of its holster and rammed the barrel between the drunkard's eyes. "Get away from me."

"Whoa! Whoa!" he quavered as he stumbled backward, a reddened circle imprinted between his brows. "No call for arms, I was just askin'."

She leaped out of her meager concealment and dashed up the pier, ramming the gun into its holster and snapping its strap in place as she went. The stern rope was cast off … the ship was pulling away … two feet from the pier … three …

Freddie took a flying leap at one of the ropes that dangled from the gunwale. Her palms burned as it slipped through her hands—she clamped her knees on it through her skirts—then her boots—

With a thump, she struck the hull of the ship like a pendulum, and the force of it nearly made her let go.

"What was that?"

"Hey! We got a passenger."

"Leech, more like. Shoot it."

"Someone'll hear."

"You idjit—folks got bigger troubles than us. Now either fish or cut bait. We gotta make some speed before someone figures out he's gone."

"Rope's too thick to cut, and a waste besides. Fish it is."

A bullet sang past Freddie's shoulder and tore through the roweling water below. A second bullet tugged at her billowing hems and with a shriek of terror, Freddie's instinct for self preservation blotted out heart and determination.

She let go of the rope and plummeted into the harbor.

Cold.

The frigid sea squeezed her chest tight and stopped her

breath. But a trail of bubbles zipped past her elbow and brought her to her senses. She pulled at the water with both hands, kicking for all she was worth, her walking skirt alternately wrapping around her legs and billowing up around her waist.

With a gasp she surfaced, slapped the water from her face, and thrashed into a turn. Ship—gun—where—

The ship with the dirty red sails was gone, somewhere beyond the wrecked hulk of a two-master just to the north. A wave picked her up and flung her into a piling supporting the dock where it had been moored.

Safe. Alive.

The pilings marched up to the muddy shoreline already exposed by the outgoing tide. Her teeth chattering, Freddie swam from post to post, her hands sliced by the purple, barnacle-encrusted mussels clinging to them, the salt water stinging in the cuts. Doggedly, she let the waves carry her closer, until she could touch the bottom. It took some doing to get her feet under her and stagger to the shore in her sopping, heavy clothes. It took even more to realize that from under the pier, the bank rose straight up, clogged with old hulls and rocks and wreckage.

Freddie slogged along the bank, under the piers and ruined wharves of the Barbary Coast, sometimes up to her knees in seawater, frightening birds and seals alike. Until at last she found what she was looking for.

A stair. Undamaged. A miracle.

With the last of her strength, she climbed one step. Two. One more. Rest. Three to go.

At the landing she sat, dripping, hardly caring where she

was or who might be looking on, breathing hard. Her muddy, cut fingers curled around the wooden step, slimy with time and tide and neglect.

The tiny, forgotten stair was sunk between two large piers built so close together that only one side of each could be used. From this vantage point, she could see the iron hull of a steamship looming over her on one side, canted over so severely its keel was plainly visible in the water. On the other side, two wood hulls of sailing ships rose and fell as the waves lifted and sank on the other. They had suffered no hurt at all.

The wind came in off the water and she shivered. She could not stay here. She must go.

But where? The church? Our Lady of the Stars. That was where Daisy had been headed. By Freddie's admittedly poor reckoning, she was closer to it than to the palace.

The palace. The authorities—Mr. Douglas, the ministers of the government—they must be told. There might still be time to save the prince. She did not know where that pathetic boat was bound, for it did not look as though it would even get out of the harbor without shuddering to pieces. What had they wanted with him? Their accents had not sounded like those of the Californios, but what did she know?

Only one thing was clear. Unless Captain Boyle had had second thoughts and gone to tell someone the prince had been kidnapped, she was still the only witness. The only one who could help him.

Right, then. She must get herself away from the waterfront. And then she must ask some respectable person to direct her back to the palace. She must raise the alarm.

She pushed herself to her feet. At the top of the steps she

found not a street or an alley, such as there was in Bath coming up from the river, but a warehouse door, which of course was locked. As she stared at it dumbly, a little boy barreled through it. He was prettily dressed in a sailor suit and a hat with a flying ribbon. He tumbled down the steps all the way to the mud at the bottom. Freddie had just tensed her legs to run to his aid as he lay there, when he … dissolved.

A minute later, he came through the door again. Fell—

Freddie bit back a whimper and got herself back down the steps before she witnessed his death a third time, and crept along the muddy beach—wider now, at least, with the receding tide.

There must be another stair. Crushed hulls had been rammed up under the piers, heaving as the waves washed them closer to the beach. Entire buildings seemed to have come down on top of others, half buried in the mud. She had to get out of here. When the tide came in, she would be crushed, too, or die of cold in her wet clothes during the night. Already the sun had fallen out of sight behind the heaps of rubble above her, leaving her in shadows.

She must keep moving. North. The church had been to the north of the Barbary Coast, hadn't it? No, that had been the Canton district. Wait. Which way was north?

Freddie tamped down the rising panic crushing her breathing, and kept going. Another stair. Another landing. She looked up. Another warehouse, this one set on stilts driven into the mud. How on earth had it survived? Another dock, whose piers had not been milled from the trunks of trees, but something more slender, more lattice-like.

And still they allowed no way up.

Was she really going to die down here?

Voices. An argument. A woman—no, two—having a disagreement in the Canton tongue. Probably worked in a flower house. But a woman might have compassion on her. The women in the streets before had not, but they could not all be like that. She could not bear much more.

"Help." Her voice was barely more than a whisper. She tried again. "Help!"

No one was listening. Or winning the argument.

"Help!" She was so thirsty, and there was no moisture in her mouth to speak. But she must get their attention.

The Colt. She would fire it—that would do the trick. But when she pulled it from its holster, seawater ran out of the barrel. Oh dear. Did guns fire when they were wet? What would happen if she tried?

No, she didn't dare risk it. She rammed it back into its water-darkened holster and looked about her. Half buried in the mud was a scattering of refuse, likely washed off the docks. She kicked at it.

Belaying pin. Broken in half.

That would do.

She threw it as hard as she could, and it arced up and landed with a thump on the dock.

An exclamation, and then two ladies leaned cautiously over the edge of the pier, which had no railing. One had white hair, the other black. Both wore the tunics she had seen on Canton ladies. Not from the flower houses, then. Respectable ladies. What were they doing down here? Didn't they know they could be killed?

"Help," Freddie croaked. "Please."

The older one gasped, while the younger gestured to her

right and down. "Get on the elevating platform and we will bring you up."

Elevating platform?

And then she saw it, halfway along the pier, where the water had to be fifteen feet deep. It looked just like one of the horizontal struts between the slender piers, until the ladies began to operate an arrangement of ropes and pulleys that had not been apparent to her before. The platform dropped to water level.

"It is too far away," she called hoarsely. "I cannot reach it."

"You must swim," the younger one said. "There is no other way up."

"I cannot." A hot trickle of exhausted tears was all she could manage. "I cannot." She collapsed to her knees in the mud.

She heard a babble of voices—a scream—and then a man's voice, urgent. Oh no! The ladies had indeed been set upon. It was all her fault for delaying them. Freddie covered her face and wept in earnest.

A massive splash made her look up in terror—they had thrown one of the ladies in! But no.

A man was churning toward her through the waves. "Hang on, Freddie," William Barnicott shouted. "I'm coming."

And before her exhausted mind could comprehend what he was doing in the water—had he drowned? Was this his ghost?—she was seized by hands that were definitely corporeal.

"Come on. Back in the water," he panted. "By Jove, it's cold. You're freezing. We've got to get you warmed up." He hauled her up against his side and then plunged into the water again.

Goodness, how white his bare feet were—as white as his shirt—

And then he was swimming, half on his back supporting her, and kicking toward the platform, which was now submerged. He sat on it and dragged her up on it beside him. A second later the platform began to rise, out of the water and into the air, a cascade of seawater coming off their clothes like some kind of reverse waterspout.

In moments she was being pulled off the platform and into Daisy's arms. "Freddie! Oh dear heaven, Freddie! What has happened to you?"

"Later," the younger of the Canton ladies said urgently. "Mr. Barnicott, run up to the last street we passed and tell the *yang-che* man to come at once. He was waiting for a fare and we shall give him one, at double his usual rate."

Freddie's mind was too befogged to be sensible of much more after that, other than two things—that Daisy's arms were tight about her, and that the old lady squeezed in on her other side did not stop haranguing the poor driver until his little steam engine gasped to a stop, and she was lifted up into the air on another elevating platform.

3:25 p.m.

"Drink this, dearest," Daisy said, pressing the rim of a cup to Freddie's lips. "Careful, it is hot."

"Hot."

"I know. You have been in a hot bath. So have your poor clothes. They should be back from the laundress at any moment. Madame Yuen's Ah Ma seems to be regarded with

130

some terror by everyone within blocks. They were promised within the hour, and it is nearly that now."

An hour! Freddie choked on the tea, which tasted of grass and childhood summers. "The prince!"

"Calm yourself, dearest." Daisy clearly did not understand, but her tone was firm. "Drink."

She obeyed. The tea was wonderful, and had the effect of clearing the curtain of cold exhaustion from Freddie's mind. "But Daisy, the prince. He has been abducted. We must find the ship that took him."

While Daisy poured another cup from a teapot as delicate as a woman's cheek, Freddie pushed herself to a sitting position. She was on a sofa in front of a pot-bellied stove that exuded warmth, wearing an embroidered dressing-gown. And sitting next to the stove on a ladder-back chair was William Barnicott, likewise wearing a dressing-gown. It only came to mid-calf, exposing his bare feet and ankles.

No one seemed to care. Not even Daisy.

Freddie averted her eyes while Daisy handed him a cup of the tea, and refilled Freddie's cup. Freddie gulped it down.

"I mean it," she said as Davey and the younger woman Daisy had called Madame Yuen came in bearing trays. "We must go at once."

"Tell us," Daisy said simply. If their adventures in the Wild West had taught her sister anything, it was to listen first, ask questions later. For which Freddie was grateful.

"I should be interested to know how you came to be in the sea and not aboard *Iris* where we left you," William said, helping himself to a delicate roll of vegetables.

"*I* should be interested to know where *Iris* has gone," Daisy put in, taking up her own cup and bowl and settling in. "The nerve of that girl to leave you!"

"Peony did not leave me. I left her. *Iris* and her crew are at the royal palace," Freddie said. "They were trying to find the prince, or Mr. Douglas, so that they could offer *Iris* to help ferry the injured to a safe place. But Daisy—" She stopped herself blurting out the reason for her cowardice with a glance at William and Davey. "I could not go. So I stayed behind."

"With the ship? It cannot moor at the palace, can it?"

"Yes indeed, on the cantilevered terrace where we were all talking the night of the ball." The ball. It seemed like a lifetime ago. "I was looking over the balustrade when I saw them—two men, carrying the prince at head and foot. So I climbed down the grapevine and followed them."

"Gracious," Daisy said from behind her teacup. "I promise that Aunt Jane will never know."

Davey offered her a bowl of dumplings in sauce. "Eat these. With your fingers. They're ever so good."

"But—"

"If you don't eat them all, you will have Ah Ma to deal with," said Madame Yuen.

"I ent afraid of much, but I'm afraid of that lady," Davey confided.

Freddie picked one up and bit into it. She may even have moaned a little as its delicious flavors filled her mouth. She ate one after another as she went on with her story. "I followed them through a door in the palace wall, then down to the docks."

Daisy made a sound, and bit into a dumpling as though to cover it up.

"Don't worry, I had my Colt. Or I did. Where is it?"

Davey picked up her harness and waggled it. "Here, drying. I already took some saddle soap to it."

"And Madame Yuen cleaned the guns," William said with a smile at their hostess. "Frighteningly handy with firearms, this lady."

Madame Yuen bowed as she took a vegetable roll herself. "You forget that our culture is a technical one. And gunpowder has been in use in even the smallest village for more centuries than anyone can count."

"Thank you." Freddie smiled at her in gratitude. "Anyway, the miscreants rolled up the prince in sail canvas or some such, and took him aboard a wreck of a ship. I am sure it cannot get far. I tried to board, but when they shot at me I lost my hold and fell into the sea."

"Mmph!" Daisy squeaked, swallowing what were no doubt a thousand questions with a bite of dumpling.

"I was not hit," Freddie assured her. "I swam to shore, but it is a maze, full of crushed ships and piers and confusion." And ghosts. She shivered. "If it had not been for these ladies hearing me, I would not have survived. So you see why we must go at once. We must find a ship that will follow them, and rescue him."

"How will you pull that off?" Davey asked. His dumpling bowl was empty, and so was the teapot. Madame Yuen picked up the latter, but waited to hear Freddie's reply.

"We are not," William said, rising. "We are going back to the island as quickly as may be, and taking to the air in my conveyance. Believe me, they are not so far ahead of us that we will not be able to spot them and mount a rescue."

Madame Yuen said, "You cannot lose time walking there. We will send you in a dragon boat."

Davey's face lit up at this prospect. "I've seen 'em, ma'am. The long boats with the dragon's head at the bow and the wings and the dual engines at the stern?"

"The very ones," Madame Yuen said with a nod. "They fly as swiftly as a gull—much more swiftly than any steamship."

And for the first time during the whole of this dreadful day, Freddie felt hope well up in her heart.

3:30 p.m.

May Lin explained their situation to the prince with as much clarity as she could force past her fear. In the course of it, he managed to sit up, wrestle himself out of his canvas shroud, and ascertain that, other than bruising that would be truly spectacular should they survive the day, he was not permanently damaged.

"I have no doubt that you were drugged, Your Serene Highness," May Lin said. "You came down that stair in the boneless manner of someone drunk or unconscious."

"You are likely right. I have such a headache as I have not felt since before the Rose Rebellion. When my doctors were poisoning me." Her eyes were adjusting now, and she could see him use the filthy steps for support as he attempted to stand. "Please call me Carlos Felipe, as you did once. Titles are of little use when one is once again in peril of one's life. And on the river we dispensed with them."

May Lin remembered those days. All too clearly. They had been all too few.

"Do your people really dislike you this much?" Lin asked.

After a pause, Carlos Felipe said, "I had not thought so, but it seems I am wrong."

"It is not the people," May Lin told him grimly. "I am afraid it is your association with Evan Douglas and me. It is your embrace of technology for the Royal Kingdom. I knew Bishop del Fuego hated a woman and an outlander in positions of trust, and I a Canton woman to boot—"

"And a witch," Lin reminded her.

"But I had no idea he would go so far as to attempt to kill me."

"Us," the Viceroy corrected her.

"Us," she agreed. "He has obviously concluded you cannot be instructed or influenced by him. The earthquake must have seemed like a gift from God, sent specifically to aid his plans for our disappearance."

"Once I am out of the way, he will send to Spain for my cousin, heaven help them all. He was cut from the same cloth as my father, only larger and lazier." He sighed. "I had not thought to face an assassination attempt so soon after the usurper's death. What do they plan to do with us? Is selling us into slavery the best we can hope for?"

"I thought that at first, but they would be foolish to let us live."

"We think this old tub is one of the prison ships. That means they'll sink it," Lin said. "It certainly cannot get even as far as the Oregon Territory. If I were the bishop, I would put out a story that the two of you ran away together, and were capsized. How sad."

May Lin could not help the chuckle that bubbled out of her. "You are as good at stories as Tia Clara."

Lin made a sound that was decidedly not laughter as a particularly large wave made the boat yaw and wallow. "We have passed through the golden gate and are in the rough part. I will be sick. Please excuse me, Carlos F-Felipe."

She staggered a few steps away, where she was miserably sick into the wooden bucket. For long, agonizing minutes it was all May Lin could do to keep her own empty stomach from emptying its pitiful contents, too, as the boat pitched and rolled. Pride alone kept her on her feet in front of him, breathing deeply, her lips pinched together.

"Who is that young person?" Carlos Felipe asked, sounding maddeningly unaffected by either the retching or the rolling of the vessel.

"She is my cousin," May Lin said simply. "My mother and her father were brother and sister. We had just discovered the relationship before you were tossed down here."

"Indeed. What has the poor child done to deserve this? Is she a political target as well?"

"The victim of bad luck. I took her with me to the meeting at the mission. A meeting that was unsuccessful, even before the earth opened up and swallowed me."

"It did what?" He sounded half disbelieving.

"I fell through the ceiling of one of the old tunnels running under the mission." She shook her head at herself. "I had thought that the widening of roads for steam landaus was important. Everything that has come after has made that seem trivial."

"It is important. But—a tunnel?"

"I will tell you the whole story if we live to see the sunrise.

But for now, if I get the chance, I will kill anyone who stands between us and safety. Lin is innocent here—she cannot be permitted to die because the church has a bone to pick with you and me."

"But you only just met," the prince said in wondering tones. "How can you feel so strongly?"

The same way I did when I first laid eyes on you, lying in Tia Clara's sickroom.

"Sometimes one heart reaches out to another, and they are knit together." Tia Clara had said that of Mother Mary once, and May Lin had thought it beautiful.

"That is it exactly. May Lin, I—"

A tremendous thud on the deck over their heads made her jump nearly out of her skin. She crouched, watching the thin line of daylight that betrayed the location of the hatch cover. "Sh! What is happening?"

"The sound of the waves on the hull has changed," Carlos Felipe said. "We are no longer making way."

"Thank heaven," croaked a small voice. In a moment May Lin felt a pair of trembling arms slip around her waist.

She hugged Lin close. "Feel better?"

"For all the good it does me. What was that?"

"I do not know, but we must be ready to attack."

"Listen," Carlos Felipe whispered. "They disagree."

From above came the sounds of a scuffle, and the hatch cover shook as someone fell upon it.

"Ye numpty!" a man shouted. "Ye cannot toss the bloody barrel down there. What's to stop the prisoners stamping out the slow match?"

May Lin's breath caught in her throat. Slow match. A fuse. That meant black powder.

Oh, Mother have mercy. They are not simply going to hull her. They are going to blow her up.

"Ye want them dead, dinna ye?"

"That's what I'm tellin' ye. They won't be dead. We have to lay it in the waist of the ship, not the *lazaretto*. Now move. No, not like that, ye stupid lummox!"

"Stop callin' me names."

"I'll call ye what I want. No, longer than that. We need time t'get over the gunwale into *Raven*, innit?"

"Knock yer block off, I will, an' leave ye here wi' the dratted fuse for talking t'me so."

"Not if I get over first. Right. One barrel ought to blow a right fine hole in 'er. Then we're away in *Raven* with a night to look forward to in Madam Della's. Lucky fer us the house ent fallen down like some."

"Come on. There's the flag. Light 'er up an' run for the grapples, boys!"

In a moment, a bitter smell filtered through the gaps in the deck above.

"Black powder," May Lin breathed. "An entire barrel of it. They want to make sure of us."

"We are going to die." Lin burrowed into her side like a chick looking for refuge under its mother's wing.

May Lin did not have the strength to lie to her. Instead, she did the only thing she could.

She hugged her tightly, kicked off the coffin's lid, and spent several precious moments convincing Lin to get into it. Once the lid was on, she reached for Carlos's hand. He tugged her down with him behind the coffin, and covered her body protectively with his.

~

Iris, en route to Rancho San Gregorio

"MRS. BOYLE, is Freddie Linden not well?" Peony Churchill asked that lady in the galley, as they rinsed cloths and refilled bowls with warm water from the boiler. They had been cleaning the wounds of the injured, but with so many, it was slow going. "I have not seen her since we lifted, and we could use another pair of hands."

Isabela came in, her bowl, too, filled with bloody water, bits of brick in the bottom.

"She is not with us, miss. Did the captain not say?" Mrs. Boyle's normally calm eyes took on an expression of horror. "Have you not been told?"

"Told what, pray?"

"Miss Freddie witnessed the prince being kidnapped, apparently, and has gone to his rescue."

There were at least fifty possible replies to such a thunderbolt, but Peony's astonished brain could only seize upon one. "And you did not think to tell me?"

Now Mrs. Boyle looked stricken. "It slipped my mind, miss, with all the injured to care for."

"She went alone? Into the city? A girl not yet twenty, a stranger?"

"Yes, miss. She was determined to go. Even my husband could not stop her."

It took quite a lot to render Peony speechless, but Mrs. Boyle had managed it. What on earth was she to do now? Their count of friends was running very low, with Daisy and

Mr. Barnicott goodness knew where, the two children who had been with them missing also, and now Freddie—

Wait a moment.

"The prince was being kidnapped?"

"So she said, miss. I did not see him, nor did the captain. But you will note that her pistol harness is missing. She had her wits about her."

Peony struggled to keep her voice steady. "Mrs. Boyle, in future, when heads of state are kidnapped and someone of our acquaintance goes to their aid, I am to be informed immediately."

"Yes, miss. But you were lost somewhere in the palace, miss. It would have been quite difficult to give you a report. However, I was wrong in not informing you the moment we made our second landing, in the courtyard."

"Yes," Peony managed to say past her pounding heart and the constriction in her throat. "Quite so. And we have no idea where Freddie might be?"

"No, miss. My husband says she climbed down the grapevine next to the terrace and ran across the lawns, but he lost sight of her."

"He was not tempted to go with her?" There. She had phrased that quite diplomatically, considering.

Mrs. Boyle looked scandalized. "Abandon ship? Your ship? No indeed, miss. That would be a dreadful dereliction of his duty."

Well, yes, she supposed it would, and here she would be with over a hundred injured people aboard, and no one but herself and Timothy to sail the ship and locate this Rancho San Gregorio. She could not fault the captain for doing his job.

But Freddie …! If she ever saw Daisy Linden again, how could she look her in the face and tell her?

And on top of that, why should the prince have been kidnapped? He had seemed so handsome and delightful and was the most divine dancer. Oh, woe! What more could possibly go wrong? Half the capital was in ruins—and now its ruler was missing.

They had been right to feel apprehensive at those bloody sheets lying in a tangle by the royal bed, and the walls open to the sky. He must have been taken mere moments before they had entered his rooms.

Young Rebecca came in bearing a bowl, which her mother took from her, rinsed, and filled. "Thank you, dear. I will come with you."

Peony turned to pick up her own refilled bowl, only to see Isabela, white-faced, staring at her. "Peonía, can it be true? Someone has taken advantage of this disaster to kidnap our prince?"

"I have no idea whether it is true or not," Peony confessed. "But Freddie Linden would not risk her life to go haring off after just anybody. Your Mr. Douglas must be informed at once. As soon as we see the injured safely into the hands of the padres at San Gregorio, we must return."

"It is Bishop del Fuego. I know it." The young woman nodded with certainty, her dark eyes snapping. "He was a supporter of the usurper de Aragon, and though that one is dead—may his soul burn forever—the ideals he stood for have not yet died with him."

Peony hardly dared ask. "What ideals?"

"Ideals that do not include women and Englishmen serving on the privy council. Steam technology. Public education for those who are not the male children of grandees. In short, anything that would drag this country into the modern age."

"And they would murder their own Viceroy for those ideals? What would happen to them all then?"

Isabela shrugged. "Another prince of the royal line would be sent from Spain. But we do not want another prince. We want our own, who has fought bravely for us and who is a good ruler. He listens. He has plans and dreams that may actually be accomplished. All he is missing is a Vicereine … and the full support of the missions."

"Well, at the moment, we must go on the assumption that he is missing, full stop." Peony did not care for the appraising look the young noblewoman had inexplicably turned on her. "And it very much looks to me as though your Mr. Douglas may need to step up and be Regent until he is found."

Isabela's eyes went very wide. "My Evan? Regent?"

"Who else?" Peony indicated the organized chaos outside the galley—the rows of the injured upon the glossy teak decks, the groans of those who needed laudanum that Peony could not supply, having none. "We have three members of the Privy Council aboard, unable to carry out their duties. Heaven only knows where the other three are. Only Evan is on his feet at the palace and doing his best to manage this crisis."

"But—but the bishop is the only one who can declare him regent."

The same bishop who might have kidnapped the Viceroy? Not much help to be found there, Peony suspected. "I think you will find that in the case of Mr. Douglas, he declares himself by his actions, and needs no man to bestow a title upon him."

Gloria had told Peony the whole magnificent story of how Evan Douglas had come to the Wild West and to the Royal Kingdom, leaving her breathless with admiration for his bravery and ingenuity. Now, the face of the young woman to whom he was engaged glowed with pleasure at this praise of the man she loved.

"Isabela, I must speak with Barnaby Hayes and tell him all you have told me. Will you excuse me?"

Isabela took her bowl out to the main salon to resume caring for the injured while Peony went in search of the detective. She found him kneeling beside a boy in the dining salon, binding up his wrist between two pieces of what might once have been a wooden spoon. When he had finished the makeshift splint, Peony drew him down the corridor to her cabin.

In as calm and succinct a manner as she could manage, she brought him into the picture, both personal and political.

"Great Caesar's ghost," Barnaby said at last, when she had fallen silent. "Freddie Linden, attempting to follow the prince, who has been kidnapped. The bishop, who acted instantly in the face of disaster, and clearly had clerics standing by waiting for the first opportunity to remove his ruler. The prince, who put down one political coup, only to be faced with another months later." He quirked an eyebrow at her. "Have I apprehended it all?"

"You forgot Mr. Douglas, the overlooked scientist from the north of England, who may now become Regent of his adopted country."

Detective Hayes nodded. "I can't think of anyone better qualified, I must say, if bravery and heart mean anything."

"So you agree, then, that we must return to the capital immediately, and inform him."

"Indeed yes. Thank you, Peony, for telling me. I had no idea all this was going on. The urgent need for my paltry abilities with first aid have kept me fully occupied."

She made up her mind in a single breath, and flung caution to the winds. "I could not bear the burden alone. I am not like you—up to my ears in Her Majesty's business. I am just a girl who likes pretty clothes, good company, and fine airships." Her voice trembled. "As An Educated Gentleman says in one of Captain Boyle's issues of *Tales of a Medicine Man* —in coming here, I may have bitten off more than I can chew."

Somehow she found herself making this confession into his shirt front, but only because his arms had gone around her.

"A woman who appreciates a fine airship is not to be discounted," he murmured.

And instead of leaping away and freezing him to the spot for his familiarity, Peony laid her cheek upon his shirt. A long sigh made his chest rise and fall.

"We only came to visit an old friend," he said, stroking her back with a comforting hand. "None of us expected an earthquake and an attempted assassination. We have all bitten off more than we can chew, my dear, Evan Douglas most of all."

My dear.

She should have been afraid to have her fears confirmed. She should have apologized for her own familiarity, taken her leave, and gone back to tending the injured. But if Peony

Churchill had one failing, it was that she did not believe in the word *should*.

Her arms slid about his waist under his worn tweed jacket, and when she lifted her chin and his lips found hers, she lost herself in the wonder of it … and the realization that in his arms, she no longer felt so afraid.

CHAPTER 14

3:45 p.m.

The dragon boat's wings folded slowly, responding to the decreasing speed of the engine, and its flying rudder sank into the waves until they were once more making way on the sailing keel. The pilot steered the vessel carefully to a rocky beach on Isla Yerba Buena that would do as a landing, and deposited his passengers.

Daisy's chignon had been decimated by the wind of their going. She braided her hair hastily while Freddie waved their thanks to the pilot, and their little party climbed the path up to the airfield. It took every ounce of courage Daisy possessed to then board William's peculiar conveyance, and not take Freddie in her arms, buckle to the grass of the empty field, and refuse to move or let her go until all this was over.

But since no one knew when it would be over, she had to make do with clasping Freddie's hand as they sat together on the rear bench. And if she insisted on holding hands for the entirety of the flight, she would dare anyone to blame her.

How close she had come to losing the one person who meant most to her in the world! And how brave William had been, to dive into the sea to fetch her sister, when it was clear to all of them that poor Freddie was in the final stages of exhaustion and could not have saved herself despite all her efforts to do so.

The dragon boat—a magnificent thing with its fierce, snarling head at the bow and its powerful steam engine at the stern—made a wide turn, laying down a long wake of foam. Then its wings lifted and its flying rudder carried it out of the water once more. It sped back to its moorage with its fellows on a sandy beach north of the Canton settlement.

Davey left off rhapsodizing about the dragon boat long enough to cast off ropes and scramble in beside William, who had the pilot's chair. "Up ship," William said cheerfully. "Or conveyance. Or whatever this is."

"I keep telling you we need a name for it," Davey told him. Then, "Cor, the city looks even worse from up here, innit?"

The propellers churned, the steam engine huffed, and the balloon bellied out to full, taking them high over the dragon boat and roughly tracking its course northward along the western shore. Within a few minutes they reached the narrow channel where two points of land squeezed the sea into the bay. Not a ship was to be seen within a mile of it.

"It must be low tide," William said, tilting his head out of the port beside him. "Look at that maelstrom. No ship would dare navigate through there."

"I hope they got out in time," Freddie said anxiously, looking down out of the other port as they passed overhead.

"It would be better if they had to turn back," Daisy pointed out. "We might have mounted a rescue on the calmer waters in the bay rather than the open sea."

"We must come up with a plan," William said, "or we will be the ones needing rescue. This conveyance is not actually an airship—it has no basket, nor any means of bringing cargo aboard once aloft."

"Did I not hear there was an airship used for training here?" Daisy asked, feeling her stomach sink that she had not thought of this ages before now. "Should we go back for it?"

"No time," Freddie groaned. "You have wasted enough already in caring for me."

"That was not wasted," Daisy said firmly. "If the only result of all that swimming and struggling is a cold, I will count it a miracle."

"Look sharp," Davey said, his head out of the port on his side, his hair blowing every which way. "We've cleared the narrows."

"I cannot go much higher," William warned them. "The winds are difficult here, and cold besides."

"And our coats are all aboard *Iris*," Daisy said. "I swear, the next time I go out to sketch, I will bring a rucksack full of enough supplies for a week."

Freddie leaned against her shoulder and looked down between Daisy's feet. "How is our little passenger managing? She did not like the dragon boat one bit."

In her airy wicker basket, the fluffy white hen was still occupied in demolishing the last dumpling from Madame Yuen's kitchen, which Daisy had saved for her. "She definitely prefers the conveyance," Daisy said.

"Wait until she sees *Iris*," Davey said, pulling in his head long enough to speak. "Lots of food aboard, and Mrs. Boyle won't be casting eyes at her. She ent big enough to make so much as a sandwich."

"I should like to see *Iris* myself, with or without Mrs. Boyle's eyes," Daisy said. "Did you notice when we lifted that the ship is no longer moored at the palace? Where on earth has it gone now?"

"I did notice," William said grimly, one hand on the vane lever and the other on the steam controls. "They cannot have left you. That is impossible. But if they have been seconded as a medical transport, which I think quite likely, is there a hospital still operating?"

"The Viceroy will know, if he is still alive," Freddie pointed out. "But please may we concentrate on finding him first?"

Had she been a betting woman, Daisy would have laid down a gold piece that Peony Churchill would have been the one flying to the prince's rescue in her beautiful ship, cutting a dashing figure as she pulled him out of the basket and clasped him to her womanly bosom. Poor prince. He would have to make do with the four of them, with no basket and no idea how they were going to accomplish such a feat.

"What kind of ship was it, Freddie?" Davey asked. "What are we looking for?"

"I wouldn't dignify it by calling it a ship. It was not that large. A ketch or lugger, perhaps? It was decked. It had three masts, and red sails, and if it manages twenty miles before sinking of its own accord, I will be surprised. I would not sail in it."

Daisy reflected that she had tried to, and been shot at for her pains.

William looked over his shoulder. "A prison ship, do you think?"

"I have no idea. What is that?"

"I have never seen one, only heard of them. In the adventure papers, you know."

"Oh, like *Tales of a Medicine Man*," Daisy said. "Those scandalous periodicals. I do not know why everyone loves them so. The world is quite dangerous enough without reading about the very worst that could happen."

William reddened, as though she had cast aspersions upon his choice of reading. Perhaps she ought to soften her remarks. "What do the adventure papers say of prison ships?"

"That they are good only for demolition. If murderers are condemned, they are put out to sea in one and sunk."

"Dear me." Freddie's face had paled. "Can we talk of something else? What direction shall we take? North? Or west, out to sea?"

"North toward the Oregon Territory, if they were taking the Viceroy out of his kingdom for some purpose," Daisy suggested, heartily in favor of changing the subject.

"Out to sea, if he's on a prison boat," Davey said with a little too much relish, bringing it right back.

"Look," William said suddenly, releasing the vane lever to point.

A thin spiral of black smoke rose on the horizon, where the sun was already nearly half buried in clouds. The sky was turning gold and orange, without which they might not have seen it.

"What are the odds that is our quarry?" William asked.

"Good enough to gamble on," Davey told him with a nod one might almost take for experience.

"Right you are." William adjusted the controls and the

conveyance banked into a gentle left turn, straight into the sunset.

MAY LIN COULD NOT HEAR.

She could see, though—as the boards and joints started above her head, popping their nails and bolts as the upper deck stripped itself away with the force of the explosion. Here, locked in the *lazaretto*, they had been safe from flying wood as deadly as thrown spears.

But only for a moment. True safety was vanishing with every board that would allow the sea to surge in upon them.

She could feel, too—the ragged pain in her throat from screams of terror—the paralyzing fear in her limbs as the final agony of the ship was revealed to them. Before her eyes, the mast plunged straight down through the hull and into the sea, dragging its burning sail with it.

"Lin!" She tried to call through the wood of the coffin, but had no idea if the sound escaped her ragged throat.

She was squashed up against the coffin, still. There was one fact to hold on to. And the reason she was squashed, she realized as her senses slowly came back to her, was that the Viceroy had a two-armed grip on the coffin, holding her against it.

Now the water roared through the destroyed gunwales. Carlos Felipe grabbed her arm and kicked at the planks of the hull behind them violently, but he was barefoot.

She was not.

They must get into the water, and they could not go out the hatch. One kick at the weakened boards with her trusty boots and one came loose—two—three. Carlos crouched behind the coffin and gave it a mighty heave out through the ragged hole.

"Lin!" she screamed as the coffin fell into the sea, then bobbed up again a moment later. Carlos grabbed her hand and dragged her through, and they both plunged into the sea. Into a cold like a living thing. A cold that seized her and stopped her breath. A cold that blinded her, deafened her as Carlos Felipe's hand was torn away.

But with a kick she forced herself to the surface. *Coffin. Must get Lin out.*

Gasping, she pushed her hair out of her face and spotted it not three feet away, the waves carrying it away from her even as she dragged air into her lungs. Carlos Felipe surfaced next to her and heaved himself toward it. He pushed off the lid and Lin popped up like a jack-in-the-box, red in the face and weeping with terror.

He shouted something, but to May Lin, it may as well have come from the bottom of the sea. And then she saw what he intended.

The coffin. It must be turned over so that they might float upon it. She grabbed the side and together they tipped Lin out into the water—her shriek of fright and outrage pierced even the deafness caused by the explosion. She grabbed Lin under her armpits with one arm, then dragged her against her chest, flailing and panicked. Carlos Felipe heaved the coffin over, trapping the air inside it. It took a struggle to get Lin up on it, until she realized what they were doing and helped them, then sprawled like a crab, her fingers gripping the sides. To May Lin's relief, when they heaved their upper bodies up on it, Lin slid to one side to compensate for the extra weight.

The coffin was watertight, so for the moment, buoyant enough. Bless the coffin maker for not shirking his duty, even for a sailor he would never meet, dead at sea.

May Lin palmed stinging seawater out of her eyes and dragged air into lungs that could hardly expand from cold. They must keep kicking. They must get clear. But for the first time, she could see well enough to glance over her shoulder at the destruction they had temporarily escaped.

Was some angry, panicked sailor even now taking aim with a pistol?

The wreck in which they had been imprisoned was sinking, blown in half by the barrel of black powder. Its keel must have broken, for bow and stern were slowly folding together like a pair of praying hands. But now, half hidden though she might be in the heaving swells that lifted them up and cast them down, May Lin could see the grave miscalculation her captors had made.

For the second ship—*Raven*, the sailors had called it—had been grappled to the stern to take their mates off the doomed prison ship. They had not accounted for the fact that water would not absorb an explosive blast. When she had assisted Captain and Lady Hollys in blowing up the old Viceroy's dam above the water meadows of Las Vegas some months ago, May Lin had had to account for this very fact.

Explosives were notoriously unpredictable, and no one had predicted that this blast would blow the starboard side off *Raven*, too. She heeled drunkenly into the prison lugger, her greater weight pressing the lugger down even as all the contents of her deck careened into the frothing water amidships. Worse, some of the grapples still held, tying the two ships together in an agonizing death.

May Lin gasped as *Raven*'s masts reached the point of no return, and she heeled further, the sails and masts tangling with what was left of the lugger's, knotting them together so inextricably that even the few sailors left alive screamed.

They were all doomed.

For there was no land anywhere in sight. Only freezing water. Even now May Lin could not feel her feet. Her strength slipped away with every wave that lifted them. Soon her muscles would stop working, and she would slip off the coffin, torn away from Lin and the prince by the greedy clasp of the deep.

Carlos's face was illuminated by the orange rays of the sun. "Hold on," he shouted at her, his voice coming from a long way off even though he gripped the coffin right beside her. "Do not leave me."

The sun slipped into the clouds, winking out even as the skies turned blood red, throwing up a distress signal that no one but the gulls would ever see.

She could not promise she would not leave him. For soon, her exhausted body would give up its spirit, and all earthly promises would be ended.

"Cousin!" Lin shouted, practically in her face. "Do not give up. William will come, I know it."

She could not remember who William was. Her mind was going in and out, like the waves. And she was so very cold.

"May Lin!" Carlos shouted. His voice was not so far away now. Halfway up from the bottom of the sea and rising. "I love you!"

Perhaps she would meet his voice again on the way down, and those beautiful words would be the last thing she ever heard.

CHAPTER 15

5:15 p.m.

Flying above the waves, Daisy could see the destruction from half a mile off. Not one but two boats were sinking, masts tangled together, men floating on bits of smashed spar, though even as William's conveyance drew overhead, she could not tell whether the men were dead or alive. The boats heaved in their final agony, swells flinging them up and then burying them, putting out the fire that had sent up the smoky distress call they had spotted from the narrows.

Whether any one else would see and come to the boats' aid, Daisy did not know. They four had one objective only: the Viceroy.

"How are we going to find him?" Freddie asked in a hushed tone that told Daisy their thoughts were running along the same lines. "What if he is imprisoned below? He may already be dead. From the blast—or from drowning."

"Blimey," Davey said, clearly torn between awe at the spectacle and disgust at how it might have happened. "Could the boats have been grappled together? Before the rigging took over the job? Look how the sea ent separating them, even yet."

"What lunatic grapples their boat to another and then blows it up?" Daisy objected. "Surely they must have collided."

"Someone has made a grave mistake, in either case," William agreed. "We will make a circuit. Look sharp. The Viceroy may have been thrown into the water from the force of the blast, and may be trying to swim."

The two boats yawed together and apart, like a creature whose jaws stretched in a fruitless groan for help. Daisy's anxious gaze combed what was left of the decks—the sails— could he be clinging to the hull?

Oh heaven—

Her stomach heaved as she realized there was a man dangling from the yards by his feet, caught in the ropes and being crushed repeatedly, even as she watched. She tore her gaze away and took refuge in the sight of the heaving waves. Some distance off, figures clinging to some flotsam were waving in frantic distress.

Sailors.

"William," she choked. "Look there. I know they intended harm. But we must try to save the living."

"Save them?" Davey repeated scornfully. "They've likely killed their prince, ent they? What do you want to save them for?"

"Because—because—" But Daisy cut herself off. "William! On that box those people are clinging to. Is that a *child?*" What manner of monster would bring a child along to witness prisoners being sunk?

"That's no child," William said tersely. "It's a girl."

"That's no girl," Davey shouted. *"It's our Lin.* Wearing her Navapai dress. And the prince! Has to be."

"But who—how—" William began.

"And *May Lin!*" shrieked Freddie. "What in heaven—?"

"Rescue first, questions later," William ordered. "Blast and bebother it, we have no basket! How are we going to get them out of the water? And what about the weight? This conveyance has never held so many."

That was one question Daisy was not about to answer. They had no choice. They must attempt it no matter the peril to the rescuers. "We cannot use the mooring ropes. We will have to tie bedsheets together, and get as close as we can."

"Too dangerous," William said. "Look at those swells. We'll be swamped."

"Can we tow them somehow?" Freddie was near tears. "They are looking up. Oh, Lin's face. I cannot bear it."

"What's the matter with you lot? Why don't you use the swing?" Davey demanded, exasperated.

William glared at him. "What are you talking about?"

"The swing. At the back," Davey said, as though William were the stupidest dunce who ever lived. "Where the steps used to be."

"Davey, if you don't make sense in the next five seconds, I'll toss you out that port," William snapped.

"Ent you been back there? Where Tobin replaced the steps?"

"What, that bit of wrought iron?"

Davey sighed. "That's a swing. To bring stuff up and down on ropes, innit? After Daisy and Freddie got down from the pinnacle cell in Santa Fe, that was one of the first adjustments he made. So's you could do another rescue if they got stuck again."

William's eyes nearly started out of his head. "Why didn't you tell me?"

"I thought you knew. Anyroad, you push a lever in the floor and—"

"Get back there and do it!" William roared.

Without another word, Davey barrel-rolled over the seat, and Freddie heaved him over the back bench into the engine compartment. Daisy crawled over into the back after him. When Freddie went to do the same, William flung out an arm to stop her.

"Not you, Freddie," William shouted. "Stay with the engine. I'll need help with the boiler if we're going to hover."

In the rear of the conveyance, where one side was made up of cupboards, and the other the sleeping compartment, Daisy and Davey crawled on hands and knees to the back. He heaved open the door.

The wind roared inside like a monster, intent on beating them to death.

"Latch the door with that bit of chain," Davey shouted.

Daisy did so, though it was a fight. Outside, the ocean heaved practically under their wheels, though they must be twenty feet above the blowing tops of the waves. Davey grasped a lever next to what had once been the back steps, and now was a kind of platform made out of wrought iron in a Navapai pattern whose significance Daisy could not remember. The boy shoved the lever forward with the strength of his entire body, and the platform began to lower, faster and faster.

"Slow it down!" Daisy cried. "The wind will catch it and hit them."

He pulled back on it with both hands and the mechanism ratcheted down the speed. Now Daisy could see the twin spools of thin rope on either side that allowed it to drop without tilting. The prince reached up, but the wind snatched the edge of the platform away from his straining hand.

"Again!" Daisy screamed forward, to William. "He almost had it!"

William adjusted his hovering and Davey tried to swing the ropes toward the three exhausted figures clinging to the box, to no avail.

Then Daisy had an idea.

"Down!" she shouted to William. "Put the swing in the water. They must go to it."

Slowly, cautiously, William brought the conveyance down another five feet. Any farther, and the waves would catch them. It might happen anyway—was there not a saying that the seventh wave was the largest?

No time to worry about that.

The prince and May Lin hauled Lin off the box into the water. She flailed her way on to the swing, her head and feet hanging off it front and back.

Davey hauled on a smaller lever and the mechanism reversed, bringing up the platform with Lin sprawled upon it. Water cascaded off her, and any second she could let go or roll or fall.

The platform locked into its dock and Daisy clung to the door frame with one hand, grasped a handful of wet wool with the other, and hauled Lin into the back. "In you go," she said, and boosted her into the sleeping compartment.

Lin was too exhausted even to cry.

"Well done, Davey," Daisy told him. "Next!"

Down went the swing. There was a pause as May Lin and the prince appeared to have an argument over who was going next, and then May Lin flopped into the water to grip the edge of the platform. She had enough strength to get her body and one of her legs upon it before Davey reversed and the swing rose into the air.

Daisy pulled her in one-handed, and dragged her forward, where she collapsed in a heap of sodden clothing on the polished planks.

"Next!" Daisy shouted.

For a third time, the swing descended and plunged into the sea. The prince pushed off from the box, which was by now nearly submerged, got himself on to it on his belly, and as the platform rose, William took the conveyance up.

A rogue wave flung the box toward the sinking boats and splashed into the platform. Daisy screamed as the prince was lifted off it. But he'd had enough strength to shove an arm through a hole in the pattern of iron. As the platform rose, he clung to it, his body hanging from it, his legs kicking.

The prince was barefoot! Daisy hardly had time to register this astonishing fact before the platform arrived and locked into place.

"Davey! Help me!"

The two of them pulled on the viceroy's chilled, unresisting form until Daisy could hook both hands into the back of the royal britches. With a mighty heave, she flung her whole weight backward into the rear of the conveyance, pulling the prince in on top of her.

She lost her breath and coughed as she got a face full of seawater.

"Off!" she said, trying not to choke.

But the prince had fainted.

"Get us out of here!" Davey called to William as he slammed the rear door closed and locked it.

"Help," Daisy gasped.

"You already are," William called over his shoulder as he flipped levers to increase the pressure in the boiler, and Freddie cranked the wheel like a madwoman. "We must get them warm. Davey, get in the bunk with Lin. Freddie, leave off doing that and share your body heat with May Lin. Chafe their hands. They will die of cold if we do not help them."

If the prince had been a larger man, Daisy might have suffocated. It was all she could do to wrap her arms and legs around him and wriggle free enough so that she could gasp for breath. She had never held a man in her arms in her life, other than in a brief hug of the farewell sort. But somehow it felt natural to allow her body to soften, to cradle the prince's chilled face between her neck and shoulder, to cover his legs with hers so that her skirts might act as a blanket. One at a time, she brought his hands up between their two bodies. The exertion alone increased her own temperature, despite the fact that she was now soaked from clavicle to boots. And soon, she was rewarded as she felt his thin cheek warm against her own.

The sound of scuffling forward told her that Freddie was attempting the same with May Lin, and Daisy could only hope that in the bunk, Davey could overcome his boy's aversion to girls and remember that Lin was both playmate and friend.

"All right back there?" William called anxiously. "We are approaching the narrows."

"I believe … so," Daisy gasped. "I do not think he is conscious yet. But his face is warming."

As though he had heard her, the prince stirred. Lifted his head as though it weighed a hundred pounds. Stared into her eyes.

"Wh-who …?"

"I am Daisy," she said soothingly. "You are quite safe. We are taking you back to the palace."

"M-May …"

"I am safe," came a hoarse whisper from nearer the boiler.

"Can you sit up?" Freddie asked her gently. "If you cannot, I am quite content here, lying down."

"Lin!" May Lin thrashed into a sitting position, struggling as though both Freddie and her robes were a prison wrapping her about.

"She's all right, ma'am," came a put-upon voice from the sleeping cupboard. "Safe as houses. I am soaked, though," he added, aggrieved. "And so is William's bunk."

The sounds of a struggle ended with Lin grunting, "Get off! You're heavy."

"That's more like it," William called over his shoulder with some satisfaction. "She must be all right if she's putting up a fuss."

Lin rolled out of the bunk and landed on the prince's back. With no more regard for him—or Daisy's breathless yelp beneath him—than if they were pillows, she crawled over them both to May Lin's side. The latter took her in her arms, whereupon Daisy got a look at the knives strapped to her forearms.

Goodness. But of course. She was a river witch.

But how very useful and discreet. Where might one obtain such a thing?

The prince's struggle to sit up in the confined aisle between cupboards and bunk brought her attention back to him with a bump. She retained the presence of mind to pull the top blanket off the bunk—only the middle part was wet—and wrap it around him. Then she moved aside so that he could share its warmth with May Lin and Lin.

"Thank you," he said. "For coming to our aid."

"I knew you would come," Lin croaked from within the circle of May Lin's arms, nearly engulfed in the blanket. Daisy marveled at how very comfortable the girl seemed in the embrace, almost as if she did not mind it.

As if she welcomed it.

"Thank Freddie for that," Davey said, lying on his stomach in the sleeping cupboard, completely unconcerned that his boots kicked on William's pillow. "She saw the prince get kidnapped. We didn't even know you were with him 'til just now."

"Thank the Almighty for Freddie," the prince whispered.

An ear-splitting sound issued from between the forward seats that expressed extreme displeasure. Freddie chuckled. "She does not like being forgotten."

Daisy pushed herself up next to Davey on the bunk. "Better hand her to me. She must believe herself to be alone. She cannot see anything from the floor."

Freddie got up and fetched the little basket with its complaining occupant from between the benches, and opened the top. "Here she is, little bird. She has not left you."

"Perdida!" May Lin exclaimed, and before Daisy could

even reach for the basket, took it from Freddie's hands. "Where … did you find her?" Her voice ran out, and the last words came in a whisper.

"Sitting on a saint's head outside the mission," Daisy said. "Do you know this bird?"

Perdida flapped her way out of the basket and landed in May Lin's lap, where she made a nest in the blanket and settled herself with an air of accomplishment, as though this was what she had wanted all along.

"She was in the tunnels with me." May Lin freed one of her hands from the blanket and stroked her feathers. "We saved each other. I lost her when the bishop's men attacked me the second time."

"I will have him executed," the Viceroy croaked.

"I should hope so," Lin said, her eyes stormy.

Daisy realized her mouth was hanging open. Clearly there were stories to be told and a great deal of catching up to do, but first things first. "Near the corner of the mission wall?" she asked. When May Lin nodded, she went on, "Then I am glad I picked her up and took her with me. One of the ladies in the Canton district gave us that little basket, and Perdida has been with us since."

"She is good luck," May Lin whispered. "Perhaps I should change her name."

"What does Perdida mean?" Lin craned her head to see May Lin's face.

"In the Californio tongue, it is *little lost girl*," the prince put in. "But now she is found."

"So are we," Lin said, snuggling into May Lin's arms. The latter rested her chin upon the girl's wet hair.

Daisy marveled at the affection between the two of them.

They seemed as close as she and Freddie, but they could not have known each other for more than a day. Another mystery that would be solved in time, she hoped.

"We are coming up on the palace," William called. "Wonder of wonders, *Iris* has reappeared. The palace courtyard is alight with torches. They must have put them out for her to land. Where has she been all this time?"

"Let us moor at once," Daisy said. "All I want in this world is a cup of tea and a change of clothes."

"And something to eat," Davey added.

"And an execution," the prince muttered, but only Daisy and May Lin heard him.

CHAPTER 16

TUESDAY, SEPTEMBER 24, 1895

9:25 a.m.

The Viceroy, as it turned out, could not bear the shaking of the earth, which was still going on every quarter of an hour or so. When he was safely aboard, *Iris* was sent aloft to the ends of her ropes, the way they had done in Bodie. Daisy was glad—for it was not the shaking that made one uneasy, but the waiting for it. Everyone's nerves were beginning to fray. As well, the bishop and his cadre of monks were still at large, and presumably with ill intent, so for the prince to sleep twenty feet in the air was highly practical.

Daisy and Freddie were already doubled up in a cabin, so Peony invited May Lin and Lin to share hers. Davey and William were quite comfortable on sofas in the grand salon. Both would have been content to sleep in the conveyance, but the wet bedding from the sleeping compartment had been borne away by a member of the household staff to be laundered and dried. The Viceroy was ushered into Barnaby's cabin, sending him out to join the other young men on the sofas.

Captain Boyle suggested that since *Iris* was now a royal airship by virtue of the Viceroy's presence, an armed guard ought to be posted at every mooring iron. But Detective Hayes shook his head and indicated the men and women outside in the courtyard, curled up in blankets on sleeping pallets, taking comfort as best they could in the fact that no roof could fall on their heads.

"Look at them," he said in a low voice. "*Iris* has been of help to their friends and families. Saved many lives. I doubt there is a man or woman in that crowd who would harm us—or him—even if they knew he was aboard."

So the night had passed as quietly as could be managed, and for a miracle, Daisy and Freddie found they were able to sleep.

In the morning, Daisy laid down her paintbrush to gaze out of the port in the salon. Despite the early hour, the soup kitchen that Isabela had organized near the courtyard gates was already busy, and was the subject of her sketch. Capably managed by the ladies of the Canton district, even now steam rose from enormous pans and kettles set on flames, and the scent of dumplings wafted into the air.

They were so kind, these ladies—so unafraid to act on their kindness. Would the Californios have done the same had the Canton district been leveled? Daisy wondered. Perhaps she misjudged them. She could not imagine Isabela looking upon the misfortune of anyone and not trying to help. But still ...

The occupants of the sofas had been up some time, talking quietly while Daisy had been painting. Now Evan Douglas entered the main salon and joined her at the viewing port, which was open. "I say, those smell good. You are up early."

"I could sleep no longer, though I did not have the heart to wake my sister." Daisy indicated her sketchbook and paints. "I am doing my best to record what I see from up here."

"For posterity?" Evan smiled.

"Perhaps. But I have noticed something odd in my view," she said, pointing. "Do you see? The harbor district all the way to the foot of the hills is now rubble. Even the mission, which I understand has stood nearly two hundred years, is a ruin. Yet on the hills practically next door, houses remain intact. If the Viceroy's personal rooms had not been on one of those cantilevers, they would have been spared like the greater part of the palace."

"You have heard the proverb about houses built on rocks and those built on sand, I expect," he said thoughtfully, gazing out toward the harbor as though tracing the truth of her words.

"I know nothing of building houses, but if I had the Viceroy's ear, I should advise him in strong language not to allow his people to rebuild down there."

"It seems logical not to take the same risk again," Evan agreed. "But look at the Canton district. It is near the waterfront, but was hardly touched at all."

"I should take further liberties in suggesting that he consult with the Canton builders, to learn what they know of dragons' eyes and swaying homes," Daisy said. "For their construction is light and airy, and moves with the movement of the earth. It is not made of brick, resisting it."

"Dragons' eyes?" Evan repeated with a smile, "If one were to take your advice, I hope one would learn what that means."

He paused, taking in the telltale view and her half-finished sketch. "There are few enough left to advise our prince."

"You, at least, are standing," she pointed out.

"One still standing, of seven," he said sadly. "Two of the Privy Council are presumed dead, one fled for his home yesterday, and three are at Mission San Gregorio, recovering from their injuries."

"They are in good hands?"

"Oh, yes. Joe—I beg her pardon, Honoria, Lady San Gregorio—is one of the most capable people I know. She is the Viceroy's half sister, if you recollect, who once shared a gaol cell with me and your papa and Barnaby. If anyone can bring them back to health, she and her padres can." He glanced down at her. "On behalf of this nation, may I say I am grateful to you and your friends for saving the Viceroy's life, and that of the President of the V.S.E."

"We did nothing more than any friend would do," she said, feeling the color flood her cheeks at the unexpected thanks. "But the prince was right to sleep aboard *Iris*."

"Yes. I believe he is still in danger, from what May Lin was able to tell us last night."

"The bishop is behind it, see if he isn't," she said baldly. "He arranged May Lin's abduction, and I'll stake my life upon his being responsible for the prince's, too."

Evan went very still. "Is that so?"

"Oh, yes. Apparently the first attempt to remove her at the meeting about the steam landaus did not work. A crevasse opened up and swallowed her, thus providing a way for her to escape. It was sheer bad luck that she ran into them again. They took her by force to the waterfront and put her on a prison ship, then the Viceroy was tossed in to join her. That cannot be a coincidence."

"The bishop," he repeated. "Of Mission San Francisco de Asis. He who oversees all the missions north of Mission Santa Barbara. The second most powerful prelate in the country."

"Yes. That one."

"It is quite true." Daisy and Evan turned to see the Viceroy crossing the salon, May Lin and Lin hand in hand behind him. "I will have him executed as soon as my men locate him."

Mrs. Boyle, who had followed them in, halted abruptly at such bloodthirsty language.

"Madam?" Evan said, his tall form tilting slightly in a bow. "How may I be of service?"

She swallowed and straightened her shoulders. "Good morning, Prime Minister."

"Prime Minister?" Daisy echoed. Since when?

"Apparently," Evan said rather sheepishly. "This is what comes of being the last man standing. Do go on, Mrs. Boyle."

That lady nodded. "I came to tell His Serene Highness that breakfast is ready in the dining salon. The Canton ladies in the courtyard have been good enough to augment our slender supplies with their good cooking."

The Viceroy turned to smile at her. "My grateful thanks, madam, to the ladies and to you. We will come."

She dipped a curtsey and Lin led the way in, where they found a simple but nourishing meal of fried fish, sausage, and dumplings with sautéed greens. One by one Peony, the crew, and the other passengers trickled in, no doubt attracted by the scent of food, to take their places at the table.

May Lin spread a napkin upon her lap and set Perdida and

a dumpling upon it, then smiled as the little hen attacked her breakfast with as much ferocity as Davey or Lin might.

"Have you found new friends in the President and her little bird?" Daisy asked Lin as they dug in to the perfectly cooked, flaky fish. "I suppose a brush with death can bring people close together faster than anything. Next you will be on a first-name basis with the Viceroy."

"I already am. His name is Carlos Felipe. But did you mean May Lin?" Lin's mouth was full, but that did not stop her. "She is my cousin."

"Your cousin?" Daisy stopped chewing.

"Yes. Her mother is my aunt. My father's sister. The one I have been looking for since I left here last January. We discovered it while we were locked up on the prison ship." The girl shoveled nearly an entire dumpling into her mouth. "These are good," she said thickly. "I forgot how much I missed them."

"My word," was all Daisy could think of to say, and not about the dumplings, either. The enormity of the chain of events that had occurred to bring the two together boggled her. Then, "I am so glad." Tears welled into her eyes. "You have found your family."

"Then why are you crying?" Lin asked, with a mighty swallow.

"They are happy tears," Daisy said. But even as she said it, she knew she was lying. Both to herself and to Lin. Yes, she was happy that the girl's long, dangerous search was now ended. But she could not help a surge of grief that no such ending seemed to be in the stars for her and Freddie. They would not give up their search for Papa for a moment... but...

She dashed the unworthy tears away, hoping no one had seen. She must not be so selfish. Not when hundreds of fathers and sons and husbands had been wrenched from the ones who loved them by the earthquake. In their quest, at least, there lay the possibility of a reunion. Many could not say as much.

To Daisy's surprise, Peony Churchill had not taken a seat next to the Viceroy when she came in. She did not even blink an eye at Perdida, who was stealthily removing a piece of fish from May Lin's plate. And as everyone exchanged stories of the previous day, it became clear that somehow, during the course of their duty as a hospital ship, Peony and Detective Hayes had drawn closer to one another.

Much closer. To the point that Daisy suspected they might be holding hands under the table.

Poor Detective Hayes. Peony would break his heart the moment a more handsome or wealthy prospect crooked his finger. But that was none of Daisy's business.

Though if the truth were told, she would rather like to be holding William's hand. He might be sitting beside her, but he was happily engrossed in conversation with May Lin and the Viceroy on the subject of cargo swings and their ability to save people's lives in a pinch.

When everyone had caught up on the momentous events of yesterday and were in possession of one another's facts, it was time to turn their attention to the immediate future.

"I will send riders to every mission in the kingdom," the Viceroy announced. "They will bear a bill of attainder over my royal seal, and the bishop's life will be forfeit. No rancho will dare give him aid, and any grandee who does so will be executed by the same sword."

Daisy's lovely breakfast seemed to congeal in her stomach.

Detective Hayes did not seem to be suffering from the same difficulty. "I beg you will not, sir."

"And why is that, pray?" the prince demanded, looking as regal as if he sat upon his own throne, instead of upon a wooden chair in his shirt sleeves, like any other refugee. "Do you wish a murderer to go free?"

"Of course not. The bishop and those who assisted in your abduction must and will be brought to justice. But think, sir. The ones who wish the two of you dead already believe that you are."

"And there is nothing to prove otherwise," Daisy said. "You were all three bundled aboard *Iris* last night in blankets. It is not likely any of the people in the courtyard saw you, much less recognized you."

William nodded. "Which gives you an enormous advantage, sir."

The prince gazed at him, then after a moment, his expression changed. Softened into gratitude. "You pulled us from the sea and saved our lives. I would be honored if you and the young ladies would call me Carlos Felipe. It saves so much time if one is to take back one's kingdom twice in one year."

Daisy could not help a smile. Really, even in shirtsleeves, the prince's charm simply enveloped you and made you want to do anything he asked. "Carlos Felipe," she said, and was rewarded with an answering smile. "I believe you must use your advantage wisely, for once lost, it is lost forever."

"What would you suggest?"

Daisy's gaze traveled around the table—to the detective, to May Lin, to Evan sitting with one arm about Isabela, to the Boyle family scattered in between them. "The wisest heads in your kingdom are here at this table. We must come up with a two-part plan. In the first part, the bishop is brought to justice. And in the second, the danger of losing your kingdom to treason a second time must be ended."

"Well said, Daisy," Evan told her with a nod. "The next question is, how?"

"A covert assassination, made to look like an accident, as mine would have been?" May Lin lifted her hands so that her sleeves fell back, revealing the sheathed knives. Her robes, Daisy saw, had been likewise laundered during the night. The fine Venetian Red wool bore not so much as a salt stain. And perhaps a red silk rose had come back with the washing, for it rested above her ear, tucked into her coiled braids.

"That is one possibility, honored lady," the prince allowed. "Though it has one disadvantage—a secret death will not act as a deterrent to others, thus achieving the second part of our objective."

"It would be very satisfying, though." May Lin sat back, shook her sleeves down, and folded her hands protectively about little Perdida's form.

"I see a third part, sir, that has not been discussed." Peony Churchill, dressed in a practical brown tweed walking suit and cream blouse, spoke up from the hostess's end of the table. "It may assist in the achievement of the first two."

"Go on," the prince said, inclining his head.

"I am no political expert—"

Detective Hayes snorted.

She raised an eyebrow at him. "Well, I'm not. My mother holds all the cards in that game." She turned her attention back to the prince. "Sir, if you had gone down with the prison ship, as the bishop desired, what would have happened to the kingdom?"

"My fiancé would have been Regent until a new Viceroy could be sent from Spain," Isabela said with a proud toss of her head, which also bore a red rose.

"So," Peony went on, "one might assume that the new ruler would be more malleable than the one the bishop had just got rid of, coming into a strange situation and seeking counsel from a trusted source—the church."

"One might assume so," Carlos Felipe allowed. "My cousins, from what I remember as a schoolboy, are a languid lot, more inclined to call for wine than for change for the people's sake."

"So the bishop is taking a gamble with fairly predictable results," Evan Douglas mused. "Even though Ambassador de Aragon is dead, the bishop would still find supporters among the grandees, whose views have not changed so quickly."

"Yes," Peony said. "Sir, are you familiar with the English king, Henry the Eighth?"

An expression passed over his mouth as though he had just tasted lemonade, and found it unsweetened. "Indeed. We are required to study the lives of kings, and take lessons from them. In that one's case, it was several lessons in what not to do as a monarch."

Daisy was beginning to follow Peony's gentle drift. "But in *that one's* case, as well, one thing was accomplished. Leaving aside his more urgent reasons for an heir, he did manage to break with Rome."

"And become head of the church himself," Peony finished with a nod at Daisy.

A silence fell as the prince took in the magnitude of this suggestion.

Captain Boyle laid down his napkin. "It seems to me, sir,

that your greatest peril comes from the bishops and missions wanting to retain control of your kingdom. They are willing to let you out on a rope just so far, but no farther. As long as you are subject to them—or to the king in Spain, for that matter—you will never be permitted to take your country on a voyage of its own."

"I am subject to no man," the prince said grimly. "Even the King of Spain has not dared to interfere in our affairs in two hundred years."

"As long as gold is funneled through the church to the mother country," May Lin put in. "If that were to stop, you might see ships full of soldiers on the horizon."

"They are no match for the airships that would be sent to meet them," Carlos Felipe riposted. "Though at the moment we only have one."

"The question is," Peony said, bringing his attention back to her, "would the people stand up for you if you were to break with the church?"

"I do not know," the prince said after a moment of thought. "Every rancho is tied to a mission. They are like two halves of a coin. Neither can function without the other."

"But is that truly so?" Isabela asked thoughtfully. "If the missions were to be removed, we would not have a padre to give the sacrament on the Lord's Day, or to heal the hurts of the families. Those offices, however, may be performed by others if they are properly trained. But if the ranchos were to be removed, the bishops and padres would die."

Evan chuckled. "They are no longer quite so good at managing farms, cattle, and orchards as they were two hundred years ago."

"But the people take their religious life seriously," the

prince protested. "If I were to break with the church, I and every subject would be excommunicated."

"As King Henry was," Freddie put in. "But he seemed to overcome that."

"Once he dissolved the monasteries, there was no one to tell the people they were excommunicated," Peony said. "It was painful, but as the third part of a strategy to prevent treason, it is a possibility."

The prince was already shaking his head. "My mind cannot encompass such a thing."

"The people already believe you are a prophet of God," Evan said to him. "Your dreams, your visions—I know that some of them were triggered by the ergot with which you were being poisoned earlier this year. But some, I believe, were true. And if I, a scientist, believe in your dreams, sir, then there is a good chance that many of your people will, too."

The gaze that Carlos Felipe turned upon Evan held an uneasy mix of gratitude, fear, and hope. "Let us set all that aside for now," he said at last. "We must first apprehend the architect of all this misery, Bishop del Fuego. How are we to go about doing that, if we may not dispatch soldiers into every corner of the kingdom?"

"The soldiers have their own families to worry about just now," Daisy pointed out.

"You can find him, Daisy." Davey appeared to be torn between giving the hopeful Perdida the last dumpling, or eating it himself. "You and Freddie are good at that." His sense of fairness prevailed, and he cut the dumpling in half.

"Detective Hayes is the professional," Daisy said hastily. Going up against churchmen who had already proven they would kill in God's name was not exactly what she was in this city for. "He is an agent of the English crown, with knowledge much greater than ours, and he has been in this country before. Covertly, as it were."

"But a woman may go nearly unobserved," May Lin put in softly. "Perhaps I might assist by taking you to the tunnels. Bishop del Fuego seemed awfully familiar with them, and they may lead us to whatever secret refuge he is using now that Nuestra Señora de las Estrellas is in ruins and he cannot return to the cathedral without being recognized."

"I will do what little I may, Daisy, if it will help," Peony said. "I have seen with my own eyes how you put two and three together to make five squared."

"But—" *But Papa.* How were they to take up their search now? Hire a boat in which to pursue him? Lean on William's kindness once more and prevail upon him to fly them to wherever the ship with a woman's name had gone? Was it better to remain with Peony and hope that in return, she would offer her ship for the pursuit out of the goodness of her heart?

She met Freddie's gaze.

"We cannot leave now," her sister said softly, as though these questions fluttered in her mind, too, seeking a way out. "Not when so much is at stake, and we have only the slenderest of clues as to where Papa has gone from here."

"Find the bishop?" Daisy said quietly. "Overthrow a kingdom? And then Papa?"

"*Iris* is at your disposal for any or all of those things," Peony said. Clearly she had ears like a cat.

In May Lin's lap, Perdida finished the half dumpling and blinked up at Daisy in contentment.

A laugh bubbled up as Daisy realized she had already made her choice. "*Carpe* dumpling," she said to May Lin, whose eyes glowed with humor. "Let us go at once, while the bishop still basks in the comfort of believing himself both clever and safe."

CHAPTER 17

TUESDAY, SEPTEMBER 24, 1895

11:20 a.m.

Daisy no longer considered Freddie's leather harness for the Colt revolver outlandish or unladylike. In fact, as she gazed into the dark mouth of the tunnel and felt the ground move restlessly under her feet, a woman's arming herself to the teeth seemed very sensible indeed. If she had a knife in a sheath at her wrist, concealed under the gaily embroidered sleeve of the Californio blouse she wore, she might feel more capable of stepping into the dark.

Inches from their feet, the water whispered against the bricks where the tunnel gave on to a narrow strip of muddy sand. At high tide, they would not be able to enter. Where had the tide been when May Lin's abductors had brought her to the pier above them? Daisy had forgotten to ask, what with trying to keep May Lin's directions and descriptions of docks and ladders in her head.

"Oh, Daisy," Freddie whispered. "There are people in there."

181

Davey turned, his eyes wide. "Who? How do you know?"

Freddie flushed scarlet, and Daisy's stomach clenched as she realized what her sister meant. Whatever spirits had revealed themselves to her must remain her secret.

Something with four legs skittered on the bricks, and something else squealed. Daisy clutched the Thaxton pistol in her pocket more firmly, her thumb as close to the hammer as possible without actually drawing it back.

"Only rats," Freddie said weakly. "Let us go on before we all lose our courage."

"Remember what May Lin told us. At the top of this tunnel is a gate in the mission wall. The wall is offset, in a zigzag, to allow for a door. If someone comes in from the top, we may get into trouble, but we must try to find a clue as to the bishop's whereabouts. This is the last place he was seen."

"If someone comes down, Freddie will have to shoot them," Davey said cheerfully. "Dead men tell no tales."

"You have been reading too many of those lurid adventure tales," Daisy said reprovingly. "Hush, now. We do not want to advertise our presence."

Cautiously, they proceeded into the dark. Before she slung it to her back, Daisy reached into her rucksack and withdrew a moonglobe. She held it up just in time—Davey, a few feet ahead, jerked to a halt before he tripped over the body of someone lying curled on his side. Beyond him, two women looked up, their eyes bleary and hopeless, bundles of valuables forming their pillows.

People, homeless now, had taken refuge in this tunnel. Was that a sign that it was less likely to collapse? Daisy could only hope so as she nodded politely and proceeded farther in, stepping around a recumbent person or small groups every dozen feet or so. After a stretch of a quarter mile with no one in the path, Daisy was almost ready to hope that there would be no more.

At which point she saw another.

Only … he did not look as though he were sleeping. Nor did he look like the townspeople, dusty and frightened. As Davey leaned over him, she lifted the moonglobe and saw that he was a monk, lying partly across the gutter. A trickle of water ran in the groove under his body, and had washed away part of a dark stain.

Daisy reached for the boy's thin shoulder to pull him away. "Dead. Not long ago. Maybe yesterday." With a glance at Freddie, she silently asked, *Is his the spirit you saw?*

Freddie shook her head.

"No wonder nobody's sleeping up this far. His throat's been cut." Davey sounded only a little subdued. But then, he had been on the streets for over a year before he had met them in Georgetown. It was likely he had seen this much and more. "P'raps he refused to do what the bishop wanted, and was sent to Heaven to collect his reward."

Daisy shivered in a dank breeze that followed them up the tunnel from the waterfront.

A breeze.

"Do you feel that?" she whispered. "The air is moving. I believe the door at the other end has been opened."

"Low tide," Freddie whispered. "Perhaps that is when they go back and forth—unless they have a prisoner to put on a boat."

Daisy doused the moonglobe in her pocket. "We must hide."

But where? They could hear faint footsteps now. Two men

for certain, possibly three, coming down a staircase without fear of being heard. There was not a single hiding place, for the walls of the tunnel were rounded and smooth.

"What are we going to do?" Davey whispered hoarsely.

"Take hands." Daisy grasped his hand and reached back to feel Freddie's fingers slide into hers. "We must retrace our steps, quickly."

Davey felt along the wall, stubbed his toe on a raised brick, and choked back a curse. "And then what?"

Hide behind a family taking refuge here? No, that would probably frighten them even further. And they might turn them over to whoever was coming.

"We pretend to be sleeping, like the others. Come. Quickly."

They shuffled down the tunnel until the sound of low conversation told her where the last small group huddled. Daisy pulled Freddie and Davey down with her, pushing them between herself and the curved wall. Freddie curled up in a ball and Daisy tugged her sister's skirts into a bundle where she might lay her head.

She would not think of what had been running over these bricks before their arrival, or of anything but clutching Davey's thin form to her chest and gabbling a mental prayer for their own safety.

Soon light flickered in the tunnel, and she could hear the distinctive slap of sandals. There were three, she was sure of it. Even this far down the tunnel, sound carried. She could hear them speaking to one another in the Californio tongue, and a moment later the sounds of shuffling. Then a grunt, as though the body of the deceased monk had been lifted, and several lines in Latin. A blessing for the dead?

The sandals slapped on the bricks once more, with the precision of men carrying a heavy weight and trying to be sure of their footing. They staggered down the tunnel toward them.

Closer. Twenty feet away now. Daisy buried her head in Davey's shoulder and tried to look as though she were sleeping, not hiding. Davey was so tense his body trembled, and Freddie lay motionless, face to the wall, her knees bent to accommodate Daisy's head upon her skirts.

As they passed, something landed on Daisy's hip, and she nearly came up off the floor with a bloodcurdling scream. It took everything she had to beat down her terror as the monks brushed by them, the hems of the robe of the nearest one brushing her back. The sound of their going faded along the tunnel, murmurs rising among the little groups of people in their wake.

"Disposing of the body with this many witnesses?" Freddie breathed. "They are awfully confident."

"We cannot stay here. We must go."

As they climbed to their feet, something clinked on the bricks behind her. Daisy pressed a hand to her chest to still her galloping heart and shook the moonglobe into life.

"A coin," Davey whispered, picking it up. "Did you drop it, Daisy?"

She shook her head in wonder. "They are so confident in their power that they are dispensing alms. While carrying a dead body."

Davey had no qualms about pocketing the coin. "Let's be off, before they come back."

With the moonglobe lit once more, their clothes brushed off as well as might be, they met no other obstacles, not even other refugees. The tunnel terminated in a set of stone steps, which Daisy would have thought would have been destroyed in the earthquake. But this particular tunnel must be built on firmer ground, for only pebbles turned under their boots as they mounted toward the daylight. The door, still open, told them the monks expected to return this way.

"I wonder if those were May Lin's abductors?" Daisy said as they slipped out to the street, and it was safe to speak.

"How many monks know about that tunnel?" Davey asked. "All of them? Or just the bishop's men?"

"We cannot know," Daisy said. "We must hope that they will return to the bishop. When they come back, we will follow them."

"We may not get another chance," Freddie agreed. "It was difficult enough convincing William and Detective Hayes that we could do this at all. We must not return empty-handed."

Davey surveyed the deserted street, filled with treacherous heaps of rubble, some of which had fallen into a crevasse that split the paving stones from one side to the other. "See, there? Across the way—that bit of wall is left standing.. Enough to hide behind, innit?"

A luxurious house of more than one floor and what must have been a courtyard was now a heap of rubble as tall as two men standing one above the other. But the broken wall gave them shelter, and Daisy was even able to poke a brick out of its mortar. It fell on the far side, leaving a rectangular hole with an excellent view of the gate.

"Do you think May Lin and Lady Isabela and Lin have reached the school airfield yet?" Freddie wondered aloud.

"They must have," Davey said, craning his neck to study the sky, though the palace was too far away to see if the airship that had been moored at the Viceregal Society of Engineers was aloft.

With it and *Iris*, May Lin and Evan could widen their sphere of assistance to the injured, and ferry twice as many to mission hospitals within range. An additional benefit was that they could test the loyalty of the padres in each location. Of some the Viceroy was certain—at San Luis Obispo de Tolosa, for instance, Isabela's home. And San Gregorio, where his half sister lived. But of others he was not so sure.

The Viceroy, his presence still a secret, flew with Peony and her crew, and Isabela had been giddy with delight at being asked to accompany May Lin as navigator, with Evan, her fiancé, as chief engineer. If the plain little vessel remained in royal service, soon they would have to name it. Isabela favored *Mariposa*, while May Lin had suggested *Rosa*, a subtle tribute to the women of the rebellion. Daisy thought it a difficult choice, but it was not hers to make.

Hers was this present task.

"You are not to engage them," the Viceroy had said bluntly, when it became obvious that only Davey would go with Daisy and Freddie. "You are simply to find the bishop if you can, and report back."

William had been frantic at the thought of the three of them on their own in the damaged, suffering city. But he and the contents of the rear compartments of the conveyance were badly needed by the injured, so he had extracted a promise from all three of them that they would not take even the smallest risk in their attempts to locate the bishop while he stayed behind to perform his medical duty.

Somehow Davey had managed only to nod, so that he

would not break a verbal promise to the man to whom he was devoted.

Mrs. Boyle had found them a small canvas rucksack and filled it with food and water. After yesterday, she was taking no chances that her guests might starve in a tunnel. Daisy, who agreed with this point of view completely, carried it. Isabela had foraged within the palace to locate clothing that might be worn by a Californio woman working there. The more that Daisy and Freddie could pass at a distance for women of the city, the better. They wore black skirts with a wide flounce at the bottom, trimmed with colored ribbon. Their blouses were embroidered with red roses and yellow sprays of acacia and green leaves, not cut as low as Isabela's, but with a modest ruffle at the neck.

"In the language of flowers, acacia signifies concealed love," Daisy said as they dressed.

"I know," Isabela said. "You are concealed for love of our prince and our friends."

Perhaps she was right.

"Wrap this in your sash, and tie it at the front, so," Isabela instructed once they were dressed, handing both Daisy and Freddie tiny bottles made of brown glass.

"What is it?" Daisy asked as her waist was wrapped in red silk and knotted, the fringes hanging down nearly to her knees.

"Acid," Isabela said briefly. "Should you need to throw it, avoid getting it on your skin."

Dear me. Daisy felt the tiny glass shape pressing into the small of her back even now, as she watched the mission gate from behind the damaged wall. *A knife in a wrist sheath would have been much more efficient.* But their little party attracted no attention in the damaged streets, and she did appreciate having a secondary, more concealed means of protection.

She and Freddie had arranged their hair in braided coronets like Isabela's, but with no hat or bonnet. No one cared about hats or bonnets, anyway. When a city was literally thrashing in pain, protecting one's complexion from the sun was the last thing a woman had time to think of.

Movement caught her eye, and she sucked in a breath through her teeth. Davey peered around the jagged end of their hiding place, Freddie leaning behind him. Together they watched three padres in rough wool robes emerge from the gate, close and lock it, then proceed solemnly, their heads bowed and their hands tucked into their sleeves, up the middle of the road, skirting the edges of the crevasse.

"Davey, stay out of sight, but keep up," Daisy whispered. "Freddie and I are about to go into mourning. Seeking a relative. Or something."

She clasped her sister's hand and passed her free arm about her shoulders, as though consoling her on a mutual loss. They followed the padres, two girls among many. Some were at work on the rubble of houses with their surviving family, attempting to clear rooms. Some sat upon broken walls, weeping for their dead. Men and women alike carried stretchers hastily assembled from tree branches and clothing, in the direction of the palace. Word had gone out that the injured were being conveyed to safety by air, and any worries about flying in the face of God had apparently evaporated in the more present danger to those they loved.

The padres led them two blocks north, then three west, up a steep hill crowded with elegant houses and trees that had once sheltered them graciously, but were now fallen on lawns and through roofs. From the corner of her eye, Daisy glanced at Davey, who kept up by dint of leaping over walls and scrambling around heaps of fallen brick, lending a quick hand where he could and trotting on when he could not. At length the monks reached a house that seemed to have suffered less than its fellows, though no one seemed to be in residence. Daisy tilted her face in toward Freddie's, walking slowly past the corner, as the monks looked around, then proceeded through a gate in the wall.

They did not lock it behind them. A flash of brown hair and dusty boots among the bougainvillea told her Davey had taken advantage of this oversight and slipped inside.

"After them," Freddie murmured. "We cannot lose them."

The gate let them into a garden, where fallen trees littered the lawn. Glass from broken windows sparkled in destroyed flowerbeds. Davey waved from behind a small stone building that might have been a greenhouse or a gardener's shed, and they ran across the grass.

"In here," he whispered when they joined him.

Freddie squeaked, "They'll have seen us." The building possessed windows, half covered in a creeping vine with trumpet-shaped yellow flowers.

Davey shook his head. "Entrance to another tunnel. Come on."

Whose house had this been? What madwoman would go down there to face who knew what?

Daisy had no idea of the answer to the first question. As for the second? She took a deep breath, adjusted the rucksack, and stepped inside the shed's low door.

She did not know what to expect, but an orderly stack of small, narrow objects wrapped in burlap was very low on the list. "Davey, what are you doing?" she whispered. "Is that a trap door?"

"Yes," he said, unconcerned about the stone slate that lay partly across a hole in the rear of the shed. Daisy approached it cautiously to see a ladder going down into the darkness.

Tunnels were all very well, but she preferred the ones where at least she knew where they went. Was this the point at which they ended their labors for the day and went back to the palace to tell the Viceroy what they had seen?

Behind her, Freddie gasped, and Daisy whirled to see that Davey had unwrapped one of the bundles. "Davey, stop that at once. We have no time for satisfying your curiosity. We must go before we are—"

He pulled away a length of cotton that formed an inner wrapping, and Daisy forgot what she had been going to say.

"Is that … gold?" Freddie whispered.

"It's heavy enough." Davey lifted the ingot, about six inches long and four inches high, with both hands.

"Put that back at once," Daisy managed. "Are those bundles *all* gold?"

"Must be." He covered it up like its fellows. Quite a number of others were set under the windows, larger and with odd shapes, unlike the neat stack of ingots. "What kind of person stacks gold in their garden shed?"

The earth trembled again, and the slate that covered the tunnel's mouth scraped as it moved.

"Never mind," Daisy said nervously. The shed could collapse upon them at any moment, to say nothing of what might happen in the tunnel if they did not make up their minds. "Some eccentric rich man's gold is not going to assassinate the prince. Our task is to find the bishop and not allow ourselves to be distracted. Those monks are our best lead."

So. Not back to the palace, then.

She stifled a sigh of regret, turned, grasped the ladder, and placed a boot on the first rung. *Once more into the breach, my friends.*

CHAPTER 18

1:35 p.m.

Peony tripped on a broken corner of brick and staggered like a drunken sailor before she got her feet under her.

"Are you all right, miss?" Captain Boyle, holding the other end of the stretcher, looked over his shoulder in concern.

"Yes, quite all right." She shook her head at her own clumsiness, and managed a smile at the young girl with the broken leg who was their patient. "I'm so sorry, darling," she said to her. The child might not understand her language, but it appeared she understood the apologetic smile, and pale with pain though she was, returned it weakly.

Peony and the captain took her into the *asistencia* at Mission San Rafael Arcángel. The captain remained to settle a large man whose pain was clearly more than he could bear while Peony trotted back to *Iris*, up the gangway and along the corridor to her cabin.

She knocked and waited.

"Come in." The Viceroy turned from the viewing port, where she noted he was taking care to stay out of sight.

She closed the door behind her. "May I bring you anything, sir?"

"The head of the bishop on a plate?"

She swallowed at the grisly image. "We will find him."

He made a vague gesture of frustration and returned to his contemplation of the town outside, where people came and went from mission to airship with supplies and the injured. "I should be in the capital, organizing assistance for those whose homes have been destroyed. I should be out there in the square, doing what I can to help. If nothing else, I ought to be assuring the people that they need have no fear."

"That will be difficult when chimneys are falling and wells are drying up."

The pain in his face seemed to grow deeper. "I meant to say, no fear of their government failing them." He sighed. "But I suppose I cannot even say that, if I am to hide in ladies' chambers for fear of assassination. If I could just tell someone that their injury will be cared for, I would be happy."

Peony took a firm grip on her patience and made up her mind. "Then go out to the saloon and do so, sir. We are many hands short and every pair is valuable. It is no good your hiding in here if you want to help. Besides, even if someone does recognize you, they may think it is simply the laudanum."

"Do you think so?" His face brightened, and she tried not to smile at someone so happy to be a hallucination.

"I do. Wash your hands and come with me."

She left His Serene Highness in Mrs. Boyle's competent care. Immediately, that lady set him to work preparing the injured for transport to the *asistencia*. It would do him good to consider others before himself and to be bossed by someone else for a change. Then she picked up several empty baskets that had contained bandages, to return to the mission. They had moored in the town square, so it was not a very long walk.

Despite its imposing name, the neat two-story church was small and did not even boast a steeple. Which was probably a good thing, for there was nothing to topple and kill anyone standing below. Water trickled in a stream down a hill behind the building—another good thing, for lack of water would increase the death toll all by itself.

"May I offer you a drink?" Detective Hayes—oh goodness, she had kissed the man, surely she could think of him by his first name—emerged from the trees with a jumble of bottles in his arms, their glass tinted every color, from the brown indicating whiskey to the blue of medicine to the ruby red of a container for vanilla and almond extract. A bucket dangled from his good elbow, sloshing with every step. "I have just been to the spring and filled every bottle I could find. It is good water, and so cold it will chill your teeth."

"You have been using your arm," she accused him, seeing no sign of the sling. She set the baskets on the ground and began to fill them with bottles of water. "You know the padre at San Gregorio told you not to. Your shoulder will never heal if you do not rest it." The bottles cooled her hands. They would be most welcome in the infirmary. "And thank you for the offer. I will have some later."

"I must use my arm," he told her once they had delivered the water to the padres, and had returned to *Iris*.

The Viceroy barely looked up, so soberly was he listening

to Mrs. Boyle's instructions on the wrapping of bandages about the head.

"It is so stiff it might just freeze in one position," Barnaby went on. "Selena Chang in Bodie told me it was better to use it than not, and I trust her."

Peony had met Mrs. Chang, and found her terrifying. Trustworthy, but not the sort of woman one ought to argue with. Rather like her own mother, from whom she had not heard in some time.

"You must do as she said, then," Peony allowed. "Come, let us see if we can find some more bottles and buckets. The refectory would be a good place to look, and I am sure none of the padres has time to pursue the errand."

They had perforce to go through the church, with its unusual star window above the door. As they paced up the short nave toward the exit on the right side that would take them into the closed courtyard and the refectory, Peony paused at the altar rail.

"Offering a prayer?" Barnaby said in a low tone. "How surprising."

"I do not see why it should be," she said, making certain that her shoulder did not bump his healing left arm. Really, she ought to have chosen her location better. They stood here like a bride and groom waiting for the minister. "That poor child the captain and I took into the *asistencia* a little while ago could certainly use our prayers, and her frantic mother as well."

A moment passed. Then he said. "Forgive me. You are quite right."

But in that moment, as she gazed at the altar and the carved figure of the Archangel Raphael above it, she realized that something was *not* quite right. Footsteps sounded in the nave, and she turned to see the padre who had shown the way to her and Captain Boyle and their stretcher bearing the child.

She dipped a curtsey. "Padre." They had lingered too long. Other injured people required their assistance, and the water would have to wait.

He inclined his head. "Senorita. I am in need of prayer myself." He gazed at Raphael for several moments, then sighed as his gaze fell to the empty altar.

She might be imagining things. There was probably a reasonable explanation. But curiosity got the better of her. "Padre, may I ask you something?"

"Of course, señorita. I owe you and your crew much more than an answer to any question."

"Are we needed immediately?"

"No, my child. I did not come for you, I came for a moment of refreshment in the house of God."

"Ah. Then perhaps you might tell me what normally rests there on the altar?"

He glanced at it, then smiled. "You are wondering where the gold chalices and plate are. How observant of you."

"Were they damaged during the earthquake?"

"It is a miracle, certainly, that Rafael himself seems to have preserved them. And our bishop has apparently realized that further preservation is in order for all the missions. He has commanded that all the gold altar pieces, as well as our gold reliquary containing the finger bone of Saint Sebastian, and our ingots in the treasury, be sent to San Francisco de Asis for safekeeping. Two monks charged with that task left at dawn this morning."

"San Francisco?" Barnaby said in surprise. "But that

mission is in ruins. San Rafael Arcángel was hardly touched—for which we and our passengers are thankful. Surely your valuables are safer here."

The padre looked worried, then smoothed his brow with what seemed to be an act of will. "It is not my place to disobey a directive from my bishop, señor."

"Do you obey him in all things?" Peony asked.

"All things spiritual," the old man responded carefully. "According to my conscience."

"What of the Viceroy?" she went on innocently. "You obey him in all things temporal?"

"Indeed," the padre said. "But he is more than a temporal ruler. He is anointed of God, a prophet, and I am at his service if he should require even the smallest of offices from me." He met her gaze. "Even here in this village, I have heard of you," he said unexpectedly.

"Have you?" Her stomach clenched. Those words never meant anything good.

"You are a friend of the Minister of Magnificent Devices, are you not?"

"I am," she answered. With an airship at her back, she could hardly deny it.

"As am I." Barnaby's expression had shuttered, as though he were readying himself to act. But not, surely, against this innocent old man with his hands tucked into the sleeves of his brown robe?

The padre nodded. "Mission San Rafael Arcángel declared for the side of the Viceroy during the Rose Rebellion," he told them quietly. "We sent food and supplies to the rebels, and did our best to assist our prince in keeping his throne." He lifted his chin with dignity. "I was very nearly unchurched for it, but I would not change my stand."

"Well done," Barnaby said with a quiet smile. "For we fear that the war is not yet over. Yesterday, in the midst of the destruction of the earthquake, the very bishop of whom we were just speaking attempted an assassination of the Viceroy."

The padre gasped, and his face paled.

"He was not successful," Peony hastened to reassure him. "The prince is well." *And not fifty feet from you.* She wished she could tell him that, but she could not risk the word getting out through the mission network, which seemed to be very efficient.

"And the bishop?" the old man asked, struggling to speak. "What of him?"

"We do not know," Peony admitted. "We have been flying the injured to every *asistencia* we can reach. I am afraid we are behind in our news since this morning."

The padre's gaze moved to the altar, bare except for an ornately embroidered cloth that reached the floor on both sides. "As am I," he said. "Thank you for your confidence."

But the worried look did not leave his eyes, even as he saw them out and raised his hand in blessing.

MAY LIN CALLED, "UP SHIP!" and an eager group of little boys rounded up by Lin cast off ropes as though they had been doing it all their lives, instead of just this afternoon for the first time. As her young cousin joined them in the navigation gondola, May Lin had to smile at their awestruck faces falling away below, forming an oval of admiration in the square outside the Mission de la Exaltación de la Santa Cruz.

"I remember the first time I ever saw an airship," she said to Lin and Isabela at the navigation table. "I had never seen anything so beautiful. I think I must have been ten then."

"So old?" Isabela said. "But I thought they were common in the Texican Territories."

"Not in the river canyons. They cannot moor below, and there are few trees on the mesa tops to tie up to." May Lin set her course north for Mission Santa Clara de Asis, the nearest to possess a hospital. "At ten, I knew more about steamships and how to sink one than I did about air vessels. I learned quickly, though. My mother took me to see my father in San Antonio not long afterward, and I spent most of the voyage in the engine room."

"I should have done the same," Lin said. "I can operate William's conveyance nearly as well as he can, now."

"I cannot say that I feel an affinity for engines," Isabela confessed. "But I do like navigation. Reading clouds and land forms, as you have taught me. Feeling the currents of wind and allowing the ship to resist or respond to them."

Weather was too mercurial for May Lin, though she had learned to read the skies out of necessity. "Some must fly, I suppose, and some must navigate, and some must make certain that the ship is capable of flight."

She preferred the first and third duties. At the moment, Evan had the third while she acted as captain. The little school ship was small enough that if she leaned back, she could see through the viewing port up into the engine room where, from the change she could hear in their pitch, Evan was tuning the engines with enough steam pressure to take them over the mountains.

"What was your opinion of the padres at Santa Cruz?" she asked once Isabela had completed the plot of their course. "Are they loyal to the Viceroy?"

"I do not think so," Isabela said bluntly, laying down the compasses. "The padre did not look me in the eye, and avoided our questions."

"The altar pieces are missing, too," Lin put in. "Just like Mission de San Carlos Borromeo de Carmelo." The syllables rolled off her tongue like music. Isabela had been coaching her.

That young lady nodded. "If they are also gone from Santa Clara, I will begin to think that the bishop is stockpiling gold out of more than simply a wish to protect it."

"Santa Cruz was hardly damaged at all," May Lin reflected aloud as Evan reported the engines' status through the speaking horn she angled the vanes to take them higher. "The only reason we have passengers from there is because of the fire that broke out in the refectory. Though I am sorry for the two men. They are in pain, no doubt because of the quantity of butter spread upon their burns instead of ice."

"There is no ice at this time of year. They ought to have used cold water." Isabela's tone was slightly absent. "What would he want gold for? The bishop, I mean."

"Wars are expensive," she blurted, then backed away from that terrible thought. "We are merely guessing. Let us see the state of the altar at Santa Clara. Perhaps the pieces at Santa Cruz were merely being cleaned."

Lin snorted, and it was clear Isabela thought the same, but

was too well bred to actually make such a sound. Once they moored in the enormous courtyard before the cathedral at Santa Clara and had discharged their duty to the burn victims, Isabela took Evan's arm and led the way into the equally imposing church. May Lin's skin prickled as she paced down the nave after the couple, Lin's hand in hers. She wanted to tuck her hands into her sleeves, and find comfort in the sheaths of her knives.

Isabela genuflected at the bare altar, then rose to give them a significant look. There were too many people in the church to speak, so it was not until they were outside on the steps once more that she said, "Evan, I am afraid. Here, not only are the altar pieces missing, but the statues over the altar as well. I have been here before, and there were six—one of Saint Francis, one of Saint Claire, and four apostles."

"I do not like this at all. They were solid gold?" Evan's tone was quiet. It was clear he had been thinking since they had shared their suspicions with him.

"Yes. In fact, the— Look." Isabela's voice rose as she pointed. "Why is that crowd gathered around our ship?"

"We had better find out before they start stoning it."

Their strides lengthened and they arrived in the shadow of the fuselage in time to see a padre step on to the gangway, only to spring off, startled, as it bobbed under his weight. He had not realized that the ramp was not actually touching the ground.

"Padre," Evan called. "We are so sorry to have kept you waiting. Will you come aboard?"

The man stepped back, drawing his dignity about him like a cloak. "Minister," he said, leaving off the Prime. "Lady Isabela." He did not address May Lin or Lin at all.

This was not unusual among the less enlightened of the

churchmen. In fact, May Lin rather preferred being beneath their notice. It was safer.

The padre frowned up at the little ship's coated canvas fuselage above his head. "I never thought to see such an abomination here."

"I am certain that when they recover, your burned brothers will be grateful for their speedy delivery into your care," Isabela said pleasantly. "How may we assist you, padre?"

"We have received the message from our holy bishop about the safekeeping of the most precious artifacts of our church," he said ponderously.

"Yes," Isabela said. "At Santa Cruz, the padre has already dispatched men to San Francisco de Asis with their plate and candlesticks."

"One man may carry them, if he rides a mule," the padre said in a tone that implied Santa Cruz was insignificant and probably ought to be using silver. Or even clay. "But the valuables at Santa Clara de Asis are priceless, to say nothing of heavy. We had thought of sending a wagon, or even calling for the train, but when we saw this—this—"

"Airship," May Lin supplied.

"—vessel, it was revealed to me that God had sent a better solution."

May Lin gazed at him. Hypocrite. An abomination until he really needed it, and then it was God's will?

Evan nodded. "It will not fly in the face of God, then, to bring His most precious symbols aboard and fly them to San Francisco de Asis?"

"Indeed not. The mighty God of heaven uses even these unworthy vessels—" He spread his hands to include himself. "—in His service. But your destination is not the cathedral."

"It is terribly damaged," Isabela said. "Has the bishop given more explicit instructions?"

"Yes. Accompanied by four of our brothers, you will take the plate from this church to the house formerly occupied by His Excellency Augusto de Aragon y Villarreal."

May Lin felt a tingle of shock. Lin looked up to see what was the matter, as her fingers had tightened involuntarily around the girl's hand. No one called the traitor de Aragon by his former title or even his name. He was always referred to as *the traitor*, or *the usurper*. The padre in charge of the rich and influential Mission Santa Clara had just shown his hand in grand style.

Evan said, "With all respect, padre, de Aragon's former home is in ruins."

"Not that one. His summer home on the island."

"I'm sorry?"

"*La isla de los alcatraces*," the cleric said impatiently. "The island of the pelicans. You will take our artifacts there, and when you have done so, the brothers will assist you in collecting those that have come from the other missions."

"But padre," Isabela protested, "we are ferrying the injured to every *asistencia* within reach. Lives are more important than—"

"Nothing is more important than God's work," the padre thundered.

May Lin admired Isabela for bearing up under the onslaught. And really, she must protest no more. For until now, May Lin had had no idea that de Aragon had a summer home on the island, which lay between the Canton community on the west side of the bay, and several fishing villages on the east. Pelicans notwithstanding, it was not the most welcoming of places, with dangerous currents and only a few hardy trees able to grow on its rocky plateau.

It was, however, an excellent place on which to stockpile enough gold to finance a political coup and then some. One could see one's enemies coming from a long way off.

Isabela curtseyed. "I beg your pardon, padre."

"Of course we will assist," Evan hastened to reassure the cleric. "In fact, if your men are ready, we can begin loading now."

An hour later, the little ship wallowed in the air as it lifted. In the hold, four grim and muscular monks stood guard over a dozen packing crates, the longer of which May Lin assumed contained the statues. It had taken two men to lift them.

Isabela shook her head as she plotted their course northward, her curls moving softly upon her neck. "We could buy a small country with the gold we are carrying." The monks could not hear, but she was clearly taking no chances in case they decided to leave their post and roam about the ship. "I do not know whether to laugh at what they have entrusted us with, or go into hysterics."

"It is a king's ransom," Lin said, her eyes sparkling with the joke.

May Lin was not laughing. A king's ransom, indeed.

A new king, from Spain, with a well-paid army to ensure he took the throne.

CHAPTER 19

3:20 p.m.

Daisy was quite certain they had been walking for ten miles at least, their heads bent so as not to knock them on the tunnel roof. A kink was surely forming in the small of her back. It had taken perhaps a quarter of a mile to catch up with the three monks, who lit their way with ancient pitch torches that must have been staged at the bottom of the garden shed's ladder. No newfangled moon-globes for them, apparently. She, Freddie, and Davey stayed well back, in the darkness, keeping the monks in distant view and doing their very best not to be heard.

It wasn't easy. Some of the noise they made as their boots turned over bits of loose rock or slid on an uneven piece of the floor could pass for echoes. She hoped. But they could not speak, only follow as best they could.

The floor of the tunnel had changed within about a thousand feet, turning from brick to solid stone. If they had maintained their previous direction, they had passed under the

Canton district and were now somewhere below the waters of the bay.

No, she must not think of that. She must concentrate upon the wavering light and the three black shadows far ahead, and make sure they were not seen. If she thought about the sheer weight of the water that might be lying upon the roof of this tunnel—provided her sense of direction had not been completely turned around—she would run back the way she had come, screaming.

Perhaps—if she ever saw daylight again—she might ask one of the Canton ladies. Who had bored this tunnel such a distance? And why? For was it not much easier to build a boat and cross the bay than to engineer a tunnel and walk?

Periodically Freddie would suck in a breath through her nose and clutch Daisy's hand even tighter. Once she even choked back a whimper, at which point Daisy realized they were not alone. Yes, there were the monks, but Freddie could sense there were others here, too. Others who had been here a long time.

The poor darling. She was being very brave. Daisy was not the only one who wanted to run away screaming. Only Davey, in the lead as the three of them held hands so as not to lose one another in the dark, seemed unaffected by either water or ghosts. His task was to pursue, and pursue he did, with a light step that slowed more and more the farther they went.

When Daisy was certain she could walk no longer and would simply curl up against a curved wall and wait for the sea to break in the roof, the padres began to talk among themselves. Since they had been silent before this, Daisy's flagging spirits perked up at the possibility that they might have reached their destination.

Any destination. She would be perfectly happy to climb out and discover said destination to be nothing but a rock in the middle of the sea, festooned with sea birds, if only it meant getting out of this tunnel.

The torch seemed to levitate, and she realized their guides were climbing. Steps? A ladder? Then the torch plunged to earth and went out.

Utter blackness descended.

They heard the sounds of shuffling. One stone scraping upon another. A *clunk*. Then silence.

"I'm hungry," Davey said in a normal tone.

Daisy nearly jumped out of her skin. "Shh!"

"No need," the boy said. "They've gone topside, innit? Can we have some of that food? We'll need to wait a bit, won't we. Let them get out of earshot before we climb up."

The acrid scent of the extinguished torch tickled Daisy's nose as the smoke drifted down the tunnel to them. "Very well. Quite right. Here is the moonglobe."

From the rucksack on Daisy's back, Freddie pulled a small lidded basket containing cold dumplings wrapped in a damp cloth, another full of cut vegetables, and a short length of what appeared to be bamboo containing slender sticks of meat that had been dried. The meal was both satisfying and restorative, and when they had eaten half and tucked away the other half in the rucksack for later, and finished a jar of water among them, Daisy felt almost courageous.

"Davey, go up and see if you can move the stone." She raised the moonglobe as he scampered up stone steps so steep they were nearly a ladder, refusing to think of what they would do if they could not budge the stone.

But in a moment they heard the scrape of its motion, and in a moment Davey whispered, "All clear. Come ahead."

Daisy and Freddie emerged into a cellar. A set of steep steps made of wood led to a perfectly normal door with an iron latch. All around them were boxes and baskets full of everyday things—potatoes, onions, root vegetables, bottles of wine. Bars of gold. Explosives.

Davey pounced on a crate whose lid had been pushed to one side. "You could blow up a house with these," he whispered in delight. "Black-powder bombs!" He put two of the rounded, palm-sized explosives in his pockets. "When you pull the pin, it ignites them."

"Davey!" Daisy tried to remonstrate about stealing, but really, bombs seemed like an excellent idea. She was tempted to palm one or two herself. But it appeared ladies had to make do with a pistol and a tiny bottle of acid.

"Where are we, do you suppose?" Freddie whispered. "Fascinating as all this gold is, I shall die if I cannot see daylight in the next five minutes."

Was it still daylight? Daisy had lost all track of time. It could be midnight, for all they knew. And they could be in a fishing village, though that did not seem likely. Fishermen did not possess cellars the size of this one. Or ingots of gold.

There was only one way to find out. "Let us go up," she whispered back. "Be very quiet."

Davey, who had more experience in this type of work, lifted the latch silently and inched open the door. He leaned down to whisper, "Scullery. Clear."

The scullery gave on to a butler's pantry, which led to a kitchen the size of the main saloon on *Iris*. All empty. The kitchen was in use, however, for a fire crackled in the hearth and a steaming kettle sat upon the hob. And on the far side of the room were three horizontal windows deeply set in the stone wall, in front of which, outside, plants swayed in the breeze.

Daisy stood on tiptoe to see over the foliage while Freddie drank in the sight of the sky. "We *are* out in the bay," she breathed. "Look, that is the Canton district, straight across from us."

It felt as though they had walked halfway to Santa Fe, when in reality it was only to this island, a distance that couldn't be more than a mile.

"Come," Freddie said urgently, dragging herself away from the sill. "We must conceal ourselves until we find out what this place is."

"And why the monks came here carrying gold they keep in a garden shed," Davey added.

Next to the hearth, something creaked. Daisy stifled a gasp. Was someone coming down the corridor? Were there rats?

A panel that she had mistaken for a cupboard swung outward.

They were discovered! Trapped in the room ten feet from the door of the butler's pantry. Daisy fumbled for her pistol and pulled it from her pocket, raising it and pulling back the hammer with her thumb in one smooth motion. Freddie unsnapped her holster and did the same with the Colt.

A girl of about their own age ducked out of the low aperture, carrying a painted china pitcher. She was dressed in black silk, knife pleated at the hem in a flounce of wondrous abandon. As she turned to close the panel, Daisy saw the back of her bodice, embroidered with flowers in matte black thread, so that they stood out against the shine of the silk. Her brown hair was dressed simply but elegantly in a French braid about her head like a coronet. She closed the panel, making it invisible again, and turned.

To see two pistols aimed between her startled, long-lashed brown eyes.

She gasped, nearly dropped the pitcher, and clutched it with both hands against her chest, as though it might stop the bullets.

She said something rapidly in the Californio tongue.

No one moved. Daisy had absolutely no idea what to do next. Shoot her? That hardly seemed fair when she hadn't done anything wrong. Tie her up and toss her in the tunnel? Interrogate her in some mutual language?

The girl's gaze focused upon the short barrel of Daisy's weapon. "I say," she said in an accent one might hear in a ballroom in Mayfair, "is that a Thaxton single shot?"

3:45 p.m.

"Isabela—Evan," May Lin said to them as the little ship labored through the skies northward, "with all due respect to bishops and padres and God himself, and much as I like pelicans, I am not going to take all that gold in the cargo hold to *la isla de los alcatraces.*"

"Certainly not," Evan agreed. "I came in here to say the very same. We will take it to Honoria at San Gregorio as fast as this little tub can carry us."

"She is not a tub," Isabela said indignantly, patting the nearest steam pipe as though the ship might have taken offense. "*Mariposa* is beautiful."

211

"She is called *Rosa*," Lin objected. "We already decided."

Isabela lifted her chin. "Very well. She is Madame la Presidente's ship to name. But I will call her *Mariposa* in the privacy of my own thoughts. Whether butterfly or rose, we must send one of her pigeons at once to let the Viceroy know what we suspect."

"Quite right, darling," Evan said. "If there is paper and ink aboard, I will write a message."

Your Serene Highness,

It has come to our attention as we transport patients that the Church is stockpiling gold. Every mission we have visited today has sent its gold to the city at the bishop's command. Ostensibly it is to protect the people's treasures following the earthquake, but even missions with no damage have been charged with sending their altar plate (and goodness knows what else) to la isla de los alca-traces. It is our feeling that the summer house of the traitor, which has been deserted since his death, is to be the secret repository of enough gold to finance another revolution—or at least the installa-tion of another viceroy.

Miss Churchill must convey you with all speed to San Gregorio. We have the Santa Clara treasure aboard with four burly monks to guard it. We will need Honoria's help to overcome them upon landing.

Your servant,

Evan Douglas

The pigeon flew off, the late afternoon sunlight sparkling on its bronze wings and propellers, while May Lin encouraged little *Rosa* to do what she had not been designed to do, which was to fly as fast as possible while weighed down with so much. Built for the flight education of cadets, she lacked the more powerful engines, ornate rooms, and comfortable cabins that a pleasure craft like *Iris* possessed. But she made up for her spartan interiors with obedient controls and a sensitivity to weather that May Lin had fast come to appreciate.

If she ever got the chance to return to the river canyons, a ship like *Rosa* would be her choice of conveyance. Small, plain, light, and unobtrusive. She might even be able to land her on the largest terrace at Mother Mary's village, if the river were low.

But now she must think of a different landing. San Gregorio would be within sight shortly and they needed a plan. "There are no viewing ports in the hold. The monks will not know that they are not on the island until they disembark," she mused aloud when Evan returned from releasing the pigeon. "Is it better to coerce them out and then lift? Or take them prisoner with Honoria's help, and leave Santa Clara's treasure on the rancho?"

"What are we going to do with all that gold?" Isabela said. "Float about with it until it is safe to come down? No. The second plan is the better one."

"I agree," Evan said, not surprisingly. Isabela was no fool. "I wish we could let Honoria know, but the pigeons have no codes for fixed locations, only other ships."

"She will deduce it herself when the monks emerge from the hold and incite a riot," May Lin said dryly.

The prince's half-sister was a shape-shifter like the ones in the Navapai tales, going about as a man as easily as a witch or a spy—or a lady of quality, for that matter. These days, Lady San Gregorio or not, thousands of acres and hundreds of men at her command or not, she hardly stepped out of her own doorway without being prepared for a fight.

As they came in on a long, highly visible approach to the field nearest the hacienda, the ocean glinting a mile away to the west, Lin pointed. "Look. Can you see *Iris*, just coming over the hills behind us?"

"Excellent." May Lin angled the vanes and leaned into the speaking horn. "Release the pressure, if you please, Prime Minister. We will take her down."

"Evan, if you don't mind," came the dry voice as the pitch of the engines changed. "At least until we're out in public."

By the activity in the field as they floated down, Honoria had already deduced that the unexpected sight of two familiar airships coming toward the hacienda, not the mission hospital, meant that something was amiss. As *Rosa* settled gently among the long grass and wildflowers, May Lin could see two dozen men ranged along the fence looking as though they were watching the spectacle, every one with a very modern piece of weaponry strapped to his hip.

The lady of the manor met them at the foot of the gangway. "Evan," she said, giving him a hug. "Isabela."

"May Lin! Sister!" Ella, the lady's companion and true love, ran straight into May Lin's arms. "Something is wrong. You must tell us at once, before *Iris* lands. But who is this young person?"

Lin dropped a respectful curtsey to both ladies. "I am Yang Lin-Bai, May Lin's cousin."

"Then you are my sister, too." Ella, loving and irrepressible as ever, gave her a smacking kiss. "Now, out with it."

May Lin did not mince words as she told them of what they suspected. "The prince is aboard *Iris*, not the injured. I should like to have our unwelcome passengers dealt with before he gets here."

"Certainly," Honoria said with the kind of grin that had made the rivermen turn pale. "Escort them out as though there is nothing wrong."

"And if they decline?" Isabela said.

"Shoot them. They are traitors to my brother. A quick end is too good for them, but if they do not put up a fight, they may be guests in the gaol."

"You have a gaol?" Lin blurted.

"I do now. Ella, dearest, see that there are pallets and food laid in the cellar. We will be as courteous as the padres allow us to be."

May Lin hustled Lin and Isabela out of the field and behind the fence as Evan released the wide gangway to the cargo hold and the four monks, blinking in the sunlight, came down. They were surrounded by San Gregorio's men before their sandals buried themselves in the golden grass. When the monk in the lead swung a meaty fist at his escort, he was felled by half a dozen bullets before it could connect.

The three remaining monks fell to their knees, confused and disoriented. Clearly, they had no idea where they were, and a stay in the cellar would not enlighten them.

Thus it was that when *Iris* descended into the field in all her splendor and Peony, the Viceroy, and her crew descended, it was to find the Lady of San Gregorio and her guests forming a welcoming committee. No one was the least bit concerned that a body was even now being conducted to the mission church for final offices and burial.

The Viceroy embraced his sister and Ella, and received smacking kisses in return.

"We have news," Peony said as she rose from her curtsey.

"As do we," May Lin said.

"Come into the house," Honoria told them, indicating the way through the orchard to the *estancia*. "It seems we must have a council of war. Again."

"Wait." May Lin counted heads swiftly. "Peony, where are Daisy and Freddie?"

"And Davey?" Lin added. "Is William still here at the mission?"

"He is," Ella said. "I will send for him."

Peony spread her hands. "As for the Lindens, we do not know. We came straight here as soon as we got your pigeon."

May Lin felt her blood chill in her veins. "They have been gone since this morning. Has no one heard from them at all?"

CHAPTER 20

3:50 p.m.

"I will ask the questions," Daisy said firmly. No one standing in the kitchen moved, though Davey's eyes were wide as his gaze moved from herself to Freddie.

He had never seen them holding firearms, Daisy realized, his two young ladies from Bath. Which was not surprising. In Georgetown, they had not yet acquired any. Not until Bodie, and he had not been there. Until yesterday, they had been paying a civilized call upon Peony's acquaintance in the Californias. Until yesterday, they had been searching for Papa. Until yesterday, they had been hobnobbing with royalty, not pulling said royalty from the sea and trying to stop people from being assassinated.

"Never mind the Thaxton—who are you?" Freddie said to the girl in black, bringing them all back to the main point.

The girl lifted her chin. "I am Elena Pilar de Aragon y Valdez." The syllables rolled off her tongue with a grandeur that before this, they had only heard used by Carlos Felipe.

De Aragon! That was the name of the man Evan Douglas had told them of. The man who had tried to kill the Viceroy earlier this year, so that he could take over the kingdom as Regent and begin an invasion of the Texican Territories. But before she jumped to judgement of this strange girl, it was best to check the facts.

"A relative of the man they call the traitor?" Daisy asked coolly.

While her chin remained high, two spots of color burned into the girl's cheeks. "I am his niece. His sister was my mother."

Was. "Do you wear mourning for your uncle, then?" Daisy persisted, with a touch of disdain.

"Certainly not." She did not move, but her voice conveyed her contempt. "He is responsible for my mother's death. And his lackeys for my continued imprisonment here."

Imprisonment? A hundred questions crowded Daisy's tongue, but from somewhere in the house came the sound of a door closing, and male voices. Pilar drew a breath of alarm.

Daisy gestured at the secret staircase. "Open that, if you please. We must not be seen."

"I should say not," the girl said. "They do not know about it, and I prefer to keep it that way."

One elegant finger found a rosette carved in the oak mantel over the hearth, and the door popped open. Davey scampered past their unexpected hostess and through it. Daisy and Freddie followed, the girl and her still empty pitcher bringing up the rear. With a click, the door closed behind her.

On any other occasion, Daisy would have been fascinated by the tight little stair, which offered landings through which it appeared one could look into various rooms through peepholes. Narrow corridors ran this way and that, presumably between the walls.

"The door at the top," the girl whispered, by which helpful information Daisy realized that she could likely put away her Thaxton and stop expecting her boots to be grabbed and pulled out from under her.

They emerged into a suite of rooms that were full of light and air but not much else. A bed, nightstand, and a wardrobe in the bedroom. A sitting room that held a table with a pair of chairs. No rugs, no comforts, no personal items of any kind except for a trunk at the foot of the bed and a framed daguerreotype of a woman upon the table.

"Now," the girl said, "you will tell me who you are, what you were doing in the kitchen, and how you got here."

"You're really a prisoner, miss?" Davey said, having prowled over every inch of the two rooms in something under a minute. "Why?"

"Your name, sir?" she asked instead. "You may call me Pilar."

"I'm Davey Fletcher, Miss Pilar. From Georgetown, and before that, er, England."

"I am indeed a prisoner, Mr. Fletcher. You are the first company I have had in a year. Will you introduce me to your friends?"

Davey rose to the occasion admirably. "This is Miss Daisy Linden and her sister Frederica, from Bath. They are looking for their father, who is lost." He frowned. "At least, they were looking. Just now we're trying to keep the Viceroy from being killed."

"Keep him from being killed?" She whirled to confront Daisy. "He is not dead?"

"No indeed," Daisy said. "At least, not when we left him this morning. But not for lack of trying. Yesterday they put him on a prison ship and sank it. But we saved him and our friends who were with him."

Pilar pressed a hand to her chest and sat on the uncushioned window seat as though her knees had given out. "Felipe is not dead. Oh, thank heaven and all the angels."

Felipe?

"The bishop does not know," Pilar said, as though she were talking to herself. "None of them know. Oh, why does he hate him so much?"

"The bishop seems to object to his elevating a foreigner and a witch to positions in the government, among other things," Daisy said. "Airships seem to be a difficulty, too. There is so much gold in the basement of this house that we suspect he is stockpiling it for some terrible purpose over and above deposing the Viceroy. So you are a royalist, then, Miss er, Pilar?"

She must be. One did not first-name princes unless one knew them very well—or had saved their lives.

"I am nothing at the moment," the girl said bitterly. "I cannot even offer more than two of you a chair. But under normal circumstances, yes, I was a perfectly loyal citizen of this country. I knew Felipe as a small child. Once he returned from his education in the mother country, and I was out in society, I was present at a ball or two, and danced and talked with him. I helped Mama with a grand fiesta at Rancho San Juan Bautista on his first progress about the country after his father's death." She looked away. "Not that he would remember the particulars. I suppose one moonlit night looks much the same as any other."

Daisy could imagine that every young lady of quality in the entire country had flung herself at Carlos Felipe's head. It would be difficult to distinguish one from another, although this girl could not be said to be quite like anyone Daisy had ever met. She was as regal as Isabela, yet spoke with the plummy tones of Peony Churchill.

"Were you educated in England?" she asked.

"Yes, I spent four years there. Mama was determined that my marriage prospects should be wider than what the Royal Kingdom offered. She was a bit of a maverick. Her brother the usurper hated her for it."

"What's a maverick?" Davey wanted to know, perching next to her on the window seat, leaving the dining chairs for Daisy and Freddie.

"It is a steer—a male of the bovine sort—that does not run with the herd, but takes its own way."

Davey seemed delighted with this information. "We're all mavericks, then," he said to Freddie. "A herd of mavericks, ent we?"

"I think we must be," she told him with a smile. "But Miss —Pilar—why should you be imprisoned, if your uncle is dead?"

"I am a pawn in a greater game," the girl said, her lips tight. "First the bishop held Mama and me here to ensure my uncle kept the terms of their traitorous agreement. After my uncle's death in the Rose Rebellion, when we thought we would be set free, that monster kept us here still. My mother caught a chill that turned into pneumonia, and all he did was permit his monks to bring blankets and soup."

Pilar's expression turned murderous. "She died because of his neglect."

"But I still do not understand—" Daisy began.

"I am the last of the de Aragon bloodline—the oldest in the country," Pilar said with a sigh. "I would not have been … had not my aunt killed herself and her two children in shame at what her husband the traitor had done."

Shocked to the core, Daisy pressed her fingers to her lips. Davey looked fascinated. "How did she kill herself?"

"*Davey,*" Freddie choked. "And now, Pilar?"

"I, a mere woman, am not worthy of actual conversation with these men of God, you understand, even in chapel. Sunday evenings from six until seven I dine with the bishop, so he is forced to speak to me. I am a sinful temptation, you see. Otherwise, no one tells me anything. But once I discovered the secret stair, I was able to learn much more than I—or they—ever dreamed."

"Such as?" Daisy prompted.

"Such as everything," Pilar said proudly. "As I said, they believe our prince, with all his progressive ideas and forward-thinking ways, to be dead. They will call another member of the royal family here from Spain to rule. I will be forced to marry him," she concluded, her spine wilting. "No matter his looks or his character or age." She shuddered. "Apparently we are to produce golden children and usher in a new age of piety, obedience, and glory."

"How appalling," Freddie said, then covered her mouth. "I do beg your pardon."

"Oh, no, I feel the same way," Pilar said on a sigh, her rage burning out as suddenly as it had ignited. Or perhaps she was simply very good at pushing it deep inside.

"Why haven't you escaped?" Davey said. "It's a bit far to swim, but there must be boats coming and going, innit? Or you could—"

"Mama and I have been over every inch of this island attempting to find a way of escape. We must have got too close, because after she died and was buried with all pomp and circumstance next to the well in the garden—" The rage lit in her eyes again at this insult. "—I was brought back to our rooms and locked in. I wish I knew what we had seen or discovered, but I don't."

"Another entrance to the tunnel, maybe," Davey said. "That's how we got here."

Pilar stared at him. "What tunnel?"

"A tunnel runs under the bay from over there." Daisy pointed out the window on the west side, to see the sky turning a strange color over the hills. A curious greenish yellow, like a bruise after two or three days. But it was too early for sunset, wasn't it?

"We followed the monks through it," Davey said eagerly, and Daisy dragged her attention back inside the room. "There's a lot of gold in a garden shed at the other end, and a lot of gold here. Bombs, too." He pulled one out of his pocket to show Pilar.

"A tunnel," Pilar repeated, staring at the bomb but not seeing it, as though she had received a great shock. "All the way to the city."

Her breathing deepened, her face flushed, and Daisy realized that a rage such as they had not yet seen had surged back to the surface.

"I might have saved my mother's life," she said in a voice hushed with fury. *They* might have, simply by taking her on a pallet to the *asistencia*. They told me a boat could not come, because there was a storm. Or the tide was too low. Or the boatmen wanted too much pay. Excuse after excuse as to why they would not help."

Daisy exchanged a glance with her sister across the little table. Pilar had seemed perfectly pleasant—for a girl who had been locked up for months. But perhaps there was another reason she was imprisoned, and not because of some dynastic marriage, either. Perhaps she was simply mad.

"I am sorry for the loss of your mother," Freddie said gently. "We lost ours last year. We believe she died of grief, following my father's abduction."

Pilar seemed to control her emotions with a great effort. "Abduction?"

"Papa was an engineer," Daisy said. "Many men with such skills were abducted from the Territories to build the old Viceroy's great dam, to the south. Papa lost his memory following a beating. After the Rose Rebellion, he seemed to remember enough to attempt to travel. We have been hunting down clues, from Georgetown to Santa Fe to Bodie to San Francisco, trying to find him."

Hearing that she was not alone in tribulation seemed to calm Pilar. "Then we must see you on your way as soon as possible."

"What about you?" Davey said. "You can come with us."

"I?" Pilar shook her head. "Of what use am I? No one even knows I am here."

"Carlos Felipe is on Peony's airship," the boy reminded her. "You could ask him to help you."

Her face flushed. "He would enjoy an airship. But he has more important things to do than look after one insignificant girl. I saw from my window what happened to the city yesterday. The task ahead of him is enormous."

"And yet this house appears completely untouched," Freddie said wonderingly. "Is it a fortress?"

"No, just a house. A large one, meant for diplomatic affairs and entertaining and spying on its visitors," Pilar said, "but still a house. I do not know why it is intact when half the city is not."

"You could go home," Davey persisted, trying a different tack.

"I have no home to go to. Not really. My cousin on the Valdez side will have inherited it following my mother's death, and it is not likely his wife will appreciate a penniless spinster about the place. Not one bearing the de Aragon name. They are royalists, too."

Daisy fought her growing impatience at this willingness to discount two perfectly rational suggestions. Did she really want to marry a horrible stranger and produce golden children? "So you prefer to rot here at the bishop's beck and call rather than do something to help yourself?"

Pilar drew herself up. "How dare you!"

"Quite easily," Daisy retorted. "We have crossed this continent at considerable risk to our lives, and at every step we have found that people are willing to help if they are only given a chance. If you know *Felipe,* then of course you must appeal to him for assistance. It is the only sensible thing to do. In return, you must tell him why the bishop is doing all of this. What his plans are. You have firsthand knowledge, where we do not."

"You are very blunt," Pilar said icily. "One might almost say rude."

"At least I have not given up on my own life," Daisy snapped. She took a breath to calm herself. "Now. Lay aside your airs and self pity. Let us be friends and help one another, for goodness sake."

Pilar seemed to struggle with this suggestion. The proud, ancient bloodline at odds with an honest fear of living alone in the world? "The monks are unyielding in their obedience to the liturgy of the hours," she said at last.

Davey looked mystified. "What's that—and what's it got to do with anything?"

"Those are the old prayers," Pilar said to him. "Matins, Lauds, Compline, Vespers." When he still looked blank, she shook her head. "It is not important. What matters is that when they are at prayer, I may come and go. They were at None when we met in the kitchen. I had come to get hot water to wash with. I hope that when they see the kettle, each will think one of the others forgot and left it on the hob."

"How many monks are here?" Daisy asked. It appeared that they were going to be friends. Relief was a whisper in her spirits. She had not been looking forward to leaving this girl in her prison to face a fate that men in authority dictated for her. Or of dragging her out of it against her will.

"Monks? At least a dozen, plus the bishop."

"We followed three here," Freddie said.

Pilar nodded. "They come and go, presumably seeing to the gold. I always thought they used boats. I should have known when I couldn't see any such thing from my windows." She sighed and shook her head. "You are quite right that His Eminence is stockpiling it. If the people resist the installation of a new ruler after their own prince's murder, they plan to hire an army of mercenaries from the Oregon Territory to control them. On the Columbia River there are great steam-powered battleships to protect the territory from pirates out of Port Townsend. These battleships would sail southward and attack San Francisco de Asis at the bishop's command. Or at least allow the people to think they would attack, until they surrendered."

"Good heavens," Daisy said faintly. "We must get you to the Viceroy as quickly as possible. This is far more than even we suspected. He must be informed at once."

Life seeped into Pilar's face. "Yes," she said. "Of course you are right. I cannot stay here weeping over the past. Paralyzed by fear of the future. The present is too important."

"I'd say so," Davey told her. "When is the next, er, prayer? When the coast will be clear?"

"None is just over. Next is Vespers, at six." She indicated the position of the sun. "Two hours from now."

"We cannot stay here another two hours," Daisy exclaimed. "We must get you to *Iris* at once." She jumped up and walked to the window.

The city seemed so close, yet so very far away. So much water stood between themselves and their friends. Where was William at this moment? She could not even see *Iris*, though part of the cathedral that had been so badly damaged was plainly visible. She should have been able to see the airship. Was it still busy ferrying the injured to mission hospitals farther and farther away?

"They will bring me a tray soon," Pilar said. "They will unlock the door to give it to me, and again to take it away. We cannot go down to the kitchen now. They will all be there, preparing the evening meal."

"And the bishop?" Freddie said. "Does he eat with them?"

Pilar snorted. "Hardly. He is not the kind of man to scrub carrots and knead bread. I could take you along one of the secret corridors so that you might watch him in his study, plotting the destruction of this country. Writing letters to the missions demanding their gold and altar plate. Sending *billets doux* to Spain, to whatever malleable member of the royal family he can convince to come."

Daisy stood at the window, gripping her elbows in an effort not to bang her fists on the sill in frustration. They must get out of here without delay. They had the means—all they had to do was get across the kitchen, through the butler's pantry and the scullery, and down the cellar steps.

The vision in her mind of the path to freedom abruptly collapsed as she leaned to look out of the window with greater attention. "Good heavens," she said. "Does the tide normally go out so quickly here? I don't remember this happening yesterday."

"What do you mean?" Freddie joined her at the window, while Davey squirmed around to stand on the window seat and look out.

Pilar gazed over his thin shoulder. "What is happening?" she said softly. "No tide can go out that fast. Look, the island itself is being exposed. And—and—*Madre de Dios*, is that the sea bed? How is this possible?"

"Blimey," Davey breathed, goggling. "The water is all being sucked out."

Imagine the chaos in that narrow entrance to the bay. Imagine what will happen when it comes back in.

Beside her, Freddie went rigid, and swung her head abruptly to the left, as though someone had touched her without permission. Daisy distinctly heard her sister suck in a breath through her nose, as though she had prevented herself from screaming by sheer will. Daisy fumbled for her hand.

For the space of ten seconds, Freddie stared, frozen, not breathing, at absolutely nothing.

Then with a gasp, she wilted.

"Freddie," Daisy whispered. "What is it? What did you see?"

"We must get out of this room at once," Freddie said, her voice hollow. The hand in Daisy's had gone ice cold. "If the water can recede that quickly, it will come in just as quickly, and we are exposed up here. We must get into the tunnel. Now!"

"But Freddie, the monks—" Daisy began.

Her sister jerked her Colt from its holster. "You and I will deal with the monks. Davey, get those bombs ready. We have less than two minutes. Something terrible is about to happen."

4:30 p.m.

"Felipe—brother—you must not go back to the city," Honoria said urgently, her hand upon his arm.

"Let us go," Evan said. "If we have to send a search party through every tunnel after Daisy and Freddie, we will, but let us bear that risk. Not you."

They had finished their late luncheon, and now sat at the old-fashioned plank dining table, the appalling stuff they called coffee in front of them, to hold council. May Lin had declined in favor of a single glass of wine. Food was one thing, but coffee made her heart race and caused every fear she had ever entertained to attack her in the subsequent sleepless night.

The Viceroy had taken the news of his bishop's betrayal much better than he had just taken the news of the missions' gold. That the altar pieces and ingots contributed by the piety and labor of his people were now being redirected for some unknown purpose of said bishop's was simply adding insult to injury.

"I swear I will execute him myself with my father's sword." Carlos Felipe pushed away from the table and began to pace in front of the steam boiler recently installed where an old-fashioned fireplace had been. The boiler was a piece of art, in May Lin's view, with brass angels holding upraised hands to support the pipes, and the very latest in pressure gauges and temperature measurements so that it could function as hot water heater, oven, and griddle all at once.

"If you do kill him, the monks will make a second attempt at your assassination," Evan pointed out. "Or a third. Soon I shall begin to lose count."

The Viceroy paced. Up and down over the handwoven rugs. Up and down. "Very well. I will not do it myself."

May Lin allowed herself a sigh of relief, and helped Lin to an orange from the arrangement in the center of the table. The child had already consumed both the roast pork and vegetables for the main course and the flan with blackberry sauce for dessert. Honoria merely smiled at her in approval for her healthy appetite, like many around this table having once known both starvation and imprisonment.

"But I cannot stay here all day, hiding behind your skirts, sister, and those of Miss Churchill."

"I am not wearing skirts," Honoria pointed out. "And you have not been here above an hour."

"I have been hiding aboard *Iris*, doing what I can, but not what I ought," he said. His brown eyes snapped, and he straightened to his full height. "The city is in ruins. Aside from Evan and Isabela, with me in hiding there is no one to lead, to form rescue parties, to comfort the people in their time of need. I must do my duty. For them, and for my own self-respect."

"It is too dangerous," Honoria protested with a shake of her glossy head. "And the Mother only knows what del Fuego will do when he finds out you are still alive."

"Have a fatal apoplexy, one hopes," Peony said, daintily choosing a grape.

May Lin had had enough. "I agree with the Viceroy," she said. "Carlos Felipe, you have been able to help the injured, and have seen the extent of their despair. I am certain the word has already gone out that you have been doing so. Someone must give them hope and leadership, and you are the only one who can."

A chorus of arguments flew up like a flock of startled starlings.

But the Viceroy was smiling at her, and May Lin felt a clutch at her heart. *What if he is killed because you encouraged him—*

No. She was right to do so. Had she been in his place, she would have felt exactly the way he did now. "Your people admire and serve you in the sense that they admire and serve Saint Francis or one of the archangels," she said, leaning forward earnestly. "But if they see you in the streets helping with your own hands, organizing rebuilding projects, and clearing wells, you will cement their loyalty as nothing else can. No bishop will ever be able to say a word against you. They will have seen action on their behalf that speaks louder than words."

"We cannot possibly allow—" Evan began.

"It is too dangerous." Honoria repeated at the same time. "But I can see as plain as day that you are set on it." Carlos

Felipe spun to embrace his sister as she rose. "So Ella and I will go with you to the city. As bodyguards if necessary. But as support, too."

Now it was the Viceroy's turn to look horrified. "I cannot let you. What if—"

"*Let* me?" Honoria looked amused. "You could not stop me, dearest one. You forget you are surrounded by *las brujas*. Me. Ella. May Lin."

"And thank heaven for it," Evan said unexpectedly. "These are the only circumstances under which I could agree. Honoria, you've taken a huge burden off my heart. With you and Ella by his side, I can only feel sorry for the man the bishop sends to do his dirty work. Now we can get on with it."

Honoria grinned in a way May Lin had not seen in many a long month. The way she used to before the Rose Rebellion. Before the dam and her imprisonment. Her eyes held anticipation and joy. "Let us cast off ropes at once," she said.

"Our destination is the palace courtyard?" Captain Boyle asked, already on his feet.

"Yes. But we have taken advantage of *Iris* long enough," Carlos Felipe said. "We must reestablish our headquarters in the palace for the long term. First we will stop the gold coming from the outlying missions, and establish food trains instead. Send to the army for tents, that families may have shelter, and explosives, to bring down buildings so damaged that they are dangerous."

"And when we rebuild, we will not do it on the marine flats," Evan reminded him with a glance at May Lin. "The damage was much more severe there. We must consult with the Canton engineers. The architecture of Spain no longer serves us here. We would do better to adopt their methods, and build safer homes."

"Agreed," the Viceroy said. "But first things first. Let us arm ourselves and go."

So, in a late afternoon that was marred only by a peculiar sky that seemed to portend a storm, May Lin took *Rosa* up. The crew of *Iris* cast off ropes a few minutes later. This time, Carlos Felipe had boarded with them. Honoria and Ella checked their weapons and explored *Rosa* while in the navigation gondola, Lin watched Isabela and her compasses with grave attention.

They were crossing the coastal mountains when the prince said, "Lady Isabela, Lin, would you give May Lin and I a moment of privacy in which to speak?"

Isabela curtsied and vanished through the portal before May Lin could stop her—even before she could recover from her own surprise. Carlos Felipe had never wanted to speak to her alone before. On the contrary, he was never alone at all, except when he retired for the night, and even then someone slept in his dressing room should he want something.

Lin hesitated, her gaze flicking from the prince to her cousin. Looking for permission to obey a man who was not technically her sovereign.

"If you please, may my cousin stay?" May Lin tried not to sound desperate. If he was going to give her a dressing-down about something, dadburn it, he could do it in front of a witness.

After a moment, during which it was clear he wanted to say no, he nodded. "Perhaps it is appropriate that you have a family member present, as is our usual custom."

For a dressing down? Or was he going to knight her or

perform some ceremony? For what Californio ceremony did people need a family member present? Mystified, May Lin set *Rosa's* course as Isabela had plotted it, and gave him her complete attention, one hand still on the helm.

He looked down a moment, as though marshaling his words. "Do you remember what I said to you yesterday, as we were about to drown in the sea?"

She had been deafened by the explosion of the barrel of black powder. Only now was her hearing coming back to normal.

When she shook her head, he said, "Then let me say it again." He took her hand in his, and removed the other from the helm so that he held both of them. "I love you."

It hadn't been a dream, there in the water, clinging to that coffin and half drowned already. May Lin stared at him, as unable to move or speak now as then, only for different reasons.

I love you.

"We are never alone, so I am taking advantage of these few minutes to put my heart before you," he said in a low tone. His eyes were deep and so brown, and filled with hope. "Yang May Lin, will you marry me? Will you become my vicereine, and rule at my side? Will you help my people as only you can, and bring them out of this disaster with me?"

She could not speak. The vision his words built in her mind was too vast, too astounding, for words. She—a witch—born on the wrong side of the blanket, the daughter of a Canton engineer and a Texican cowboy—become vicereine of this nation?

"The church will never allow it," she croaked.

"I will deal with the church as I deal with the bishop," he

said grimly, and she believed him. "Even if I must break with it. Only you and I matter. The marriage we will make. The family we will have. The country we will build. Together."

Did you say these things to Gloria Meriwether-Astor? The treacherous thought crept in like a tattletale.

Oh yes, she'd had the whole astonishing story from Ella, who had been lady's maid to Gloria during the events that had incited the Rose Rebellion. The very man who stood here now, imprisoning her hands, had proposed to Gloria, a married woman, and required that she annul her marriage for his sake, to boot.

I love you.

Fool. It would not work. Could not. She was not accepted in the city now. If he should announce an engagement, there could very well be riots in what was left of the streets. Marry a witch? Had it been anyone else in this position, she would have laughed in disbelief.

"May Lin?" His voice was gentle. And then, her entire body resounded with the shock as he bent and kissed her.

Kissed her as a lover would. The kind of kiss that could draw the very soul out of a woman's body. For a moment, she fell into it, fell and spiraled and drank the ecstasy of it, drowned in it—

I love you—

Drowned—she was drowning—

With a gasp, she broke the kiss and moved back just enough to let cool air flow between them. She pulled her hands from his and gripped the familiar spokes of the helm, as though to find her balance.

"I care for you, Felipe," she said. "I do, truly."

Already he had gone still, as though bracing himself. "But?"

"But it would never work." She looked into his eyes. They were of a similar height, so she only had to look up a very little. "The Rose Rebellion was won in part because of *las brujas*, but that does not mean the kingdom would accept one as its vicereine."

"They will," he said. "In time. When they see how very suited you are to rule."

Oh, how little he really knew her. "They have seen what you and Evan have allowed them to see while I have lived here," she said quietly. "The quiet engineer. The respectful councilor and advisor. The obedient teacher. But Felipe, I have killed men. I have destroyed Californio riverboats and feasted afterward. I have taken lovers."

He blinked, and she steeled herself to say more.

"You must give your people a vicereine who is one of them, my dear one. Choose a bride from among the grandee families, and cement their loyalty forever."

"I do not want any of those girls."

"You have not given them a chance." And then she was inspired by an idea. "The city needs nurses, and money, and female leadership. Let it be known that the daughters of the *estancias* are wanted for their loving charity. Choose from among those girls. The ones who get their hands dirty to help you will have the qualities you are looking for."

"I don't want them," he said again. "I want you."

She shook her head.

"You are refusing me?" His voice cracked, and her heart cracked with it.

I love you.

"I must," she said miserably. "And more than that, I must leave."

"What? Leave? May Lin, you cannot leave me. I need you now—more than I have ever needed anyone in my life."

"I will help you until we have dealt with the bishop." The idea that had been no more than a wistful hope now bloomed into full possibility, like a rose moved out of the shadows and into the sunshine. "When this is finished once and for all, I am going back to the river."

"No," he whispered. "You cannot."

"It is my home." She touched his cheek. "It is my freedom. Until this moment I did not realize how much I missed ... both."

"I would never take your freedom from you," he cried, and with a pang she saw how much she had hurt him. "You may visit Tia Clara and the ones we love whenever you like."

A ghost of a smile touched her mouth. "Certainly. I and my trunks and at least a hundred retainers will ride your magnificent *Silver Wind* as far as the railroad tracks go, then in ceremony and state we will travel in wagons to the landing at Santa Croce. And then what? Squeeze everybody aboard a riverboat so that Mother Mary and Tia Clara can feed and house all of us?"

"Put like that, it does seem ridiculous," he admitted after a moment. "Tia Clara would have a fit, and Mother Mary would probably shoot half of them on principle."

"It is impossible. All of it. You know it is."

His head came up, and those beautiful brown eyes, full of love and pain, captured hers once more. "Then let me come with you. The bishop believes me dead anyway. We'll go to the canyons together, be married by the padre at Santa Croce, and never come back here again."

If he had struck her, she could not have been more shocked. Or appalled. "Felipe—"

"I love you, and I think you love me, and how else are we to be happy?"

But sometimes there was more than one way to be happy. Look at Honoria and Ella. Look at Isabela's sister Beatriz, illuminated with joy at the prospect of becoming a nun. Over his shoulder, she looked at Lin, sitting on the iron steps that led up to the main deck, her eyes wide and her hands clasped so tightly in her lap that her knuckles had turned white.

Was she afraid that May Lin would say no—or yes?

There were other paths to happiness, though the price to give up the one offered her seemed almost too high to pay.

Almost.

"You cannot run away from your inheritance," she told him. "Leave the kingdom to the bishop and your horrible slouchy cousin? You would never do such a thing, and I would never respect you if you did."

"Never?"

She shook her head, and one of her braids came loose to fall over her shoulder. In the moment it took to pin it up, she repinned the blood-red rose as well.

He did not miss the gesture. "So you will not marry me?"

It took every ounce of strength she had to look him in the eyes. "No, my dear. I will not. I am going home."

His mouth trembled, and he looked away. "With your little cousin, our witness?"

"If she will come. Will you, Lin? Will you come with me and make a family, just us two?"

A pleat formed between Lin's brows. "You mean you're not going to be a princess?"

"I'm afraid not," May Lin said. How ridiculous it sounded. "Did you want me to be?"

Lin gave a decided shake of her cropped head. "I'm glad you said no. I left this city once before, and I can't leave it again soon enough."

May Lin surprised herself by smiling. "Can we deal with the bishop first?"

"We'll go right after?"

"Yes. The moment this is done. But will you miss Davey and your Mr. Barnicott and the Lindens?"

Lin levered herself off the steps. "I will, but they can come visit. If what you say about the terrace in Mother Mary's village is true, William's conveyance ought to fit nicely on it, with room to spare. And he doesn't eat very much, for a man. Davey, on the other hand…"

May Lin laughed out loud this time. Davey was a growing boy. And the sooner she got Lin into Tia Clara's capable hands and got some proper nutrition into her, the better May Lin would feel.

Carlos Felipe had not taken his desolate gaze from her. "In that beautiful head, you are making plans already that do not include me."

"It is what women do, my dear," May Lin said. She dared to take his hand. Deep in the night, she had imagined these brown fingers playing upon her own body. Someone else would have that pleasure now. She shook the thought away. "But we never forget those we leave behind, do we, Lin?"

"No," her cousin said, cheerful now that a decision had been made. "And we always look forward to seeing them again."

The Viceroy squeezed her fingers, then froze with a quick intake of breath as he gazed over her shoulder. "May Lin."

She whirled, her other hand closing on the helm. "What … *What is that?*"

The three of them pressed themselves against the viewing port. They would pass over the ruined palace in a moment. And beyond it, the bay—

"The water—" Carlos Felipe rasped. *"Madre de Dios!"*

For the bay had emptied as though it were a tin tub. And now, the very air seemed to shake as though thunder had sounded. The sea leaped at the rocks at the entrance to the bay, striking them with titanic force, pouring through the channel, howling back into its bed, sweeping everything before it. The sea, now as tall as a mountain, relentless as a rudderless ship, bearing down—

Five hundred feet in the air though they were, May Lin screamed as the weight of the entire ocean crashed against the defenseless islands, against the rubble of the city, against the chaos of the Barbary Coast, and completed the destruction the earthquake had begun.

CHAPTER 22

5:04 p.m.

Freddie kicked open the cupboard door with one blow and Daisy cried out. She had never seen her sister use violence in her life. They burst into the kitchen, stunning the monks into immobility.

"Out of the way!" Daisy shouted, leveling the Thaxton at the monk standing in the door of the butler's pantry, a crock of butter in his hands.

"Save yourselves," Freddie cried, ramming him out of the doorway with her shoulder when he did not move.

He gaped at Pilar and shouted something in the Californio tongue, dropping the butter and lunging at her. Davey stuck out his foot and he fell across the threshold like a sack of flour. As nimbly as a mountain goat, Pilar leaped over him and they were through.

Pandemonium broke out in the kitchen as they ran through to the scullery and hauled on the door to the cellar.

Locked.

Freddie screeched in rage and terror. She aimed the Colt at the lock and pulled the trigger.

The roar of the gun was deafening in the enclosed space, and the two monks that had run after them into the butler's pantry shouted in terror and fled back the other way.

The door blew open and Freddie plunged down the steps. By the time Daisy and the others reached her, she had the stone off the entry to the tunnel and was already halfway down.

"What—?" Pilar began, her eyes huge. Daisy could hardly blame her. Freddie shooting the lock off a door? The heaps of gold in the cellar were less astonishing.

"No time!" she shouted, and pushed Pilar toward the steep stone stair. "Davey, you next."

"But why—what did Freddie—"

"Get down!"

Davey swiped an ingot off the pile and staggered with it to the hole, but Daisy pulled it from his hands and flung it on the floor. When she practically trod on his head coming down after him, he scrambled down in earnest, swearing with increasing inventiveness on every step. Her feet had just touched the ground when she heard a sound the likes of which she had never dreamed could be possible.

A hundred Colts fired in a small room.

Thunder.

A train running straight into the side of a mountain.

All of it at once.

Only by the tearing in her throat did she realize she was screaming, yet she could not hear herself. The concussion to the air around them was dreadful, and stunned, she watched as sunlight, pure and ethereal, shone down through the hole like a benediction she could not understand.

And then the water came in like a torrent.

"Run!"

She grabbed Davey by the shirt and yanked him after her until he got his feet under him. Then she wrestled the moon-globe from her pocket. In a state of utter panic, they pelted up the tunnel as though the very gods were after them, and every one wanted them dead.

What had seemed like ten miles earlier today was an endless nightmare now. Half crouched under the low ceiling, crashing into one another, breathless with fear, they ran and ran until Daisy's lungs gave out and she had to stop and clutch her side.

"I cannot—"

"Come on, Daisy," Davey urged her. "The floor is an inch deep now. We'll drown if we stop."

"Moonglobe," she gasped. "Take the lead."

The very presence of the water acted like a goad to her feet. How had she not noticed it? She could only imagine an entire ocean trying to get in through that well in the cellar, a weight that would burst the tunnel from within if it did not first collapse on their heads.

Running ... stumbling ... gasping for breath ...

Just as she thought she would go utterly mad from fear and anticipation of her own dreadful death, the angle of the tunnel floor changed. Now it was dry. Could it be—?

"Nearly there," Davey panted. "A little farther."

Pilar was weeping softly. *"Mama ... Dios mio, mama ..."*

Daisy pushed her from the back. "Do not stop. Keep going."

The sight of the ladder, so homely, so *there* for them, was like a miracle. Daisy would have fallen to her knees in thanks if the fear had not urged her forward. They went up it so fast it danced upon its feet—and here was the shed—and the air—and the light—

Daisy fell to her knees and kissed the grass.

Davey pocketed the moonglobe as he ran across the lawn. "Look!"

She pulled herself to her feet, half afraid another wave was coming that would engulf them for certain this time. From behind a tumbled stone wall, clinging to it like a life raft, all of them panting as though they'd never get enough air in their lungs, they looked down the slope to the bay.

"*La isla,*" Pilar croaked, pointing. "It is gone. All gone."

The island itself still stood in the midst of an enraged sea, but everything on it had been scoured away. Its flat top was as clean as a wood table—no summer house, no trees, no driftwood. The sea heaved and ran still, as though trying to make itself comfortable in a bed that was a little too small for it. But as they watched, large seabirds, disturbed and flung into the air in alarm, began to settle upon the wet expanse of the island.

Claiming it. Making it their own.

Daisy gripped Freddie's hand and met her eyes. "How?" was the only word Daisy's lips could form.

Her sister gulped. "P-Pilar, your mother. Was she … a lady of forty or so?"

Pilar's wet, horrified gaze turned to her, and she seemed to be translating Freddie's words, trying to find their meaning. "Yes."

"Did she wear … gold earrings? With … rubies?"

Pilar gasped. "How did you know?"

"She—she appeared to me in a vision. Said we must get out at once. She— She saved—" Freddie choked and could not go on.

White as his shirt had once been, Davey dragged his gaze away from the scene of destruction below. "Your mum saved our lives?"

In Pilar's brown eyes, horror was slowly being replaced by the dawning of joy, like the rising of the sun. "She said— As she lay dying, she said she would never leave me. That she would love me to eternity."

"That she does," Freddie said with such conviction that Pilar's eyes filled with tears.

"I wish I could have shared your vision. Seen her one last time."

Freddie gripped her wrist. "She will always be with you. Love like that snaps its fingers at death. Your mother was a woman of rare character and bravery. And so are you."

Pilar began to cry, but it was not from grief, Daisy was certain. It was from joy, and relief, and a comfort that perhaps she had not known since her mother's passing.

"Daisy, can we have some more of that food in your rucksack?" Davey wanted to know.

Trust a boy to bring them out of the realms of angels and back to the needs of the body. By the time they had emptied the rucksack and pillaged its contents, and Davey had put the bombs and the moonglobe in it for safekeeping, Pilar had begun to recover.

"I can never thank you," she said, slipping an arm about Daisy's and Freddie's waists as they stood once more at the tumbled wall. "You have saved my life in more ways than one."

Each time they looked, the sea seemed to settle a little more, and more pelicans gathered where the house had been. The bay was covered in flotsam—crushed boats, the roofs of houses, trees—all heaving restlessly in the chaos.

Below, the area of the city nearest the water, where the streets and homes had suffered the most damage, was a wilderness of everything the dreadful wave had brought in, knocked down, and carried away. No one could have survived it.

And yet, near where they stood, where the ground began to rise and where some houses had been built upon the rock, people had emerged and were beginning to clear the streets. Carry the injured to safety. Mourn their dead.

Pilar turned to Daisy. "We must help them," she said.

"What can we do?" Davey wanted to know. "I want to get back to William and the others."

"We can—we can—" Wildly, she looked around. And then her eyes widened as she looked up at the house, set in its damaged gardens but still standing, its doors and roofs intact. "Why, this is my uncle's house. How did we come to be here?"

A tunnel from the traitor's official residence to his summer house, where he could safely keep his sister-in-law and niece prisoner, and no one would ever know. A garden shed full of gold, waiting for transport to the safety of the island. Daisy wondered that they had not guessed its ownership long before this.

This same conclusion seemed to strike Pilar. "We will turn the house into a hospital. Come, let us begin in his own neighborhood, and bring healing where once there was only greed and destruction."

"But we have no doctor, or skill at nursing," Freddie protested.

"There are doctors in the Canton district," Daisy told them. "Pilar, you are right. If you and Freddie go down and encourage people to bring their injured here, I will clear rooms. Goodness knows there look to be enough rooms to house a village. Davey, you go to the Canton settlement and beg them to send a doctor."

"Aye, miss." He scaled the wall and scampered off down the street.

Pilar and Freddie smacked the dust off their skirts and followed. Daisy mounted the steps to the door and tried the handle.

Locked.

"Oh, for heaven's sake." She couldn't very well shoot the lock, for they would need the door. The verandah was wide, and here were windows. She heaved on one, and with a screech, it slid up. Swinging her legs inside, she stood and trotted over to the door, which she unlocked.

Now. Light. Rooms. Beds and cushions.

She thrust back the heavy silk drapes and the last of the afternoon light illuminated the dusty furniture.

And glinted off the fuselage of an airship.

With a gasp, she craned to see it more clearly.

Not *Iris*.

Daisy had never seen it before, but she'd heard of it. The school ship. The one whose name they were still arguing over. It was circling slowly, as though looking down in horror, unable to think what to do next.

She had no idea who was at the helm, but it had to be

someone they knew. Maybe even William, who could pilot such a thing.

No—no—wait, it was leaving!

Daisy flew up the stairs to the bedroom, tore a sheet off one of the beds, which threw up a cloud of dust that got into her throat and her eyes.

Quickly!

The bedroom window gave on to the roof. Daisy pushed up the sash and squeezed out. Without a care for the pitch of the roof or the consequences if she should fall or any of the remonstrances she would be screeching at Davey if he tried such a thing, she hitched up her skirts and staggered up the tiles to the wing that overlooked the slope. With no trees left to shelter the house, she was in plain view from the air.

She hoped.

She shook out the huge bedsheet and began to flap it up and down, as though it were a rug to be shaken out.

See me! Come help us! Please be a friend—we need you!

The ship floated still in the direction of the bay.

Hesitated.

And then Daisy distinctly heard the pitch of the propellers change in the preternatural silence that had descended since the sea had gone mad. The little ship put her shoulder into the turn and began to come about.

5:40 p.m.

"May Lin! Look!" Lin grabbed her sleeve and dragged her over to the starboard side viewing port. "Those people are signaling us."

May Lin allowed herself to be dragged, her mind still not

able to comprehend the horror she had just witnessed. A city already suffering, already damaged in ways that might take years to repair, had just been attacked again. Had she been that kind of woman, she might have thought God was inflicting punishment upon the kingdom for the evil of its churchmen. But that was foolish. Mere wishful thinking. Her mother would say the city had been built on the eye of the dragon, and in irritation, the dragon had blinked it away.

Clearly something about this location was prone to exaggerated acts of nature. The sooner people made homes elsewhere, the better.

On a rooftop up on a hill, where trees lay helter-skelter yet houses remained standing, someone was on the roof waving a sheet for all she was worth. Someone in a black skirt and embroidered blouse. A Californio woman.

And yet—

May Lin leaned in until her nose touched the viewing port's pane. "Good heavens! That's Daisy Linden!" She leaped for the helm. "Evan?" she called into the speaking horn. "Isabela!"

"We are here," Evan said, sounding a little dazed. "May Lin, did you see...?"

"Yes, I saw. And now I see Daisy Linden on a rooftop on that hill twenty degrees north, signaling us like a madwoman. Coming about!" She adjusted the vanes horizontal. "Full speed. Can you see her?"

"Yes!" Evan called, life and strength coming back into his voice. "Where shall we moor?"

"In the garden," Carlos Felipe said into the speaking horn. "It is the traitor's residence. How have they come to be there?"

"We will soon find out."

Daisy somehow got down off the roof without killing herself, and was standing on the grass ready to catch the ropes when they settled a few minutes later. When they had shut down *Rosa*'s engines, they ran down the gangway.

At which point Daisy broke down completely and flung herself into May Lin's arms. "I have never been so glad to see anyone in my life," she sobbed. "The sea—did you see the sea? What it did? Did you see it?"

"We saw," May Lin said, awkwardly patting her back. "Where have you been all this time? We thought you were dead."

"If not for poor Pilar's mother, we would have been." Daisy hiccuped and attempted to gain control of herself. Completely oblivious of the fact that she stood in the presence of royalty, she hauled up the ruffle of her skirt, exposing half her petticoat, and scrubbed her face. "We have been in the tunnel—oh, there is so much gold—where is the Viceroy?"

"Here," Carlos Felipe said, who had been right in front of her the whole time. "I am very glad that you are not dead. But who is Pilar?"

Daisy's face crumpled in a spurt of temper. "Oh, if that isn't just like a man. You danced with her, you goose—Elena Pilar de Aragon y Valdez." The name rolled off her tongue with every bit of the grandeur that Isabela employed with her own. "She's been imprisoned on that wretched island by the wretched bishop for almost a whole wretched year! And did anybody know or care or do the least thing to help? No!"

The Viceroy gawked at the disheveled, tearstained termagant, leaning practically into his face with her hands on her hips. May Lin was seized with the urge to shout, *Brava!*

"Pilar? de Aragon? A year?" he repeated in increasing astonishment.

"Impossible!" Isabela's face had gone slack.

"Not in the least impossible!" Daisy snapped. "Oh, goodness. Come along, all of you. Davey has gone for a Canton doctor. Pilar and Freddie are down in the streets, encouraging the people to bring the injured here to this house. Now we may bring them aboard the ship and take them to a proper *asistencia*. Don't just stand there, come and help!"

To decline or even hesitate would be like shouting into a hurricane. Carlos Felipe raised his eyebrows at Evan Douglas, as though somehow it was his fault that such a harridan could shout at him. Smugly, May Lin extended her hand in an *after you* gesture. In order to follow Daisy, they had to pick up their pace to a run. Halfway across the garden the latter waved at a nondescript stone shed. "There are bars of gold and church plate in there. We will have to see about returning it."

In a shed? Well, May Lin supposed as she jogged along in Daisy's furious wake, it was as good a hiding place as any.

At the bottom of the hill, they found Freddie and Pilar coming toward them. Each carried a child, bloodstained and one clearly unconscious. Behind them staggered a man carrying a woman—the children's parents?

"Freddie—Pilar!" Daisy called. "Help has come. Let everyone know to take the injured aboard the airship."

"There are so many," Freddie said as they joined them. "We cannot help them all."

"We may make a beginning," Pilar said firmly. Her cheeks were flushed with exertion, her crown of braids loosening and making a glossy halo about her face. Her eyes lit with warmth at the sight of the Viceroy, alive and well. "Hello, Felipe."

The man holding his wife gasped in sudden recognition, and attempted to bow. The Viceroy stopped him and said a few comforting words to him.

Then he straightened. "Hello, Pilar." His gaze took her in as though he could not quite believe she was real. "I am sorry I did not know you were imprisoned by the traitor your uncle."

As though her relations were her fault! May Lin met Daisy's incensed gaze.

Pilar lifted her chin proudly, yet when she settled the child in her arms, it was with infinite tenderness. "I may have been my uncle's pawn in the beginning, but the bishop was behind a larger plan all along."

"She has information for you," Daisy put in. "About the bishop and his plans. But never mind that. He is drowned and I am glad. Come along before this poor man drops his wife."

"Here," Pilar said to the Viceroy. "Take her."

Carlos Felipe blinked as the little girl slid into his grasp. Pilar darted into a broken doorway and emerged with … not another child, as May Lin had expected, but a chicken. It was red and dusty and cowered in her arms as though it feared it would be fed to the wolves.

"Is that for our dinner?" the prince asked, clearly half believing she was mad.

After a year of imprisonment, May Lin could hardly blame the poor girl if she were both mad *and* hungry.

"Certainly not!" Pilar said in some exasperation. "I happen to like chickens. And pelicans. And gulls and all manner of sea birds. She is *not* to be eaten, and is as worthy of being saved as these dear children. Now do stop talking and go. Once they are settled, there are half a dozen more down at the cross-roads who need help to reach your airship."

"*Si, señorita.*" May Lin could not tell if the prince was affronted or simply bowing to the inevitable.

He hitched the child higher and turned obediently to do as she asked … and to begin with one small kindness the work that lay ahead for his kingdom.

WEDNESDAY, SEPTEMBER 25, 1895

11:20 a.m.

By the power vested in me by God and His holy saints," the padre at San Gregorio Mission said in English, out of consideration for the groom, "I pronounce you husband and wife together. What God has brought together, let no man put asunder. Prime Minister, you may kiss your bride."

To the applause of everyone in the mission church, Evan bent to kiss Isabela, who returned it with such enthusiasm that Daisy blushed. But her father, leaning on a crutch on the bench closest to the altar, beamed with pride and love, and took her mother's hand as though he, too, remembered the joy of their own wedding day.

In the midst of destruction and death, Evan and Isabela had made up their minds that the lengthy progresses and ceremonies of the old world would not be part of the new—at least as it applied to them. While their friends surrounded them, and the Viceroy himself gave his blessing, they would seize the moment and be married without delay.

The wedding feast was held in Honoria's apple orchard immediately after the ceremony, the branches heavy with fruit providing a good omen for the couple's life together. Not that Daisy was an expert in these matters. But after Emma Makepeace had had her happiness so cruelly snatched from her, she could not blame Evan and Isabela for dispensing with tradition and getting on with the business of living … and loving.

As for herself, she had awakened that morning with the conviction that if they did not take up their search for Papa, the business of their own lives would be delayed indefinitely in helping others recover theirs in the damaged city. It had been a mere five days since their arrival in San Francisco de Asis, and yet she felt as though she had aged twenty years.

A message had come yesterday from Madame Yuen via the Canton doctor. Her grandmother had learned the name of the ship on which Papa had departed. Since then, she and Freddie had had not a single chance to act upon that information.

Not until now.

The *Barbara Carol*, bound for Port Townsend in the Canadas, had departed on Saturday, when Daisy and Freddie had allowed themselves to be entertained by the Viceroy instead of attending to their business. They had been in the same place on the same day and not even known it. A lump formed in her throat at the thought. They were now four days behind Papa. How far could a steamship travel in that time? Had the dreadful wave swamped every ship for hundreds of miles along this coast—including the dreaded steam battle-ships patrolling the mouth of the Columbia River? Or had

Papa reached his destination before the wave rose, and vanished among the melee of criminals and pirates on the docks?

If Daisy had been afraid of Papa's attempting to navigate the Barbary Coast before, it was nothing to what she felt now.

She gazed at her sister over the bouquet of Queen Anne's Lace, roses, and mint on the trestle table, which they had picked together as supper was being laid out. At the head table, Evan was toasting his bride with a glass of golden wine sent by the padre at San Rafael Arcángel specifically for the occasion.

"The judge from Bodie, Freddie … did he not go to Port Townsend to bring law and order to the place?"

They had been quietly talking over their options under the sounds of merriment and the clatter of cutlery on plates. In Freddie, too, there seemed to be an urgency, a knowledge that decisions must be made, and sooner rather than later.

"Judge Wilson Bonnell," Freddie remembered aloud. "All he wanted to do was to work in his garden, but they begged him to take the post in Port Townsend. He and his family moved there from Reno, and that is all I can recall about him."

"So perhaps conditions may have improved slightly?" Daisy hardly dared to hope.

"We will not know until we arrive. We must go at once, Daisy. As much as we want to help the prince and May Lin and Evan and Isabela here, it is not our place." In the dappled sunlight beneath the apple trees, Freddie looked pale, and fragile in a way she had not been in Bath. Daisy felt a stab of guilt. The simple fact was that the Royal Kingdom was not good for Freddie. She had almost died twice now, and they hadn't even been here a week.

Oh, for a single day in which to sit in their own orchard, where nothing bad would happen! Perhaps they might even keep chickens. Daisy had become rather attached to little Perdida, who last night had been riding about on May Lin's shoulder, tucked up under her ear. How comforting that must be. At the moment, the little white bird was attacking a fallen apple, while May Lin kept a watchful eye upon her. The red hen that Pilar had rescued from the abandoned house had followed Daisy and Freddie this afternoon as they had picked the flowers. Now she circled Perdida, looking for an opportunity to poach a bit of apple.

Perhaps Pilar would be too busy to look after her. She ought to go with May Lin and Perdida, no matter how much Daisy wished the red hen might go with them.

The sooner they took up their search, the better. But when she broached it to the others at the table, this perfectly reasonable plan met considerable opposition.

"Go to Port Townsend?" Peony Churchill repeated, pushing the fronds of the ostrich feather upon her enchanting hat out of her eyes. "Now? How will you get there?"

At which point Daisy belatedly realized that of course Peony could not be expected to cart her and Freddie about indefinitely. Their paths must diverge sometime. Despite a nagging distrust of Peony where men's hearts were concerned, it was difficult not to like her—and heaven only knew she had been of immense help, both to herself and Freddie personally, and to the kingdom at large.

"Of course I do not expect that you and your crew would be willing to go as well," she said. "I am immensely grateful that you were able to bring us this far."

"To own the truth, I have not had a moment to think past

the next five minutes, let alone where our next destination ought to be," Peony confessed with a glance at Captain Boyle a few places down the table. "But I do know that two young ladies ought not to go to Port Townsend. The stories one hears are enough to curl one's hair."

"But that is where the *Barbara Carol* was bound," Freddie said. "She may have made port already. Now that Evan and Isabela are married, and the Viceroy is safe, we have not a day to lose."

"Daisy and Freddie will not be alone." William laid down his knife and fork. After his labors of the last two days, he too was looking thinner and more careworn. But his quiet words made Daisy's heart swell with gratitude. "Davey and Lin and I will take them to the Canadas in the conveyance. It will not be as comfortable as *Iris*, nor as swift, but it will get us all there safely."

May Lin turned from her affectionate contemplation of Perdida. She and Lin, who was sitting beside her, exchanged a glance.

"I am not going," Lin announced around a bite of blackberries in cream—her second helping. "May Lin is my family. She is going back to the river canyons, and I am going with her."

William's face went slack with astonishment. "The river canyons? What—"

"Carlos Felipe proposed to my cousin yesterday, aboard *Rosa*," Lin said. "But she doesn't want to be a princess. So we are going."

May Lin choked on her lemonade, and snatched up the colorful square of cotton Honoria had placed as a napkin.

Daisy glanced at the table under the next tree, where,

thank goodness, Pilar had not heard. She was sitting with Isabela's family, with whom there was a distant connection on the Valdez side. Daisy strongly suspected that she and the Viceroy might be well suited, if they could stop arguing long enough to see it for themselves.

Lin was not finished with tactless speeches. "We will make our home with Mother Mary and the others. And I will put this place behind me for good."

Daisy had no idea who Mother Mary might be, but Peony seemed to have an inkling. "Good heavens," the latter said faintly. "You declined an offer of marriage from a prince in order to return to the witches?"

"Would not you, in my place?" May Lin had herself under control now. "Even you must admit he and I do not belong together. And let us be frank—the kingdom would not stand for it."

"I do not know either of you well enough to admit any such thing," Peony said with surprising gentleness. "But I do admire your knowing yourself and the kingdom so well. When will you go?"

"I will try to find my *mecaballo*," May Lin said. "If I do find it, Lin and I will depart on it immediately afterward."

"And if you don't?" Davey asked. "We saw it outside the mission. The sea may have got it."

"If it did, I will second one from the palace guard, or make do with a train," May Lin told him. "It is safe enough." She allowed her sleeves to fall back just enough to reveal the leather sheaths strapped to her forearms.

"Then this is our last meal together?" Davey asked on a plaintive note of realization, looking between them.

"Maybe," Lin told him. "But when you come to the river to visit us, we can have lots of meals."

Davey brightened. "We can?" He looked at William. "Can we?"

William nodded. "But first we will apply ourselves to helping Daisy and Freddie find their father. I have no objection to leaving early in the morning. The conveyance is moored over there at the mission, and there is nothing to prevent our going."

"But—but—surely there is no need to be so precipitate," Detective Hayes protested. "The prince will need you, May Lin. And Daisy, what about your friend Pilar?"

As predicted, that young lady had finished her dinner and had now got up to confront His Serene Highness about something—the supply trains? Or perhaps the clearing of rooms in the palace, where the Viceroy intended to make his headquarters. Rather shamelessly, Daisy listened more closely. Ah, no—she was lobbying for the padre at San Rafael Arcángel to become the next bishop. Really, the girl showed amazing powers of organization and foresight that Daisy could only admire.

She returned her attention to Detective Hayes. "I have no fears for Pilar. She has nothing to return to, and an abundance of people and tasks to help her reestablish her life. She will be happy in helping to make things better for the people."

"The people ... and the Viceroy," Peony murmured innocently, with a glance at May Lin.

But May Lin did not seem to hear her. Instead, she stood. She took Lin's hand in one of hers, and with the other, lifted her glass of golden wine to Daisy and Freddie. "To safe journeys, then, and the people we love safely in our arms again."

Daisy's lips trembled, and tears started unexpectedly in her eyes. She stood and lifted her glass to May Lin, and then to William, who rose to his feet across from her.

"To the people we love," he said softly, and touched his glass to hers.

"And finding them," Davey put in, clinking his glass of lemonade with both of theirs, and Lin's.

And finding them. In the distance, over the roof of the mission infirmary where even now the San Gregorio monks were caring for the injured, Daisy could see the red and buff stripes of William's balloon.

We are coming, Papa. She sent a prayer, a hope, into the bright September sky. *Wait for us, and in just a little while, we will be a family again.*

She touched Davey's hair, and he leaned into her side. William's eyes crinkled, glowing with the things he would never say in public, but which she could feel in her heart like the warmth of a fire.

We will be a family, Papa. All of us together.
Soon.

THE END

AFTERWORD

Dear reader,

I hope you have enjoyed *The Engineer Wore Venetian Red*, and our continuing adventures in the Magnificent Devices world via this mystery series. It is your support and enthusiasm that is like the steam in an airship's boiler, keeping the entire enterprise afloat and ready for the next adventure.

You might leave a review on your favorite retailer's site to tell others about the books. And you can find print, digital, and audiobook editions of the series online. I hope to see you over at my website, www.shelleyadina.com, where you can sign up for my newsletter and be the first to know of new releases and special promotions. You'll also receive a free short story set in the Magnificent Devices world just for subscribing!

Daisy and Freddie's adventures will continue in Mysterious Devices Book Five, *The Judge Wore Lamp Black*. Welcome to the flock!

Warmly,

Shelley

Aster (novella)

Iris (novella)

Rosa (novella)

The Mysterious Devices series

The Bride Wore Constant White

The Dancer Wore Opera Rose

The Matchmaker Wore Mars Yellow

The Engineer Wore Venetian Red

The Judge Wore Lamp Black

The Professor Wore Prussian Blue

The Lady Georgia Brunel Mysteries

"The Air Affair" in Crime Wave: Women of a Certain Age

The Clockwork City

The Automaton Empress

The Engineer's Nemesis

The Wounded Airship

The Texican Tinkerer

The Aeronaut's Heir

The Regent's Devices series with R.E. Scott

The Emperor's Aeronaut

The Prince's Pilot

The Lady's Triumph

REGENCY ROMANCE as Charlotte Henry

The Rogue to Ruin

The Rogue Not Taken

One for the Rogue

A Rogue by Any Other Name

PARANORMAL

Corsair's Cove

Kiss on the Beach (Corsair's Cove Chocolate Shop 3)

Secret Spring (Corsair's Cove Orchard 3)

Immortal Faith

ABOUT THE AUTHOR

Shelley Adina is the author of more than 50 novels published by Harlequin, Warner, Hachette, and Moonshell Books, Inc., her own independent press. She writes steampunk adventure and mystery as Shelley Adina; as Charlotte Henry, writes classic Regency romance; and as Adina Senft, is the *USA Today* bestselling author of Amish women's fiction.

She holds a PhD in Creative Writing from Lancaster University in the UK. She won RWA's RITA Award® in 2005, and was a finalist in 2006. She appeared in the 2016 documentary film *Love Between the Covers*, is a popular speaker and convention panelist, and has been a guest on many podcasts, including Worldshapers and Realm of Books.

When she's not writing, Shelley is usually quilting, sewing historical costumes, or enjoying the garden with her flock of rescued chickens.

Shelley loves to talk with readers about books, chickens, and costuming!

Shelley loves to talk with readers about books, chickens, and costuming!
www.shelleyadina.com

www.ingramcontent.com/pod-product-compliance
Lightning Source LLC
Chambersburg PA
CBHW032118180726
48284CB00002B/605